KAT SINGLETON

FOUNDED ON GOODBYE

Founded on Goodbye

Printed in the United States of America.

Cover Design and Formatting Images by Ashlee O'Brien with Ashes & Vellichor
Edited by Christina Hart of Savage Hart Book Services
Formatted by Victoria Ellis of Cruel Ink Publishing
Cover Image: Regina Wamba
Cover Model: Jackson Walker

DEDICATION

To Ashlee,
Founded on Goodbye wouldn't be what it is if it weren't for you.
Thank you for being as passionate
about Nash and Nora's love story as I am.
You nailed the aesthetic.
Love you forever.

EPIGRAPH

"RATHER THAN *LOVE,*
THAN *MONEY,*
THAN *FAME,*
GIVE ME TRUTH."

-HENRY DAVID THOREAU

1

NORA

"Why me?" The question lingers in the air between the two of us.

The silence causes me to take a long, nervous pull from my straw, and I swish the water around in my mouth before swallowing.

I use this moment to take a good look at the woman sitting across from me. She can't be much older than my twenty-one years. I'd guess she wasn't a day over thirty, but it's hard to tell in Los Angeles.

There are so many plastic surgeons out here, she could be forty-two for all I know. Her hair is cut in a short, polished bob, the platinum blonde color of her hair appearing natural.

Monica takes a long breath, her narrow shoulders lifting and falling in a fluid movement. I can hear the annoyance in her sigh just before she says, "Why not you, Nora?"

Her comment spins in my head. She has a point; any girl would love the opportunity she's giving me. I'm just not sure *I'm* the girl to accept the offer.

Monica's phone chimes from where she has it laid out on the table. She says nothing as she picks it up and starts rapidly typing away at it.

While her fingers hit speeds I didn't know were humanly possible, I look around the swanky restaurant. At the plants cascading down the black wall located behind her.

It's loud enough inside that the two of us have had to speak up to be able to hear the other. Patrons around us are drinking cocktails named after literary heroes out of copper mugs. This is the nicest space I've been in since packing all my bags and moving out to California.

When I got the text from my agent—AKA my best friend Riley—to meet Monica Masters in an hour, I didn't believe it at first. Monica is *the* right-hand woman to music icon: Nash Pierce. I thought this meeting might give me the opportunity to be one of the dancers on his upcoming world tour. It turns out, what Monica wants from me is a bit more complicated.

When Monica's nails finally stop tapping away at her phone, she looks at me once again. "Look," she starts, lifting her perfectly manicured hand to call our waiter over for the check, "there are thousands of girls who'd jump at this opportunity in an instant. I don't particularly need you; you were just my first choice."

Her cell phone continues to ping next to her as she exchanges brief words with the waiter. When she looks back at me, the look on her face screams business.

"How did you even find me?" I use the question as a diversion, to get my thoughts together. If she were to look under the table, she'd see the incessant tapping of my foot against the shiny floors, my nerves getting the best of me.

Monica studies me a moment, only looking away to hand the waiter her credit card. A few moments pass before she speaks. "You have a large following on

Instagram. It seems people gravitate toward your life. That's exactly what I need. I need people to give a damn about you."

I gulp, her words simmering in my head. I think about my followers, or friends as I like to call them, on Instagram. Somehow, I have amassed over a hundred thousand of them. My following had started to grow after a news company featured my senior showcase on the air—a contemporary number that set the small town I lived in ablaze.

I try not to think of the showcase, of the reason they featured me.

When I moved to LA, I was just a simple small-town girl with big dreams. The same kind of dreams that most people in LA have. In my case, make my passion for dancing a career.

When I snagged a position in an up-and-coming dance company, my follower count kept increasing. Once I realized people were interested in that type of content, I started posting videos of me free styling to popular songs; and after that, my following skyrocketed.

It still feels odd that I share my life with so many people. If I accept Monica's offer, there will be double—maybe triple—the amount of people looking at my life. I'm not sure I'm prepared for that, but then again, her offer is a one-way ticket to pursuing my dreams.

I just have to sell myself in the process.

I try to swallow past the lump of nerves in my throat. "I need some time to think about this."

Monica's eyebrows raise. She probably thought I would have jumped at the opportunity. She doesn't know I swore I wouldn't be a cliché when I moved to LA. I didn't want to sell myself to achieve my dreams. And what she's offering is a complete sellout. A sellout I find myself highly considering.

Her nails tap against the table. "You can have a day. Rehearsals for the tour begin next week and if you happen to say no, which I'm not sure why you would, then

I'll need time to screen other girls and meet with them. We have auditions on Saturday. If you say yes, you'll be expected to be there."

My eyes flick back to the plants hanging on the wall behind her. Staring at Monica for too long makes me incredibly nervous, and right now I'm just trying to keep my cool. "You haven't given me many details on what this gig will entail except that you're *literally* hiring me to break Nash Pierce's heart."

My hands move all over the place as I recount the conversation we just had. People are probably staring, but I'm too deep in my thoughts to worry about that. What she's proposing to me is crazy.

"Which, while we're on the topic," I mutter, "why do you even think I *can* break his heart? He's Nash Pierce and I'm, well, not on his level."

The waiter hands Monica her card back before scurrying off. I don't blame him—the look on her face makes me want to run away as well. Monica is known for being one hell of a ballbuster in Hollywood, and after meeting with her today, I can confirm what the tabloids say about her are true.

She's terrifying.

"Have some self-respect, Nora," Monica chastises.

I want to shrink down in my chair at the tone of her voice. It makes me feel like a child. It's how my mother used to talk to me and my sister when we did something wrong.

"You're stunning," she continues. "The dance videos you upload show just how sexy you are. You're very talented to be able to dance like that. If I didn't think you were up for the job, I wouldn't have gone through all the hassle to look at every *single* one of your Instagram posts and take the time out of my *very* busy schedule to meet with you."

"Then answer me as to why you need to hire somebody to break his heart?" I lean across the table, my elbow almost bumping the drink in front of me.

"I think it's pretty obvious that his new self-titled album lacks the, let's say *emotion* that his debut album had. He wrote *Back to Yesterday* after his first love broke his heart. The fact that those songs were so raw, it reached his fans in a special way, highlighting every bit of his feelings through that heartbreak. Those feelings were the steppingstones for what made him the music icon he is today."

She takes a moment to fire off another message on her constantly pinging phone before she goes on.

"While this new album has been sitting at number one for a few weeks now, it isn't reaching the fans the way we need it to—to have lasting stardom for him. And much to the dismay of Nash's inner circle, he refuses to let any girl get close enough for him to even possibly fall in love, let alone feel anything. At this point he's got nothing to inspire his music." Monica leans back in the brass chair, her arms folding over her chest gracefully.

I stir the ice cubes in my drink with the fancy straw, mulling her words over. "What makes you think I'll be able to get close to him, then?"

Monica laughs. "Oh, hon, I'm not positive you'll be able to." She reaches across the table to put her hand on mine. Her brown eyes look me dead in the eye as she continues to speak. "It'll be hard, and it'll take time, but we just need someone to inch their way in close enough to make any of this a possibility. My bet is you're just the girl for the job. With those sweet hazel eyes and kiss-me lips, it'd be hard for any guy to say no to you, even if that guy is Nash Pierce."

She must be certifiably insane to think a girl from small-town Ohio is going to break *Nash Pierce's* heart—better known as the music god of my generation. But I humor her because she does paint a pretty picture.

"So, you hire me as a dancer for his new tour, expect me to get close enough to him to make him fall in love with me, and if somehow it *is* possible for me to make that happen, I'm just supposed to break his heart? All so he can write and perform better songs?"

Monica gives one fervent nod of her head. "Exactly. Heartbreak sells, sweetie. And Nash needs someone to break his heart again so he can connect with his music. It'll need to be one hell of a broken—"

"*If* he falls in love with me."

A baby cries in the background; it's shrieking loud and interrupting the hip atmosphere of the restaurant.

Monica's eyes flick to the area where the cries are coming from before bringing her brown-eyed gaze back to me. "For starters, I don't like being interrupted." She taps her nails against the screen of her phone and stares me down like she's planning my demise.

I bite the inside of my lip before mumbling out an apology.

"Like I was saying..." Monica sits up straighter, flipping her blonde hair over her shoulder. "The team isn't putting this whole thing together with absolute certainty that he will fall for you. We don't know if you have what it takes to slither your way into Nash's heart, but you were my first choice, so the offer is on the table. We might even choose a few of you to try to be more efficient with all this."

She shrugs, as if it is totally normal that Nash Pierce's team is going behind his back to *hire* girls to come in to break his heart. It makes me feel kind of sad for him.

"Just so we're clear, this is not to be discussed with anyone, whether you accept or not. Understood?"

I swallow nervously. "I understand."

Monica pulls a large stack of papers from her purse. "Here's the NDA. You can't discuss this with anyone but me or your agent, whether you accept the terms or not."

My eyes rake over the words on the paper. I have no idea what any of this legal jargon even means. Before I can get my thoughts together, Monica sets a pen in front of me.

Picking it up, I look over the document in front of me. The pen feels heavy in my hand as I sign on all the lines she points to. Deep down I know I should probably have this looked over by a lawyer or something, but I'm still trying to process what she's offering to think about anything beyond it. I do know I have no problem keeping this a secret from everyone in my life but Riley. I'm happy we faked her being my agent so she could be my loophole in this whole thing. There's no way I could make this decision without discussing it with her first.

"So, what will it be, Ohio?" Monica leans across the table, her body language making it apparent she's two seconds away from leaving.

My head spins with all the details she's given me. I want to make dancing a career like I want to marry Chris Pratt—very badly. There's nothing I want more than to be successful in this industry. But am I willing to chase my dreams at the cost of somebody else's heart?

"What's in it for me?" I finally ask.

Monica hums, a smile upon her face. "Name your price, darling."

2
NASH

"Hell no," I snap, strumming out a few chords on my guitar to drown out her voice, making it known the conversation is over. Unfortunately, my manager is persistent and doesn't give a rat's ass if I'm done with the conversation or not.

"It's already been decided, Nash. I was just letting you know as a formality. Two days from now we'll be holding auditions for this tour's backup dancers."

I still refuse to look at her, instead staring down at my guitar, until I see two death trap shoes step in front of me.

I sigh, my fingers falling from the fret board as I look up at my manager, Monica Masters. By the look on her face, she's annoyed by me, but if we're being honest, that's the normal look I see from her.

"I said I didn't want fucking dancers. It's me and my band up on stage. There's no need for dancers," I huff. I managed to sell out arenas on my last tour just fine without dancers. I don't know why she's being such a pain in my ass about them this time.

I'm not doing fucking dancers.

Monica sighs, swinging her huge purse from one arm to the other, almost taking out a guitar in the process. She glares at me, and if looks could kill, there's a good chance I'd be dead on this floor right now.

I've taken a backseat to planning my upcoming tour, not having it in me to form too much of an opinion on anything to do with it. But I do have a strong opinion on this. I don't want to perform with dancers. I want it to be me and my band—no one else.

Speaking of said band, two parts of it walk into the studio as Monica stares a hole through my forehead. Troy raises his eyebrows behind Monica's back when he notices her stance. We've all learned by now that when Monica has her foot tapping, she's about a minute shy from having you by the balls.

Well, they all seem to understand this. Unfortunately for Monica, I employ all of them, and I can tell her no whenever the hell I want. Like right now, because there won't be dancers on *my* tour.

"Nash, the whole team has decided," she says smoothly, enunciating every syllable. "You *will* have dancers. Now it's up to you if you would like to show up at auditions on Saturday or not to choose them. But you're going to have dancers whether you like it or not."

Her phone rings at the perfect time, giving her the opportunity to walk out the studio, her obnoxious shoes thumping against the padded floors during her exit.

Poe lets out a long whistle. "What's up her ass today?"

Troy laughs next to him, spinning his drumsticks between his fingers. "Does Monica ever *not* have a stick up her ass?"

I shake my head at the two of them, letting them continue their banter as I adjust my guitar and imagine firing Monica for the umpteenth time in my life. Just as I focus back on my guitar, playing some of the chords to the song we'll be working on, the rest of the band walks through the studio doors.

My band consists of the best of the best. Troy on the drums, Poe on bass, Luke on rhythm, Landon on keys as well as various other instruments. Then we have my backup vocalists: Josh, Elton, and Leo.

All the guys taking their spots in the studio now have been with me since I started my solo career. Some of them, like Poe and Landon, I met when I was part of the boyband: Anticipation Rising.

Three friends from middle school and I had decided to perform in a talent show on a dare. Little did we know, there was an agent in the crowd as a spectator that night.

The next years went by in a whirlwind. One minute, we were nobodies; the next minute, our faces were in every teen girl's bedroom—and *our* teenage years were spent under a microscope.

Some of us grew up fine despite all odds. Others, like me, were still fucked up from the whole ordeal.

Now, at twenty-four, I can barely take a piss without the paparazzi following me in. Privacy is nonexistent for me, and the more I want to create music *I* love and believe in, the more the people who pretend they own me push back.

Take my current shitty situation for example. I know, and they know, that I managed to sell out my first world tour—a *stadium tour*—without fucking dancers. I don't need them, *clearly*, and fuck if I know why they're so hell bent on having them this time. But I'll be damned if I stand up there and sing songs I know are complete shit while girls—and probably guys—parade around me, half-naked and twirling and shit.

Fuck. That.

A rough hand squeezes my neck, and I look up to find Poe standing next to me. "You ready?" he asks, stepping back and running his hands through the mop of hair on his head.

I nod, forgetting about the dancers and putting my head where it should be—with the music. "Let's start with *Love Me Like You*," I instruct.

Everyone takes their spot in the studio, preparing their instruments and looking to me for confirmation.

I count us in with, "One...two...one, two, three—"

As I get lost in the song, everything else fades away around me. We run through good chunk of the setlist before calling a break for lunch.

Wiping the sweat from my neck, I look to my band. "Meet back here in an hour."

They nod before filing out of the room, leaving me and Poe in the studio alone.

"How do you think it went?" I ask him, unscrewing the cap to my water bottle while following him to a couch.

Poe sighs, plopping down onto the brown leather. He runs a hand over the stubble growing around his mouth, avoiding my eyes for a moment.

Unease builds in my chest. "Spit it out, Poe."

"Nash..." he begins, his hands falling tiredly next to him, slapping against the stiff leather. "The band is doing everything they need to, but it still feels off."

"Then the band isn't doing everything they need to," I counter, shaking my head to move the long piece of hair blocking my sight.

He rolls his eyes at me. "No, man. It's *you*. You aren't in it anymore. Not like you used to be. It seems like you don't even want to be here. I see it, the band sees it, and quite frankly, I think everyone sees it but you."

I tap my hands against the counter in front of me, anger bubbling inside me. "I don't know what the hell you're talking about."

"Look, I've known you since you were a teeny bopper dancing in sync with your adolescent friends. You're like a younger brother to me."

All I can do is let out an irritated sigh. Poe isn't much older than me, but I let him have his moment as he rattles on.

"That's why I'm going to be real with you when I say you need to get your head back into the music. Hell, your heart needs to be in it, too. Because there'll be tens of thousands of fans cheering you on at this tour, and they deserve someone giving their all to it. Someone who gives a fuck about what they're doing."

Annoyed by his words, I roll my eyes. I'm sick and tired of everyone telling me this bullshit. "What's up with everyone being on my ass about my heart not being in the music anymore?"

Poe shrugs, pulling at the label on his water bottle. "You seem like you don't want to be here."

I let out a resigned sigh, because he's right. I'm exhausted by the life I live. I don't exactly *want* to be here. I don't know where the fuck I want to be. Nothing matters to me more than the fans and the music, but right now it doesn't feel like my life revolves around either anymore.

I'm controlled by numbers and corporate assholes who wouldn't know how to write a bridge if it slapped them in the fucking face. When I went solo, I left the group because I wanted to be my own boss. I wanted it to be *me* who had the final say in things.

To get where I am now, I had to cut ties with three of my best friends. I left them high and dry when I sold the front-page story on how I, Nash Pierce, was leaving Anticipation Rising.

The only way I could live with myself after doing that to my friends was knowing I had to do it if I wanted to control my music. Because *I* wanted to be in control of *me.* Now, as I let out a half-hearted laugh, I can't help but think twenty-year-old me was incredibly naïve.

Here I am, four years later, hating myself and my job at times because I'm doing the exact opposite of what I'd set out to do. I can barely take a piss without someone telling me when, where, and how to do it.

My mind tracks back to my last tour. Things were so much simpler then. I was allowed to perform a setlist completely written by me. Songs I was *proud* of. Not the cookie cutter shit I perform now that are written with one purpose only: to top charts.

“Do you?” Poe’s voice breaks through my thoughts.

I look up confused, forgetting what he said. “Do I what?”

He gives me a dejected look. “Do you even want to be here?”

I snicker. “Well, I mean, I wouldn’t mind cutting to the part where I’m underneath someone tonight.”

Poe straightens on the couch, resting his elbows on his thighs, and the leather underneath him groans with the quick movement. “Cut the shit. Your whoring-around bullshit isn’t going to hide the truth.”

It’s my turn to get angry with him. I’m annoyed he’s not taking the fucking hint to drop it.

“Yes,” I lie, “I want to be here.” I stretch my arms above my head. “Now, I’m going to go eat before I continue to work my ass off for the *fans* paying to see this tour.”

I push past one of my best friends, not bothering to look back at him. I don’t want him to see the lies written all over my face.

Nothing feels more like home to me than a stage in front of thousands of fans. Nowhere else could ever compete with that.

I’m just bitter that when I stand up there this tour, I’ll be standing up there as a washed-up version of myself that I can barely tolerate to look at in the mirror anymore.

It doesn’t feel like I’m performing for myself or even my fans at this point. It feels a whole lot like I’m performing for my label and the people trying to run my life.

And I fucking despise it.

3
NORA

"Excuse me, *what*?" Riley shrieks, her voice screeching through my car's speakers.

"Jeez, Riley," I say, reaching for my dashboard to turn the volume for the Bluetooth down. "You just about busted my eardrum!"

A car honks behind me before it whips over into the next lane and speeds right past me. People in LA traffic are *so* friendly.

"I'm sorry, Nora, but you can't expect me to be silent when you tell me you're going on tour with Nash freaking Pierce!"

"Well believe it," I tell her. "I have to go to auditions, but it seemed like kind of a done deal."

"Remember us common people on your road to fame," she jokes, muttering something quietly to someone on her end of the line.

"By the way, I had to give Nash's manager *all* of your info," I add nonchalantly, hoping she doesn't freak out.

"What?" she screeches, clearly freaking out.

"I know, I know. But you were listed as my agent and when she said she'd get in contact with my agent, I panicked."

"What happens when she finds out it's a total fake?"

I shrug, forgetting she can't see me. "We won't let that happen."

She sighs. "It'll be fine. Everything will be fine, because again, my best friend is going on *tour*!"

I laugh, still trying to process that fact myself. "We'll talk more about it at home," I say, merging into the right lane.

"Hell yeah, we will. I want all the dirty deets! You have to tell me how wonderful this will be for you before I have to start processing the fact that you'll be leaving me."

I swallow, trying to figure out if I plan on telling my best friend the *real* reason I'll be going on this tour.

"Okay, tell me *everything*," Riley says, speaking through a mouthful of food. She's sitting across from me on our living room floor, her legs crossed in front of her.

Finishing my own bite of food, I hold up my finger. After swallowing, I give her a shrug, unsure of where I should even begin. Today was totally unexpected and I still don't know how to properly put into words what Monica is asking me to do. "Well, you know how I was shocked to hear from Monica."

When we first moved out here, Riley and I decided to put her down as my "agent" in my bio, thinking it made me sound like I was already a somebody, even if it was just an act. Then again, nearly everyone in LA is putting on some act or another.

Riley didn't check it very often, as the inbox was pretty consistently empty aside from spam. That is, until a few days ago—when Riley received an inquiry from Nash Pierce's manager.

We thought that was spam too at first. Who wouldn't? But it goes without saying we found out it was very real. A little too real, I'm realizing, the more I think about it.

Riley nods, loudly slurping a noodle into her mouth in the process.

I recount to Riley everything Monica and I talked about before she dropped the bomb on me.

Riley wipes her mouth with a napkin at the same moment her brown eyes pop wide open. She throws down the napkin and shoots up from where she'd been sitting. "I've got an idea!" she yells as she disappears into her bedroom.

After Riley gets out a whiteboard and insists on making a pros and cons list, I look at her solemnly.

"I just don't want to be a shitty person by agreeing to this. I don't want to be anything like *them,*" I admit.

Brief flashes from high school come to mind. I try to not think of the person—the people—that made the end of my senior year hell for me and those I love.

My past is something I rarely talk about anymore. I tried to leave every tragic thing that happened in high school back in Ohio. But that doesn't mean I ever want to do something where I have to question my own morals. And getting close to someone to intentionally hurt them is a great way to have me questioning everything.

"I'm dead serious. You deserve to chase your dream, Nora. You've been through a lot. You risked a lot to be in the position you are now, and this is literally your dream we're talking about. You can't pass up the opportunity."

"Follow my dream, while agreeing to try and break somebody else's heart, what a *great* opportunity," I say sarcastically.

Riley plops down next to me with a sigh. She leans her head on my shoulder, the both of us looking forward. "You said it yourself; you don't think you'll even get the chance to break his heart."

"That's true," I tell her, thinking her point through. I highly doubt he'd be interested in *me*. In reality, I most likely won't even have the chance or opportunity *to* break his heart. He's Nash Pierce. He won't spare me a second glance.

Every magazine makes Nash seem like a raging douchebag. A playboy. Someone not looking for anything remotely serious. From personal experience, though, I know the labels others can push on you without knowing your true character at all. I know how wrong they can be. And part of me wonders if Nash Pierce is really the kind of guy everyone makes him out to be. Riley gives me a serious look, her hands dangling in front of her. "If you do, then we'll figure it out then. There's no part in worrying about it right now."

Lingering in the silence for a few moments, staring at the list in front of me, I come to my final decision. "I'm going to do it." The words come out way more confident than I feel.

Riley jumps up, a beaming smile on her face. "My bestie is going to be famous!"

Meanwhile, I just hope this tour will end with me not hating myself for the things I've done.

4

NASH

I groan as I pull sunglasses over my eyes, a headache wreaking havoc on my brain. Looking to my right, I find a mass of people waiting outside the building where auditions are being held. The location we chose was supposed to be secure. Only the people auditioning were supposed to know where they were taking place. But here we are, with a hundred screaming fans outside the door I'm supposed to be walking in.

I rub my temples, hiding behind the tinted glass for a few seconds longer. I know I'm late, but I woke up this morning with a raging hangover and no desire to come here at all.

The screams outside the SUV window do nothing to help ease the tension in my head. I'm two seconds away from telling my driver to take me back home, to let Monica and anyone else decide which dancers to hire for the tour.

But I'm already here. And if I'm going to have other people sharing *my* fucking stage, I might as well have a say in who it'll be.

Unbuckling my seatbelt, I look over at Sebastian, one of my security guards. "I'm ready."

He wastes no time opening his door, the roar of the fans drowning out any other sounds around me. My eyes track his movements as he rounds the front of the car and then stands like a brick wall in front of my door.

I stare at the dark hair on the back of his head for a few moments, giving myself one last chance to bow out of this shit show. I take a deep breath in before I knock my knuckles against the window three times, letting him know I'm ready to exit the car.

Sebastian swiftly turns around, opening my door and ushering me safely out of the car. The fans go crazy, their screams meshing together in one ear-piercing sound. I fall in step with Sebastian, walking one beat behind him as he directs us toward the door.

"Nash!"

"Can I have your autograph?"

"Oh my god, it's him!"

The fans are excruciatingly loud. I try to aim a smile in the direction of the noise but cameras flash in my face, so I stare at my feet, trying to hide behind my sunglasses and hat.

"Please stop, Nash!"

I used to stop and sign something for every single one of my fans. Now, that is nowhere near possible for me. Every place I go is leaked to the press and in no time there's a swarm of people—half paparazzi, half fans. If I stood outside and signed something for each and every one of them, smiled for every photo op, I'd never release another album let alone go on tour.

I just don't have the damn time.

But in the press, they call me cold and callous for no longer interacting with my fans the way I used to. The fame has gone to my head in their eyes.

What they *don't* seem to understand, is with more fame comes more responsibility.

If people want me to do the things they love me for, like write songs, I can't spend all my time appeasing them.

But I tell a fan not to grope me, and I'm the asshole.

If I don't smile because I'm late and have shit to do? I don't care about the people who support my career.

I've learned the hard way there's no way for me to win in these situations.

"Step back," Sebastian orders, scolding a fan that's slipped through the barricade.

My face is plastered all over her T-shirt. The photo is of me stripped down to my underwear for a popular brand's new line of underwear. The shirt makes me cringe.

"Move!" Sebastian yells, no longer a warning tone.

The girl begins to cry. "Nash, I love you so much."

She somehow manages to further press her body against the door. There's a good chance she's going to have to be peeled from the glass at this point.

When she adjusts her hand, she leaves behind a sweaty palm print on the door. Tears stream down her face as she begins to sob a few feet away from me.

There are still screams echoing behind me as Matt, another one of my bodyguards, walks up to her and asks her to move one last time. The crying fan doesn't move, which causes Matt to have to escort her out of the way.

As he leads her back to the barrier between me and the other fans, she looks over her shoulder and makes direct eye contact with me. "I just wanted you to see me!"

The words sit deeper in my gut than I'd care to admit. It's not that I don't care about my fans or don't want to get to know them, the problem is I can't spend all my time doing it.

Her words are still ringing in my ears as we shuffle through the entrance to the studio, the sounds of the fans outside fading as the doors shut.

"You're late."

I don't have to look up to know who it is. I've heard that exact phrase fall from Monica's lips many times before. She's lectured me so many times in my life that I'm nearly desensitized to it by now.

As I pull the hat from my head and tuck it into the back pocket of my jeans, I step closer to her. "I'm fucking here. What more do you want from me?"

Monica swivels on her heels and starts walking down the hallway. "I want you to give a damn about your own tour, Nash. That's what I want." Her words bounce against the walls of the empty hallway.

Sebastian clears his throat behind me. Not bothering to look at him, I follow in Monica's footsteps.

"Who said I didn't care about this tour? Because it sure as hell wasn't me."

She stops in her tracks, her thin shoulders moving with a deep breath. I wasn't expecting her to turn around and retreat in my direction, but in no time, she's standing directly in front of me, a wrinkle forming on her forehead. A wrinkle no amount of Botox could get rid of when she's pissed.

Her voice gets incredibly low when she says, "You didn't have to say the words. Your indifference to every *single* thing with this tour says enough. You used to be involved in tour planning. Now I don't think you can even tell me what your stage setup will be, can you?"

My teeth grind together as I flex my jaw. I let my staff design most of this tour because they're the experts on it. I was busy trying to write decent fucking songs to perform on tour, but that doesn't seem to register with Monica and probably others. They want me to be this damn circus animal that does everything.

Monica smiles at my silence. "Take some time to get your shit together before you walk into auditions. We need these dancers, and I can't have this indifferent asshole of a popstar walking in, solidifying their probably already shitty perception of you. When you walk through those doors," she points to two metal doors down the hallway on her left, "you better have a smile on your face. Understood?"

I laugh, tired of taking orders from her when *I'm* the boss. All I do is walk away, strutting by the doors that music is blasting out of as I continue down the hallway.

I keep walking until I feel far away enough from the people who are suffocating me with their expectations. After pushing through a different door, I step into a small office. There's an old leather loveseat resting against one of the walls, a desk sitting on the other. I barely notice any of those things, however, as my gaze is focused on the tiny woman staring at me with her mouth hanging open.

"Riley, I have to go," she says breathlessly. She presses her screen and then shoves the phone into the pocket of her small backpack.

The barely clothed stranger blows a piece of long brown hair from her face. She shifts her weight, causing the paper pinned to her chest to rustle in the silence.

The two of us are locked in on each other. She rakes her gaze all the way down my body then works her way back up to my face.

I snicker. "Like what you see, Rose?"

"My name isn't Rose," she bites out.

Damn, I wasn't expecting that tone from her. She looks sweet as can be, but apparently she also has thorns.

"Well, you didn't give me your name before you decided to assault me with your eyes, so I just had to come up with a nickname. The color of your cheeks is as red as a rose, *Rose*."

She takes a step back, her one foot hitting a stack of books and causing it to topple over.

The two of us look down at the array of books on the floor.

"You're Nash Pierce," she muses.

I take a few steps closer to her. "That *is* the name my parents gave me. Sometimes I answer to it."

"Cute," she whispers, her thick eyebrows drawing together.

"You think I'm cute?" I joke, resting a hip against the old wooden desk.

The stranger and I are standing only a few feet apart. I'm close enough to see the glean of sweat on her chest. My eyes flick down to her bare stomach as she pulls it in with a deep breath.

It's clear by the sweat, along with her outfit—a tight pair of shorts and sports bra—and the number pinned to her chest, that she's auditioning to be one of my dancers. And the fact that she's still here a few hours after auditions started must mean she's not bad.

"I didn't say you were cute, I said your smartass comment was cute. Which, now that I think about it, was me being a smartass myself."

A genuine laugh escapes my lips, and I don't miss the fact that there's very little I find humorous in the world anymore. "At least you admit it."

"My name's Nora."

"Nora." I play with the name, toying with the way it falls from my lips.

She takes a step toward me, her smile showing off a row of straight teeth. "That *is* the name my parents gave me. Sometimes I answer to it."

"Look who's being a smartass now," I tease, after having my own words thrown back at me.

She looks over my shoulder. "I should probably get back to auditions. Don't want to miss my callbacks." She attempts to step around me, but I reach an arm out, blocking her path.

I quickly pull my arm back to my side, not wanting my bare skin to be against hers any longer than it should. I already hate the way I felt that small touch all the way down through my body.

No longer leaning against the desk, I find I'm almost a whole head taller than her. "You're not missing anything."

Air escapes her lips in a small sigh. "Yeah, says the guy who doesn't have to audition for anything."

"They won't start without me. I'm the *star*," I say sarcastically.

Her hazel eyes narrow, staring so deeply at me it makes my skin crawl. Not because I'm uncomfortable or creeped out, because no one ever looks at me this deeply. "You didn't actually just say that. Cocky much?"

I shrug. She can call me cocky all she wants. It doesn't take away from the fact that I'm telling the truth.

She pats me on the shoulder as she steps past me. The gesture reminds of me when I was a child and an adult would pat me on the head when I voiced an opinion and they thought it was adorable in a way that felt a lot more like condescending.

"In case you didn't know, they've been holding auditions for two hours—*without* their star."

I'd be offended if there wasn't humor in her voice. Nora crosses the small office space, and I turn my body in her direction.

"Well, you could say I wasn't very enthusiastic about having dancers on my tour. I wasn't exactly chomping at the bit to get down here," I admit.

She nods, letting my words soak in. "You know, I think when you go out there, you'll see there's a lot of talent in that room. Maybe you won't be so against it then."

"Maybe."

Nora looks like she's about to leave the room, but before she does, her tiny body turns toward me. There's a cautious look on her face. "Are you...okay?"

My eyebrows raise, her words taking me off guard. "Why would you ask that?"

She plays with her hair, the long strands cascading down her shoulders. "I don't know. I should mind my own business, really. It's just...when you came in here, you looked upset. I just wanted to ask if you were okay before leaving."

My lips part but no words leave my mouth. I can't remember the last time someone asked me if I was okay. It dawns on me how sad it is that the person that has is a complete stranger.

"I'm fine. You saw nothing," I respond defensively, upset that she read me like an open book.

Her hands fly up in front of her. "I didn't mean to offend you. Forget I said anything." She retreats toward the door.

"Gladly," I reply, unsure what else to say.

Nora whistles, the doorknob squeaking as she pushes it open. "Pleasure to meet you, Nash. *Really.*" With that, she leaves the room, not even waiting for a response from me.

I should chase after her, apologize for turning into a complete asshat, but I don't.

I'm too wrapped up in the way she had way more of a pull on me than I'd care to admit. And even though I despise every small feeling she drew out of me in that insignificant amount of time we spent together, I know without a shadow of a doubt that for some reason, I want her as a dancer on my tour.

5

NORA

I bolt out of that small room as fast as my legs will take me. My nerves are already shot after that brief interaction with Nash.

He was everything and nothing like I expected him to be.

As soon as he walked through the door, I should've taken my call with Riley elsewhere, but I couldn't force myself to leave his presence. I was sucked in by his brooding attitude and the anger in his blue-green eyes.

I'm familiar enough with pop culture to know how attractive Nash Pierce is, but seeing him in person is a whole different ball game.

A. Whole. Different. Ballgame.

There's no denying how sexy he is in magazines, but in person his good looks are magnetic. The slight tan to his skin only helps bring out the light color of his eyes; a color that isn't blue or a green but a mixture in between. His caramel-colored hair fell haphazardly across his forehead in an effortless manner. The pair of jeans and old concert tee covering his body only added to his relaxed demeanor.

Nash Pierce is freaking *hot*. And I was all too aware of the way my body felt heated under his stare.

It isn't a feeling I want to persist. If I do manage to get close to him, I know I need to keep my own feelings locked up tight.

Even if the end goal is technically to get Nash to fall in love with me, I won't be doing the same. No matter how much that small interaction with him is still lingering in my head.

Gently pushing the doors open to the crowded studio, I find my bag and water bottle up against the wall. As I slide down the cold wall, I watch the chaos of the auditions continue in front of me.

When I arrived two hours early, I didn't expect the line to wrap all the way around the door. Which in hindsight was completely naïve of me, because we're talking about a *Nash Pierce* tour. Dancing backup for him is any dancer's dream.

Now, four hours after I arrived, they've narrowed the group down to about fifty people. While we were learning choreography and performing what we'd been taught, if we were tapped on the shoulder it meant they were asking for us to leave.

Luckily, I have yet to be tapped on the shoulder. Not like I'm expecting to be, though, since Monica is sitting at the long table of people deciding our fate today. I know my dancing talent has little to do with me getting a spot on Nash's team of dancers.

That doesn't mean I haven't given my all to these auditions. I've been going full out no matter what, the energy in the room only helping me to do so.

"You're fucking *killing* it out there," a guy says to me from a few feet away.

"Thank you," I say, hiding my smile behind my water bottle.

He must take my response as an invitation to sit next to me, because he plops down right next to me, his tan knee now resting inches away from mine.

Reaching his hand out, he keeps it hanging between us. “I’m Ziggy.”

After staring at his hand for a few moments, I finally take it, wrapping my fingers around his warm palm. People are usually only friendly in LA if they want something from you, so I’m hesitant to put too much weight into his introduction. Even though his brown eyes are inviting and his smile seems genuine.

“Nora,” I respond over the sounds of one of the choreographers yelling out the counts.

They have us auditioning in different groups, learning a technical routine before performing it. There are two more groups before I’m up again, and I use the time to rest and stretch my body.

I give myself a mental reminder to step up my cardio in the coming weeks, preparing my lungs for the long days of dancing ahead of me.

“Nice to meet you, Nora. So tell me, where’d you learn to dance like that? Because, *girl*, I would bet every dollar in my checking account that you’ll be dancing on this tour.”

“Stop the music!” Derrick, the other choreographer, shouts, pulling at his long dreads. “We’re going off a simple eight count here. We’re looking for you to stand out in your group. To go *all* out. Some of you are dancing like your spot is guaranteed on this tour, which is hilarious because, *honeys*, that isn’t the case. Nash is the best of the best. We will *only* have the same dancing with him.”

As if on cue, Nash pushes through the doors. The small humor he had on his face in that office is completely wiped from it now. Replacing the humor is a look of indifference as his eyes roam around the crowded room.

Every single person in here has completely frozen in time, as if his presence hit a pause button on their life. I half-expect his eyes to linger on me but his gaze dances away from my direction as fast as it landed there.

"Well, shit, he's even better looking in person," Ziggy whispers next to me. He uses his large hand to fan himself dramatically, purring softly under his breath.

Rolling my eyes, I look away from Nash and focus on unlacing my dance shoes. I don't bother to tell Ziggy I came to that same realization myself after meeting Nash mere minutes ago.

For the next portion of our auditions, we have ninety seconds to show off our personal style to the judges. They don't tell us what we'll be dancing to, other than it'll be a song by Nash.

I have the most technique in ballet and contemporary, so I opt to go barefoot for whatever song they give me. Ballet and contemporary are my favorite styles to perform, but I've been classically trained in almost everything. My two feet have been in a dance studio since I could walk, my younger sister following closely behind me.

Most of the auditions thus far have been about showing off our technique, especially with hip hop. I choose to change up the pace with my solo, wanting to show them that my style is versatile.

"Speaking of the man of the hour," Derrick hollers, wrapping his arm around Nash's neck. "Meet the musician behind our madness, Nash Pierce!"

All the other dancers in the room break out in cheers and clapping. Ziggy next to me is loud enough for the both of us. You'd think the cheers would elicit at least a smile from Nash, but they don't.

All he does is give a slight nod of his head, the nod the only acknowledgment of all the praise he's getting.

When the noise dies back down, Derrick pulls Nash closer to him by the neck, looking at him like a proud father when he can't be that much older than him. "I've worked with Nash on music videos before, but I'm so hyped to be working with him for this tour. Any wise words for the people vying for a spot on the tour, Nash?"

The room is eerily silent as a clearly uncomfortable Nash comes up with a response. For someone who has written some of the most poetic lyrics out there, he sure does take a while to begin a speech.

Finally, he answers, pulling himself out of Derrick's grasp. "Yeah." My stomach plummets when he makes direct eye contact with me and says, "Impress me." With that, he swivels, his sneakers squeaking against the floor as he walks toward Monica.

Derrick stares at Nash's back as he retreats to the table. The choreographer yells to turn the music back on once Nash takes a seat.

It takes a few minutes for the group on the floor to get back in the groove of dancing, but then auditions resume as they were running before Nash walked in. Except now, the nervous energy has increased tenfold.

Now that Nash is here, the prospect of going on tour with him is even more real.

"Any song you're hoping to get for your solo?" Ziggy questions, biting at the tip of his water bottle. The muscles in his forearm flex as he squeezes the liquid into his mouth.

Pursing my lips, my mind spins with all the songs Nash has released. I was in my senior year of high school when Nash released his first solo album.

"Anything but *Your Expectations*," I say under my breath, unease rolling through me when I think of the last time I performed to that song and the meaning behind it.

Never again.

"Not a fan of the slow stuff?"

I laugh, wishing that was the case. "You could say that."

Ziggy throws his water bottle onto his gym bag and starts stretching out his legs in front of him. "I for one would love one of his new songs. I'm a sucker for that pop-y vibe he has now."

Ziggy and I fall into comfortable small talk while the two groups ahead of us finish their routines. I learn he's a year younger than me and has only been dancing for five years. The statement causes me to raise my eyebrows, remembering how fluid his movements were when he was out on the dance floor.

Ziggy asks for some details on my life, and I give him the bare minimum. I'm not one that loves to tell everyone about the past, instead focusing on the future.

As we chat, more people are tapped on the shoulder, leaving no more than thirty of us left.

The time comes for my solo, and suddenly I feel anxious for the first time today.

Monica has pretty much promised me a spot on the tour, but the thought doesn't do anything to calm the butterflies dancing in my stomach. I try not to put too much thought into the fact that I might be so nervous now because I know Nash will be watching me dance.

I've always been the kind to put everything I have out on the dance floor. Dance has been my way to express my deepest thoughts and emotions, even when words have failed me. But now, odd feelings snake throughout my body knowing he'll be watching my every move.

Will he study me like I want to study him?

Or will his apathetic attitude turn on me?

Turns out I'll find out sooner than later as Ziggy shoves me on my shoulder, breaking me from my thoughts.

"Nora, you're up. Go!" He swats at my legs in an attempt to push me up off the ground.

Apparently I was zoning out way longer than I thought, because there are a whole bunch of eyes staring at me, waiting for me to take my spot on the dance floor.

As gracefully as possible, I stand up and walk toward the center of the room. The wood floor is cold against my bare feet, and for a brief second I worry that I should've intended on a hip-hop dance instead of the contemporary one I have planned.

Slowly, I turn my body toward the panel of people sitting at the long table. Monica glares at me as if I'm already taking up too much of her precious time.

I don't even let my eyes wander to Nash.

"Are you ready?" Derrick asks nicely, his hip propped against a large speaker.

I nod, waiting for him to thumb through the phone plugged into the speaker system.

Looking away from him, I choose to stare at my feet, waiting for the music.

Notes start to waft through the speakers, and after a few beats, I instantly recognize the song as *Love Me Like You*.

In no time, my body is moving as I let Nash's voice dictate my rhythm. Then, for those ninety seconds, all other thoughts disappear.

For just over a minute, the world fades and it's just me, the music, and Nash's voice.

6
NASH

Well, I'll be damned. Color me fucking speechless.

This girl can move her body in ways I've never seen.

I've been around dancers for as long as I've had a music career, but how she completely loses herself in the music captivates me in ways I'll never fess up to.

And nothing captures my attention like this anymore.

Her passion for dance is clear as day as she extends her body in different positions—to my lyrics. Lyrics that are personal and etched all over my soul.

I feel anger boil beneath my skin at how her love for dance is apparent in every move she makes. That same passion and love used to seep out of every lyric I wrote. It was buried in every chord I strung.

Now that love and passion is long gone. Left in its wake is nothing but desolate indifference.

But damn if I can look at anything but her body in the middle of the dance floor. She looks so small in the middle of the studio. All the other dancers line the walls, leaving so much empty space for her to move in.

My brief moment of looking away from her solidifies that every other pair of eyes in the room is also on her.

It's hard to look anywhere else but at her. She brings the lyrics to life. We're all entranced with how she uses every inch of the dance floor before her to her advantage.

Nora leaps into the air at the same moment the chorus builds up. As soon as her feet touch the floor again, she uses the momentum to spin her body around multiple times in perfect time with the crescendo of the song.

I can't look away as she folds her body to the floor, using her body to tell a story out of every lyric I wrote.

I forget how each and every one of the lyrics she tells the story to was written about my ex, the girl who broke my heart. The girl who ruined me for everyone else. Taylor is only a distant memory as I watch Nora rewrite every lyric in my head, with only her in mind now.

Shaking my head, I rid the thought as quick as it had come.

She's just fucking dancing. Her being able to take my lyrics and attach a story to them with her body isn't anything special. Any dancer in this room can do that. And I need to get that straight in my mind—right fucking now.

She just caught me at a weak moment earlier, and for some reason now, she's taking up a small space in my head when she shouldn't be. She's nothing. And I'm angry at myself for still wanting her on tour with me.

Her body lifts from the ground slowly, showcasing her flexibility as she extends her leg into the air. The song is about to end—thank *fuck*. I don't even wait to see how she decides to end her solo. I've seen enough as it is.

The screeching of my chair against the floor harmonizes with the ending chords of the song. Standing up and angling my body toward the doors, I feel the pressure of all the eyes previously on her now at my back.

"Nash, sit back down," Monica hisses, her finger pointing at my vacated chair.

"Why, Monica?" I laugh over my shoulder. "I didn't want to fucking be here in the first place. Plus—" I look at Nora in the middle of the floor, her chest heaving from deep breaths, an unreadable look on her face. We keep direct eye contact with my next words. "No one has impressed me."

"We still have more than half the list to go through!" Monica whispers the words out of the corner of her mouth, keeping a tight smile on her face.

Judging by the look on her face, she's anything but happy underneath that fake smile she's completely seething through. And once again, her anger is directed right at me.

Surprise, surprise.

Deciding to ignore her, I head toward the door. Coming here was a mistake. All the eyes on me make my skin itch. I hate that they've likely just seen a reaction out of me after watching Nora dance.

Hopefully they all thought I hated it.

But the truth is, that *no one* who leaps around like a damn ballerina belongs on my tour.

What I pray these people didn't see was that I could barely look away from her; that watching her take my lyrics and turn them into something completely different opened up a part of me I wanted to stay closed for the rest of my life.

I've known this Nora girl for upwards of an hour, and somehow she's already clawing at parts of me that have been dead for years. What's worse is that I don't think she's even trying to do it.

More often than not, women throw themselves at me. They're putty in my hands. The women around me are always acting a part. I haven't even known Nora for a full day, but the interaction with her seemed real. Too real.

And the fact that she can fucking dance like *that* has me seeing red.

I can't have her on my tour.

I can't be in such close proximity with her.

I want absolutely nothing to do with her.

But also, I want a front row seat to every single time she ever moves her body like that.

I want to watch her take words that have poured out from my heart, my soul, and put her own twist on them.

The need is new for me, and quite frankly, it's uncomfortable. I hate it.

I'm so damn lonely recently that I'm becoming all too soft for the first woman I've had a genuine interaction with.

It's fucking pathetic.

Pulling my phone out of my pocket, I tell my driver to meet me in the back of the studio. Sebastian and Matt both wait for me outside the doors, and I fall in line behind them on the way to the back door.

As I climb into the back of the SUV, lucky to have somehow avoided the frenzy of fans, I scroll through my recent messages.

As I scroll, I find three missed texts from my younger brother, Aiden. I make a mental note to call him when I get the chance. At nineteen, he's having the time of his life in college. From the stories he tells me, I'm not sure how much learning he's actually doing. It sounds like he's majoring in frat parties and sorority girls. I quickly fire off a text to him, letting him know I'll call him later.

Thumbing through the rest of my messages, I decide to text the model I met at an award show a few weeks ago. We make plans for later tonight. I don't care where we go. The paparazzi can swarm the club I take her to for all I care. I just need to get my mind off the weird experience that was the last hour of my life.

One thing is for sure: Nora will be the last thing on my mind tonight. You can sure as hell count on that.

7

NORA

"Cut the music!" Derrick shouts, falling into a cheap folding chair on the outskirts of the room.

Suddenly the large space is eerily silent as we all collect our breaths—me and the fifteen other dancers that were selected for Nash's tour included.

"Did he hate it?" Ziggy asks nervously next to me.

I shrug, using the back of my hand to wipe a bead of sweat from my forehead. My chest heaves as my lungs try to take in as much air as possible during the long-awaited break.

We're only a week into rehearsals for the tour and there isn't a muscle on my body that isn't sore from all the stress I've been putting on it. I thought I was in shape before rehearsals began, but it turns out I was wrong.

Dancing almost every day and still keeping up with strength and cardio workouts don't hold a candle to seven-hour rehearsal days. I'm utterly exhausted, but in the most exhilarating way.

The energy in the room after we learned all the choreography to the first song they taught us was unreal. I'll be dancing in a majority of the setlist, only sitting out for five of the songs.

Running a hand through his dreads, Derrick takes a moment to stare at all of us. I don't know if we were so bad that we've left him speechless, or if he's just trying to come up with some encouraging words.

It's been a long rehearsal day. It's been a long *week*—period. Nash will be joining us here soon to learn his own choreography, and Derrick wants the songs we've already learned to be damn near perfect for him. Finally, the man proves we didn't render him speechless.

"*Here For a Good Time* is the opening of every single concert," he says quietly. "We need high energy. You guys need to give it your damn all. We're running it again from the top. Get in formation."

It only takes a few seconds for all of us to get to our starting marks before we're ready to begin. Derrick has proven to be super chill, most of the time, but he doesn't do well when we linger for too long.

The beat starts thumping out of the speakers, and then the coordinated chaos follows. The opening number is complicated. There are about two minutes that we're off stage, a countdown of sorts where Nash will have a voice-over before the music starts. Then, Nash will be on stage alone for a small amount of time before we all come out.

So far, we've been practicing from the spots we'll first take once we're all out there, waiting to go through all of it until dress rehearsals.

My body moves to the bass as I give everything I've got to the number. Listing off the count in my head, I know I'm hitting every eight-count. While I skip across the floor, I place my hand in Ziggy's.

Ziggy and I, along with three other pairs of dancers, execute the portion of the song that's a mix between the salsa and hip hop. Ziggy spins me around, catching me when I fall into him. He slides, pulling my body along with him. There are three more beats before his hands find my hips and we perform the rest of our part together.

Halfway through the song, the girls skip to the back of the room. At the front, all the guys stand in a 'V' formation—the tip missing where Nash will stand—as they jump and kick to the beat of the song.

The girls are placed in the back, and from there, we mimic the same moves as the guys up front. Except when they grab each other's shoulders and sway back and forth to the beat, we continue the same movements prior. Toward the end of the song, we run back to what will be the front of the stage. Joining with our partners one last time, we execute one final salsa move before dropping down in front of our partner at the exact time the beat ends.

A slight turn of my head as we wait for Derrick's thoughts alerts me that at some point in the song, Monica walked in. Our gazes lock and I can't tell if she's pleased or not with my performance.

I also never found out if any of the other girls chosen for the tour were given the same proposition as I was. Quite frankly, I don't care. All the girls seem nice, and I don't want to question their morals like I do my own each night.

"Much better! That's the kind of energy I'm talking about." Derrick claps and looks over to Lizzie, the other choreographer.

She nods her head in agreement, joining in on the clapping.

"Now let's do it again," Derrick instructs, already messing with the speaker system to replay the song.

We perform the song three more times, all up to Derrick's liking, before the day is finally called.

I have a light sheen of sweat on my arms and legs, proof that I was giving the rehearsal my all. Walking over to my belongings, I confirm that no matter how out of breath Ziggy is, he never stops talking.

"Any plans tonight?" he asks, pulling a rag out of his backpack and wiping his forehead.

I squat down, pulling my water bottle from the side pocket of my backpack. "Not really," I answer, taking a moment to gulp down some water. After I wipe the extra water off my lips, I continue. "My plans include a nice hot bath and hopefully twelve hours of sleep. You?"

He smirks. "Oh, ya know, just a hot date."

Laughing, I shake my head at him. "I swear, you're the energizer bunny. The last thing on my mind during this tour will be dating. I barely have time to feed myself and get a decent amount of sleep to add a boyfriend into the mix."

"Ohhh, but they're so fun!" he teases, shouldering his backpack and wagging his eyebrows.

I'm about to answer him when the distinct sound of heels hitting against the floor overrides the noise of any small conversation happening.

"Nora!" Monica says, stopping in front of me and Ziggy. She gives him a brief sideways glare, motioning her head to the door in a somewhat-nice way (for her, anyway) to tell him to get lost.

"I'll see ya later," Ziggy says, offering me a curious glance over his shoulder before leaving the room.

Monica examines me from head to toe. As she crosses her arms over her chest, her handbag dangles between us, perfectly balanced on her forearm. She scrunches her nose, taking a noticeable step away from me. "You're disgustingly sweaty."

Looking down at myself, I shrug. "That's what all day rehearsals will do."

She purses her lips in response, not acknowledging the state I'm in any further. "We need to talk."

"About what?" I wipe the hair from my face, wondering what else she could want from me.

"Not here. Follow."

Her heels get back to clacking and I have to quickly grab my backpack from the ground so I don't lose her. My short legs have to up their usual pace to keep up with her. For someone wearing stilettos, she sure is quick.

The door almost slams me in the face when I follow her out, as Monica doesn't bother to keep the door open for me.

I follow her down the near-empty hallway before she brings me into a small room. It reminds me of the office I first met Nash in a week ago, even though it's a different studio.

Luckily, there's a small table in here with four chairs surrounding it. Monica takes one, tapping her fingernails against the wood of the table until I take my own seat.

"Are you ready to get started with Nash?" she asks, her back ramrod straight in her chair.

Rubbing my thumb and middle finger together, I look at her nervously. "Of course," I finally spit out, my pulse picking up speed.

"Good. He's going to be joining all of you in rehearsals soon. Your job will *really* begin, then."

I nod, trying to fully process what that might mean.

This last week, I've been able to push why I'm *really* on this tour to the back of mind. I've been able to enjoy the excitement with the other dancers of making the cut. Nash has been in a dark corner of my mind, though. Now it appears the luxury of forgetting what I've agreed to has come and gone.

"There are a lot of people counting on you, Nora. Remember that."

After taking in a deep breath, I say, "I know. I'll try my best, I promise."

Monica lets out a shrill laugh, shaking her head at me. "A little bit of advice for you: don't make promises you can't keep. You clearly haven't met Nash if you think you could promise this egregious plan will work. Nash is a bit...*prickly* these days."

I don't point out that "*prickly*" would be the perfect adjective I'd use to describe *her*.

My mouth stays snapped shut for a few moments while

my mind races with her words.

It isn't that I think the plan will work—I actually firmly believe it won't—but I hate letting people down, so I mean it when I say I'll try my best.

"Why is he prickly?" I'm shocked the question leaves my mouth, but there's nothing I can do to take it back. Judging by the look on Monica's face, she wasn't quite expecting the question either.

"You're asking the wrong questions," she answers, beginning to tap her nails once again.

I frown. "What do you mean?"

Grabbing her handbag from one of the empty chairs, she pulls her phone out. "I have to jet to a meeting. Good luck next week. You'll need it."

The meeting ends just as soon as it began, and the whole way home I wonder what the hell I was thinking when I signed up to do this.

8

NORA

I'm in the midst of eating a triple chocolate layer cake in my dream when an incessant poking persists at my face.

Groaning, I pull my blanket over my face and roll away from whatever is poking at me.

"Nora," Riley hisses. "Don't you have rehearsals today?"

My eyes pop open. Instantaneously, I'm sitting up in bed and searching for my phone.

"Jesus!" she shrieks, jumping back. "I didn't think someone that was fast asleep two seconds ago could move that fast."

"No, no, no, *no,*" I plead, my hands feeling around my bed in hopes of finding my phone.

"Looking for this?" Riley smiles, wiggling my phone in her hands.

She's already dressed for the day in a pair of form-fitting dress pants and a sleeveless blouse. I, on the other hand, am pretty sure my old dance company T-shirt has a wet spot from my own drool.

Snagging my phone from her hand, my stomach drops when I see the time. "Shit! I'm supposed to be at rehearsals in less than an hour."

I dart across my small bedroom and pull open a dresser drawer to find a pair of leggings. My hands are digging around in the drawer when she starts talking again.

"Well, I figured. Hence why *I* could be late to my job because I took the time to wake your lazy ass up." Riley smiles again, crossing her arms over her chest.

"Shut up," I mumble as I strip out of my sleep shorts before pulling on my favorite pair of leggings. "This is all your fault to begin with. I'm *never* late. But somehow you convinced me to go out last night when I was *this close*," I hold up my fingers, a small amount of space between my thumb and index finger, "to going to bed at nine."

Riley makes her way out of my bedroom, yelling at me as she makes her way into the hallway. "Please, Nora. No one our age should be going to bed at nine. Plus, you didn't seem to mind the late night when you ordered that glass of wine."

I'm too busy pulling on a sports bra supportive enough to withstand rehearsals to respond to her.

The truth is, I was trying to ease my nerves of this being the first tour rehearsal where Nash would be there. That glass of wine sounded like a great way to take my mind off seeing him again. Now I'm full of regrets as I fight this killer headache.

I somehow manage to wash my face and get my hair brushed in record time. I'm vigorously brushing my teeth when a text from Ziggy pops up on my phone.

Ziggy: Stopping to get coffee. Late night. ;) Want any?

The toothbrush rests against my cheek as my fingers glide over my screen.

Nora: You're my hero! My usual, please. In the biggest size they offer.

Ziggy: All that sugar is going to kill you one day.

Ignoring him, I spit out the minty taste and wipe my

mouth with the back of my hand. I don't have any extra time to put makeup on, so the only thing on my face is my tinted moisturizer.

After flipping off the light to my bathroom, I grab my dance bag off the chair in the corner of my room. I fill up my water bottle quickly and am out the door shortly after.

Lucky for me, karma is in fact on my side today. Somehow there's little to no traffic on my way to the studio, and I'm pushing the doors open to the building with five minutes to spare.

I find Ziggy stretching in a corner of the room, two coffees sitting next to his bag.

"Nice of you to join us," he teases.

Setting my bag down on the opposite side of the coffees, I fall to the floor next to him and take a deep breath in. I'm just happy that *somehow*, I made it before Nash *or* Monica showed up to rehearsals.

Today might not be as shitty as I thought it'd be when I woke up late this morning. But I'm still fighting a mild hangover. "I need coffee."

Without even giving him more of a response, I grab what I know is my iced coffee by how much lighter it is in color. I suck a third of the large drink down, letting the caffeine run through my body.

"Damn. Was it a late night for you, too?" he asks.

I groan, setting the coffee down and starting my own stretching. "Yes. Riley coerced me into going out. I almost overslept."

Ziggy *tsks*. "That would not be a great first impression for Nash. Especially since you're almost always early." He holds out his hands, waiting for me to place my hands in his.

Spreading my legs to match my feet with his, he begins to lean back, pulling me forward with the motion. I can feel the stretch in my thighs and lower back. He pulls harder, straining my muscles even more.

I don't bother to tell Ziggy I've kind of already had a first impression with Nash. It's not like much came from that small conversation we had. And he's right, I would have died in a pit of embarrassment if I was late to this rehearsal.

I also would've been terrified to face Monica's wrath over it.

"Yeah, well, it's the last time I let Riley talk me into going out for a while. I don't know what I'll do if the coffee doesn't make this headache go away."

Ziggy sits up, and we switch positions. My shoulder blades are nearing the floor when Nash, Monica, and someone I don't know walk through the door.

Nash's eyes pass over us briefly before Derrick jogs across the dance floor and exchanges words with the three of them.

The other dancers and I continue to stretch and warm up, waiting for Derrick or Lizzie to give us a cue on where they want us.

Finally, we're called up to start with *Here For a Good Time*. We each take our place as Lizzie walks Nash through on where he'll begin.

I'm staring at his back, taking in the pair of athletic shorts he has on as well as the sleeveless T-shirt. Even from behind, I can see the definition of the muscles in his shoulders. With his arms pulled in front of him, I can't see all of them, but I know from previous inspection that his arms are just as chiseled as the rest of him.

We manage to run through the number a handful of times pretty smoothly. I have to give Nash credit, for how much he seems to hate dancing, he catches on quickly. And, he's good at it.

During our latest run through, he only had a few errors. And those were pretty minor. For the most part, he's caught on. Which, to be honest, surprises me. I guess he still has some of his boyband-past left in him, because he can dance—and he can dance *well*.

We spend the better half of our day practicing *Here For a Good Time* until it's run from top to bottom almost flawlessly. Derrick lets us out two hours earlier than normal, telling us he's giving us a Friday reward. I think it's because we've impressed him and managed to nail the opening number, with Nash included this time, and that was his only real goal for the day.

Ziggy and a few other dancers and I are discussing our weekend plans when I accidentally bump into Nash. I swear he wasn't in my direct path the last time I looked, but somehow he's ended up here.

Judging by the scowl on his face, he isn't pleased with the small mishap. "Sorry." I smile up at him while the rest of the group continues walking to their bags. "I must've been distracted." Going to side-step him, I'm shocked when he moves to block my path.

His eyes make contact with mine for a split second before he looks over my shoulder. Leaning in closer, his mouth lines up with my ear as he says, "Pay more attention next time."

And then he struts over to the choreographers like he doesn't have a care in the world.

Asshole.

I'm on the ground, rifling through my backpack for my car keys, when a pair of sneakers lands next to my knee.

"Hey, Nora," Derrick says, giving me a wide smile. "Can I grab you for a minute?"

I nod, nervous he's about to tell me I did something wrong today.

My backpack makes a *thump* against the hardwood as I give up on my search for my keys. It turns out I don't need them quite yet anyway.

"Sweet, over here." He hooks a thumb over his shoulder and all I do is silently follow behind him. There's a sinking in my stomach as we near the corner where Nash, Lizzie, Monica, and the guy from earlier whose name I'm unsure of talk quietly.

Derrick gently grabs me by the elbow, ushering me into the small circle of people.

“Nora, meet part of Nash’s team. There’s Nash, Monica, his manager, you obviously know Lizzie, and then Tyson, Nash’s publicist.”

“Hi, nice to meet you.” I hope my words come out more confident than I feel. Pushing the hair out of my face, I look at Derrick questioningly.

“You might be wondering why you’re over here,” Derrick begins. “To begin with, I just have to say, you’re *killing* it at rehearsals. I mean damn, Nora. You’ve got so much talent.”

Oh thank god. My racing heart is a clear indicator that I thought I was about to get kicked off the tour, the proposition from Monica and Nash’s team all but forgotten.

“Thank you.” I smile up at him, trying to ease the dread that was forming in my stomach.

“She’s just doing her job,” Nash murmurs, scrolling through his phone like this is the last place he wants to be.

Derrick’s eyes narrow at Nash momentarily before he regains his composure and looks back at me. “Okay, *anyway*, I’ll get to the point. Lizzie and I have been going through the whole setlist and what we envision for the choreography for each song. As you know, we’ve told you there are a few songs you won’t be dancing to. But there is one you aren’t on that, after further team discussions, we think would work best if you were.”

Nash laughs, shoving his phone in his pocket angrily. “What team? I know nothing about this.” He looks over at Monica, clearly waiting for an explanation.

She looks him dead in the eye. “We’ve talked about this. You haven’t *wanted* to be in on any of the tour prep. Every single meeting we’ve had that has to do with your tour has been on your calendar. This is just another thing you didn’t want to be involved in, so we handled it for you.”

A line forms on his forehead in displeasure.

“We’re wanting Nora to dance with you on *Preach*.”

Derrick's words come out bluntly.

I rack my brain to think of what song that is, but it must be from his new album because I'm not familiar with it.

I nervously shuffle my feet, fully aware we're the only people in the studio at this point. "Okay, yeah for sure I'll do it." I try to throw the words out to help ease the tension, but it's no use; Nash is glaring at Derrick as if he just told him his dog died.

"*Preach* is a slow song. One of my slowest. It's just me and a guitar up there," he says through a clenched jaw.

"Oh, well, I don't have to..." I *thought* my words would satisfy Nash, but all this does is earn me a dirty look from him.

Dude, maybe the tabloids are right. He seems like a complete dick.

"You will start the song on your guitar. But you will perform a majority of it with a headset on while dancing with Nora. We want to try new things with this tour. We think your fans will eat up seeing you do a slower dance with Nora. Plus, from her auditions, that is Nora's specialty. She should be able to bring the song back to life beautifully," Lizzie offers. Her tone is soft, her eyes cautiously watching Nash.

"We've got some great ideas for the direction of it, man," Derrick interjects.

I look down at my leggings to see if there's a piece of lint or hair or *something* to distract me from how uncomfortable I am right now.

It turns out Monica has a few tricks up her sleeve to force me and Nash together, this one being performing a song with just the two of us.

"I finally relented on letting dancers on this tour when it isn't something I've done since I was in a damn boyband. She's not dancing with me to *Preach*. Not happening." There's a bite to his words that none of us miss. It's obvious this is something he's serious about.

Monica sighs, looking up at the ceiling in frustration.

"Give it a chance, Nash. If you hate it in a few weeks, then we'll talk. But try it our way."

"What if I don't want to?" His brown hair flops over his forehead as he turns his body in her direction. He raises his eyebrows in what seems like defiance as he waits for an answer.

"For fuck's sake, Nash, could you not be difficult for one part of this tour? We're trying to give *your* fans the experience of a lifetime. You should join us." Monica's phone pings from her purse, but for once I don't see her go to answer it instantly. Instead, she stays locked in a silent stare-off with Nash.

After what seems like forever, his shoulders lower. "Fine. But I'm holding you to the fact that if I hate it," he looks at me with a taunting grin, "which is likely, then we don't do it. Deal?"

Monica gives a nod of her head. "Deal. The two of you can stay back with Derrick so he can walk through his ideas." She breezes out of the room after that, Lizzie and Tyson hot on her heels.

It leaves Nash, Derrick, and me alone in here. It doesn't take a rocket scientist to distinguish that this is probably the last place on earth Nash wants to be, but to his credit, his feet stay planted.

"Okay, so here's what I'm thinking," Derrick begins, while Nash and I both listen carefully—whether we want to or not.

9
NASH

Fuck. This. Shit.

Derrick might as well be talking to a brick wall right now, because I'm not listening to a thing he's saying. I'm too busy wallowing in my anger. This is yet *another* part of my tour I have zero control of.

Most of my slower songs are songs I poured my fucking soul into. They're meant to be performed with just *me* on the stage. It's supposed to be me, the fans, and the lyrics I've threaded myself into.

Now *she's* ruined it.

And what's worse is she doesn't even realize it. She laps up every single word Derrick says like a damn dog. It's borderline pathetic.

I'm not sure how he plans on making this song better—his words, not mine—but I'm betting that, come two weeks from now, she'll have wasted all her time learning the choreography to this song.

Because while I've accepted that I'll have dancers on my tour, what I'm *not* accepting is dancing to songs that were written as a way for me to connect with my audience.

Fat fucking chance.

"Ready to start?" Derrick asks, giving Nora a look that doesn't sit well with me for whatever reason.

She gives him an enthusiastic nod, reaching over her head to stretch. Derrick averts his gaze as her perky tits jut out. Nora hasn't bothered to hide much of her body in the outfit she chose to wear today. It's the first thing I noticed when I walked into the studio today. Those athletic leggings of hers hug every curve and muscle of her legs. Forgoing wearing a shirt, she's been dancing around in a sports bra all day that's left little to the imagination.

I hate that my eyes were always on her, even in the moments she spent talking to someone other than me.

I've been wanting my attention anywhere but on her, but there's something about the way she moves that makes it hard to look away.

Derrick was right when he pointed out how talented she was. I have no idea if she's been on tour with another artist before or what her dancing resume even looks like, but it's hard to miss her talent.

No matter how talented she is, though, I still don't want to do a dance with just me and her. And I plan on letting Monica know it.

Yeah, that'll be a no for me, sir.

Yet here I am, following Derrick into the center of the studio to get this shit show on the road.

For now, I'll be a semi-good listener because I respect Derrick, but that doesn't mean I have to enjoy it.

"This is what I envision..." Derrick begins, looking over at me. "Nash, you'll be standing at the end of the catwalk, *with your guitar*," the prick emphasizes, calling me out from my previous outburst of wanting it to just be me and my guitar for this song.

"For the beginning of the song," he continues, "Nora will be behind you, her back against yours." He points to the spot where he wants me to stand. As soon as I take my place, he grabs Nora by her shoulders, gently moving her until we are back-to-back.

Her narrow shoulders fall against my back, and I can tell the exact moment she takes a long breath in. The two of us angle our heads toward Derrick, waiting for his next instruction.

"Perfect." He takes a step back, tilting his head. "I'm going to go get the song playing and walk you through what I imagine for the beginning of the song as it plays."

His shoes squeak against the polished hardwood as he crosses the space to the speakers. While we wait for him to find the song, the song I'm dreading listening to on repeat, I step away from Nora. I don't see any reason why we need to continue standing against each other while we aren't practicing.

Pulling my phone from my shorts, I scroll through the infinite number of texts I've received in a short time. Most are other celebrities wondering what's going on tonight. It's no secret that wherever I go at night, the party comes with me. I don't respond to any of them, not knowing what the hell I want to do with my night.

The quiet space is soon filled with the chords I've written. The strumming of my guitar, beginning the song. Before Derrick can turn around and find me as an unwilling participant, I step back until Nora and I are touching from shoulder to calf.

"Nash, you'll have your guitar for this part," Derrick says, stepping back toward us.

"You've said that," I breathe out, tired of him throwing my words at me from earlier.

"And during that part, Nora, you'll begin by standing still against him. As soon as..." he waits a few seconds, "*this* beat picks up, you'll quickly turn around, hugging his back."

Derrick pulls a remote from his pocket, then pauses the song. He stares at Nora for a moment until she realizes he wants her to follow his instructions.

She's silent as I briefly lose the warmth of her body. Just as quickly as I lose it, it returns. Nora is rigid against me; clearly unsure what Derrick wants her to do next. Her temple presses into the space between my shoulder blades as she looks to Derrick for more direction.

Derrick steps forward, standing directly in front of me. He reaches around me, grabbing each one of her arms and pulling them underneath my own, placing them on my chest.

"Your hands will start here," he instructs.

Her hands are warm through the thin fabric of my shirt. He spreads her fingers until one hand is splayed out over my right pec, right over my tattoo of a baby grand piano. The other hand falls low on my abdomen. My muscles tighten involuntarily beneath her touch.

Still holding her wrists, he drags each one of her hands over my body.

"What the fuck," I mumble, feeling like I'm part of some weird threesome I didn't sign up for.

"Your hands will be all over him. Remember he'll have a guitar, so you'll have to go underneath his arms and make sure you don't get in the way of him playing."

"Yeah, because I'm *so* used to being groped while performing," I add, holding my arms in the odd position.

I *wish* I had my guitar in this moment. At least it would give me something to do with my hands. Right now, they're just hanging in the air awkwardly.

"We'll get a guitar in here so we can ensure it doesn't distract him." Derrick glares at me, taking a step back.

I laugh, unaffected by the scowl on his face. "I'm used to getting mauled by fans daily, her touch is no different. It sure as hell won't distract me."

Her hands tighten on my shirt, a quick reaction to my words. "Well, that's not what you said a second ago, *asshole*."

Her little nickname for me is said under her breath, but I still don't miss it. My lips twitch in a smile at her outburst.

It appears the sweet girl I met in that small office has some claws.

Maybe this will be fun.

"I was just pointing out how I don't want you feeling me up to mess me up while I'm, ya know, still playing guitar," I respond lazily under my breath.

"And I'm just pointing out that I'd rather *not* be feeling you up." An aggravated sigh warms my back, her breath hot.

Chuckling, I look over my shoulder and make eye contact with her. "Keep telling yourself that, Rose."

"Not my name," she chides, looking to Derrick as if he has any power of turning my asshole tendencies off.

"Could we continue here?" I ask, looking down at where her hands still rest on my body. "I'd like to get this over with so I can go meet up with a girl whose hands I actually want on me."

And it turns out there's more spunk behind all her ass kissing, because she pinches me ever so slightly.

Derrick shakes his head, clearly not prepared for the two of us to be so difficult. "Sooo..." he says awkwardly, stepping closer to us once again. He pushes play on the music, talking loudly over it when he says, "Your hands will roam over him until the words begin."

As if on cue, my voice surrounds us.

Derrick continues with, "As soon as the words start, you'll step out to the left."

Nora does just as he instructs, her body now only pressed against one side of my body.

We spend the next hour going over the beginning of the song. Until the chorus hits, she's going to just basically crawl all over me in front of thirty-thousand people. *Great.* I don't know how that's supposed to entertain my fans more than if it was just me up there, but whatever. I'm attempting to be a good sport.

At least for two weeks, that is.

Derrick keeps emphasizing how sexy and sultry the song is, as if I didn't fucking write it myself.

And apparently, because it is *so sultry*, he wants the sexual tension between us to be *palpable*. Again, not my words.

We're now at the part where the chorus begins, and Derrick tells us this is the point where Nora will take it from me and do some fancy dance things to hand it to a crew member.

Then the real fun begins, because now I'm supposed to fucking slow dance with her, or as they refer to it, *perform a contemporary number*, all while I'm still singing.

I repeat: Fuck. This. Shit.

10
NORA

“Stop it right now! You did not pinch *Nash Pierce*.” Riley laughs, dipping her chip in the salsa and taking a bite.

I lean back in the booth, shaking my head. “Stop saying his first and last name, it’s weird. And he was being an asshole! Looking back, I probably shouldn’t have but—”

“But what?” Ziggy asks curiously, leaning forward on his elbows.

“But he was being an ass! I was just doing what Derrick told me to do.” Shrugging, I take my own chip and glob some salsa on it.

It’s been almost two weeks of nonstop rehearsals, my days running even longer as Nash and I practice *Preach* each night with Derrick.

I wish I could say Nash has been nicer since we’ve become *well* acquainted with each other—our hands have touched almost every location on each other’s body—but he hasn’t. He’s been as peachy as ever lately, but I don’t let him deter me. Deep down, I think he's a lot less of an asshole than he pretends to be.

"He's not really an ass to anyone else on the team. It's weird he's that way with you," Ziggy points out. "Don't get me wrong, he's not the warm and fuzzy kind of guy, but he's civil with all of us. He actually told me he liked my sneakers the other day."

Riley looks at me, and I pray she doesn't spill the beans to Ziggy about why I'm really on Nash's tour. That secret is staying between me and her. And I guess Monica. But his coldness to me does throw a wrench in the whole get-close-to-him plan.

Ziggy talks through a mouthful of chips as our waitress refills our waters. "Did you know the other day I saw him give all the cash from his wallet to a woman who was sitting outside our studio?"

Riley gasps and leans in closer, and it's painfully obvious she's hanging on Ziggy's every word.

I stay in place, mumbling a "*thank you*" to the waitress as she refills my water and walks away.

"Yep! He snuck out the back entrance of the studio, not wanting to be noticed by anyone. I was outside on the phone with my mom. She was rambling on about how she wants me to get home. Anyway, there was a woman sitting on the corner with her dog. She was holding some kind of sign, but I couldn't read it. Nash talked to her for a few minutes before he pulled his wallet out and thumbed through all the cash he had stored in there."

Riley shoves me playfully. "Did you hear that, Nora? What a gentleman he is!"

Ziggy enthusiastically nods. "He really was. There's even more! The woman wrapped her arms around him and pulled him in for a hug. I couldn't see her face, but I could see his. And he didn't look disgusted, put off, or anything by this stranger who probably could've used a bath. Not even when she hugged him. He held her for as long as she wanted. It was dreamy."

Our waitress walks back toward us, a large tray in her

hand. She props it on her hip as she hands each one of us our entrees.

I can instantly smell the cheesy goodness of my enchiladas, my stomach grumbling in excitement. I take a long whiff, ready to get down on some Mexican food.

Riley and I have been coming to this restaurant for as long as we've lived in California. We found it randomly and have since refused to get our queso fix anywhere else. I finally invited Ziggy with us last week, and he and Riley were instant best friends.

I savor the way the gooey cheese melts in my mouth as Ziggy continues to talk. *Have I ever mentioned he talks a lot?*

"Oh, and get this," he says, pausing to take a bite of his taco, while cheese falls out the back of it. "When I came out of the studio twenty minutes later, I saw one of Nash's beefy bodyguards handing the same woman a large bag of dog food and some grocery bags."

My eyebrows lift in surprise. With the way Nash has been acting toward me, I wouldn't have pegged him as the silent charity type. Maybe I was right and there are more layers to him than meets the eye. And maybe for some reason, it makes him feel better to act like an utter dick to me instead of just admitting that maybe he's not a complete douche.

"Oh my god, he's a saint," Riley swoons. She's so busy getting mushy over Nash that her forkful of rice almost misses her mouth.

I can't help but laugh, because no matter how kind Nash's gesture was, I still wouldn't call him *a saint*.

I'll let her and Ziggy continue to put Nash on a pedestal though, too engrossed in my meal to point out his constant attitude.

Luckily, the two of them fall into a different conversation, completely unrelated to Nash. I chime in every now and then, but for the most part I'm too busy shoving food in my face as fast as possible to add anything in.

"We should go out dancing tonight!" Riley says excitedly, pushing her empty plate away from her.

Completely stuffed, I mimic her. I pull my phone out of my purse, checking for the time. "Can't," I begin. "I have to be at rehearsals in two hours for the solo. Monica wants to see it tomorrow, and Nash has to decide if it's a dance he wants to keep or not. He wants to do one last rehearsal, just the two of us."

Winking at me, Riley takes a drink from her straw. "Just the two of you, hm?"

I give her the dirtiest look possible, trying to remind her with my eyes that Ziggy is sitting right next to me.

"You know, you're living every teenage girl's dream by being alone with him," Ziggy muses, clearly unaware of the daggers I'm aiming at Riley.

"Yeah, well, there's nothing more romantic than running the same routine over and over with an unwilling participant." Grabbing my check from the waitress, I slide my card in and set it on the table.

"He's not that bad." Ziggy laughs, then moves onto a new topic with Riley.

I ignore him, clearly fighting a losing battle here.

An hour and a half later, I arrive to the studio early.

The more time that ticked by, the more nervous I got at the idea of being alone with Nash. So far, all our rehearsals have included Derrick. This time, it'll just be me and Nash—and my looming task at hand is sitting at the forefront of my mind.

The more time I spend with Nash, the more time I find to see that the whole reason I'm on this tour is a lost cause. For some reason my mere existence pisses him off. He's all jagged edges and snide remarks when talking to me. Yet he'll turn around and give that playboy smile to the person next to me.

There's absolutely no way Nash Pierce will fall for me.

At this point, I'm just trying to get him to *tolerate* me. Flicking on the lights of the studio, I strip out of my jacket. I place it next to my dance bag and water bottle. The cold air hits my bare skin, the crop top I'm wearing not fighting off the air conditioning effectively.

I slide each one of my sandals off, opting to warm up completely barefoot. I make the mental note to find a way to get in some ballet practice in my spare time soon. I miss the bite of the ballet slipper on my foot, the pressure of being perfect and meticulous with each turn of my body.

Walking over to the stereo system, I select my dance playlist and begin stretching. Once I feel like my body is loose, I stride to the middle of the dance floor and begin to freestyle. It feels amazing to just let my body lead me in my movements. I've been practicing the same routines over and over for weeks now, forgetting what it's like to get completely lost in the music.

My mind goes numb as my body takes over. For the first time in what seems like forever, my mind is still. I close my eyes, relishing in the freedom I feel.

Three songs go by before I finally open my eyes.

When I open them, I immediately stop, my eyes connecting with Nash's. He leans against the barre on the far side of the room. His tattooed arms are crossed over his ripped T-shirt, his eyes staring intently at me.

I'm stuck in place. My feet refuse to do their job and move. And my eyes...my eyes can't look away from him.

For the first time since we met, he isn't looking at me with indifference. There's no hint of coldness in his gaze.

This time he's watching me carefully, burning a hole right through me. It's intense and sends my stomach into a spiral.

I couldn't tell you how long the two of us stare at each other. What I can say is that it feels like forever. It feels like his eyes are telling me a million different things, but at the same time it's like he's giving away nothing.

"You're early," I finally breathe out, my steps slowly

bringing me closer to him.

He nods, raking his eyes down my body before putting his own bag down. “I could say the same thing to you.”

He stands right next to my bag, a smirk on his face. *What the fuck, he’s smiling?*

“Yeah, well, I wanted to warm up.” I take a drink from my water bottle, my throat suddenly dry with Nash so close.

“I saw that,” he notes, looking at me with an inquisitive look. The music still blares around us, the bass rattling the floor beneath our feet.

“Why are you early?” The second the words leave my mouth, I realize that for how long I’ve been dancing, he isn’t *that* early. I open my mouth to say just that, but he speaks first.

“Well, it was either come to this early or get drunk early. For some reason I chose this.”

I nervously laugh, craning my head to look up at him. “Yeah, that would’ve made things a little complicated.”

He quirks an eyebrow at me, causing me to quickly elaborate.

“If you were drunk for rehearsals, I mean. You might’ve forgotten the steps.”

Nash shakes his head at me, taking a step closer to me. “Oh, Rose,” he says, and I try to ignore the way my heart reacts to the nickname as if I don’t hate it.

“You have no idea how many shows I’ve done drunk,” he confesses. “In fact, some of my best performances were when I was toasted.”

He quietly observes my reaction, his eyes tracing my face. All I can do is nod, thinking back to every article I’ve read on him. There’s not a lot I’ve read, but I don’t remember any of them mentioning him being drunk. Not that it should matter to me.

“Why do you think they were your best?” I ask.

He gives me a sad smile. “People like me better when I’m drunk. I’m not as *bitter*.” He says the last word sarcastically, mischief in his eyes.

I'm about to argue, but he quickly takes a step away from me and heads toward the middle of the studio. "Let's practice," he says.

And just like that, he's got his walls back up. I can tell there's nothing else I'm going to get out of him, so I don't even try. I go to the speakers and choose *Preach* from my phone. I grab the remote and walk across the dance floor to hand it over to Nash.

It's silent as I take my spot behind him. Without any more words, he presses play on the music. On cue, I turn around, running my hands over his body. The T-shirt he's got on is thin and has holes in random places. Occasionally, I feel the warmth of his skin against mine. I ignore it, continuing the routine.

I pretend to take the guitar from him, handing it off to a pretend person. When the beat picks up, the chorus ringing through the speakers, I move around in front of him. His hands find my waist, his fingers creeping underneath the fabric of my cotton crop top.

My hands reach behind me, sliding down the backs of his legs as I fall to the floor. Slowly coming back up, I blindly reach out, his hand finding my own.

As soon as I stand all the way up, he spins me away from him. I continue to lean away from his outstretched hand, extending one of my legs into the air. Then it's time for him to spin me into his embrace once again.

My head rests against his chest in the same way we've rehearsed many times, except in the moment when he's supposed to grab my neck and dip my body in front of him, he doesn't.

The music stops abruptly. Nash shoves me away from him in the next instant. "You're off," he grumbles, shoving his hair out of his face.

"What are you talking about?" I ask confused, knowing I wasn't off.

"Start over." He leaves no room for me to argue. The music is restarted, and I have no choice but to take my spot behind him once again.

We *attempt* to run through it five more times before my patience wears thin with him.

"I'm not messing it up!" I demand, pulling my ass off the floor from where he just dropped me—on purpose.

"Yes, you are," he barks, not bothering to help me up.

I let out an annoyed laugh, dusting off my bottom. "No, Nash. Hate to break it to you, but it's *you* that's off."

The asshole rolls his eyes at me, penetrating me with a condescending stare. "I should've known this wouldn't work. I said I'd give it a shot, but you can't even get all the way through without making some kind of mistake."

My eyes widen, completely in shock he's blaming this on me. I start to back up, throwing my hands in the air. "You know what, you're right. This isn't working." I turn around, giving him my back.

I quickly walk over to my bag and grab it, not even putting on my jacket before heading toward the door. At this point I'm just hoping I stuck my feet in the right sandal, but I don't take the time to double check.

"Where in the hell do you think you're going?" he yells behind me.

"You said it yourself, this isn't working. I'm tired of being blamed for mistakes I'm not fucking making. I'm leaving. Tell Monica you tried but it didn't work!" As I say this, I don't look back at him over my shoulder. I'm too upset by his constant nagging. He's managed to make me feel like complete shit in the mere thirty minutes we've been practicing.

"You can't just leave," he says, this time a little closer to me.

I spin around in the doorway, enunciating my words and looking him dead in the eye when I say, "Watch me."

I'm halfway out the door when his hand finds my waist. "Nora, hold on a second."

11
NASH

I should just let her walk out the door.

It shouldn't bother me that she's storming out as if I've hurt her feelings or as if she's pissed—probably both.

Yet here I am, quickly closing the distance between us until I meet her in the doorway.

My fingertips find the warmth of her stomach. "Nora, hold on a second."

Her stomach muscles clench under my touch. To my surprise, she turns around, angling an aggravated gaze toward me. "What is it, Nash?"

There's a small wrinkle between her eyebrows as she stares up, waiting for me to elaborate. When I don't answer her right away, that wrinkle smooths as she lifts her eyebrows impatiently.

"You can't just leave," I finally repeat, inhaling and getting hit in the face with the scent of *her*. It smells just like roses *should*. Not that fake overpowering floral scent some women wear, but subtle enough to slowly yet madly take over my senses.

She looks at me, annoyed. “Why do you care? You’ve made it abundantly clear you don’t want this dance to be part of the tour lineup. Here’s your chance, Nash. Take it.”

She isn’t wrong. Two weeks ago, I hated the idea of doing this dance, but I can’t deny that the work we’ve put into it has paid off. What we’ve created...it works, and it works well. I have no doubt my fans will love it. I just hate that it feels so intimate to share this dance with her.

I bare my soul—the naked truth of myself—to my fans when I get on stage and sing my own lyrics. And now, sharing the stage with her and only her in a dance that drips of sex...well, it’s fucking with my head.

I hate the feeling of not being in control of my head.

I’ve been there before. I fell so deeply and passionately in love with a woman that only used my love for her against me. I have no desire to ever do it again. Sex at this point doesn’t even feel intimate to me. It’s a means to an end. Dancing with Nora feels intimate, though. It feels so much more intimate than when I’m inside of a girl. And that has all my alarms ringing.

“Are you going to answer me?” I can tell by her tone that she’s growing more irritated with me by the second. The problem is, I don’t want to answer her question truthfully.

My grip tightens, making me realize my hand is still placed on her waist. I pull it back, shocked I was even touching her for that long. I typically hate touching or being touched by people—a side effect of being groped by fans every time I come in contact with them.

I barely let women touch me when they get me off, only letting them touch what is needed. But after two weeks of having Nora touch me, and my hands roaming over her body repeatedly, it hasn’t bothered me in the slightest.

Even if I’ve made it seem as if I’ve hated it. It’s all been an act.

“Yeah, well, maybe the dance doesn’t suck as much as

I thought it would." I scratch my head, watching as her attention focuses on my bicep.

She pops a hip out, looking at me with an amused look. "Are you saying what I think you're saying?"

Nervously looking around the room, I avoid her question for a moment. "I'm saying I'm technically your boss and thinking about what's best for my tour, and this dance might be it."

Taking a step closer to me, she looks up at me confidently. "Ask me nicely, *boss*."

I try not to roll my eyes at the way she easily throws my words right back at me. She's one of the only people who has the balls to do so. Typically, everyone but the people closest to me fall at my feet, acting as if every word I utter is gold.

Tracing along her naked shoulder, I think my words through carefully. I lean in closer to her, my lips just millimeters from the shell of her ear. When I look down, I'm almost positive I can see her thumping pulse beneath her fair skin.

"A little tip for you, Nora. I don't *ask* for anything, and I sure as hell won't ask for it nicely."

She sucks in a breath, her collarbones jutting out with the movement. I revel in the fact that my words can cause that kind of a reaction from her.

Stepping away from her before I do something I regret, I make my way to the middle of the dance floor once again.

I spin the remote in my hands, watching her gather her thoughts. "Now, come back over here and let's practice this dance that screams sex but isn't near as fun as fucking."

Nora sets her bag back on the dance floor, slipping off her sandals once again. "We're just dancing, they'll see that."

I chuckle, running a hand through my hair. "Keep telling yourself that."

Not humoring me with a response, she makes her way

to where I stand. Without a second glance, she takes her spot behind me.

I can her feel her shoulders against the middle of my back, and I allow us a split second of silence before pressing play.

We make it to the end of the routine easily, making it to the most complicated part we only learned a week ago. The very end of the song has more technique than I'm used to, something I'll have to adjust to while also making sure I'm singing.

She launches her body at me, wrapping her legs around my middle. From there, her body falls backward. I can feel the strength in her legs as she holds onto me tightly, unable to depend on me holding her there as my hands skirt down her middle.

Her palms meet the wood and she lets go with her legs, effortlessly rolling onto the floor. I reach out and grab her hand, pulling fast enough that between my effort and her jumping she soars into the air.

Catching her by the waist, I lift her above my head. The last words of the song are being sung as I lower her, her body dragging against mine.

The music stops briefly before it picks back up once again, the song being left on repeat. Except this time, neither of us move to do it again. We're lost in a fleeting moment, almost every inch of our bodies touching.

My fingertips are still resting against her ribcage. I can feel every inhale and exhale she takes. Her hazel eyes stare up at me, the fluorescent lighting not doing the unique color of them any justice.

"How was that?" she asks, her hands tightening on my biceps.

"Can't say I hated it," I answer, slightly out of breath. I'm shocked by how straining this has been. I have a personal trainer, Zach, who travels on tour with me. He makes sure I'm hitting the gym five times a week, even if most of the time it means I'm hungover and pissed. But somehow, this dance is still kicking my ass.

She laughs, noticing we're still touching in the next moment and stepping away. Lifting the bottom of her shirt, the shirt that isn't even long enough to cover all of her toned stomach, she wipes at her face. "After your attitude a couple of weeks ago, I can honestly say I never thought I'd hear you say that."

I shrug. "Yeah, well, I'm allowed to change my mind. Things change."

Nodding, she gives me a taunting smile. "Oh, yeah? What changed?"

You.

"I like making money. And what we're doing with this dance," I cock my head toward the rest of the dance floor, "that'll sell."

"Am I going to have thousands of screaming girls jealous of me during those three minutes?" she asks, expertly securing her long hair into a bun at the top of her head.

"No. They'll be jealous of you for three minutes and forty-six seconds. You ready for that?" I ask, reminding her right down to the second.

In truth, I wish more people would've prepared me for fame. For what extreme fame entails. I can't go pick up my coffee order without cameras snapping in my face. Or without complete strangers asking me extremely personal questions.

Nora shrugs haphazardly. "Obviously. I'm just doing my job, after all. There's nothing going on for them to be jealous about."

You have my attention, I want to say. *That's something not many people get, and millions would be jealous of.*

I make sure I have her attention before I speak. "If I look at a model I'm shooting with for more than two seconds, the Internet goes crazy, wondering if she's my secret girlfriend or hookup. Those women get blasted by the media. Rabid fans come out of the woodwork and point out every single flaw of these models who are just doing their job. Be prepared, Nora. We may just be working, but once people get a glimpse of what we're doing, you'll be next."

The truth sucks, and more often than not, the women I hook up with *want* the spotlight. They seek me out to be the girl on my arm for a night. I let it happen. It's better having the media think I'm a playboy than being in the position I was in years ago after my breakup with my ex.

I'd much rather them think I'm a heartbreaker than the one with the broken heart.

I have to hand it to her; she doesn't look nervous from my words. All she does is glance up at the ceiling briefly before clapping her hands together. "Let's run it again."

So, we do. We do it over and over until I'm confident I could do it in my sleep.

The two of us eventually fall to the floor in exhaustion, our bodies landing next to our things. It's silent except for the both of us gulping down our waters now that we've sat up. My shirt disappeared five tries ago and the cold wall against my back is doing wonders in helping to bring my body temperature down.

Nora tosses her empty water bottle on top of her bag, her head falling back and resting against the wall. "I think we nailed it," she gets out between heavy breaths.

I nod, finishing off my own water. Wiping my lips, I look over at her. "I'll tell Monica the dance stays."

Nora's eyes light up, her teeth peeking out with a wide smile. "I don't know her that well, but something tells me she's going to be shocked by your decision."

My head falls a few feet away from hers, a smile on my face. "I'm sometimes hard-headed with her. She'll probably be shocked and ask me if I have any ulterior motives."

She pushes my shoulder teasingly. "*Sometimes?* I'd put money on all the time."

Running a hand over my mouth to cover my smile, I shrug. "I'm a moody popstar. Comes with the territory."

Nora pulls her legs in closer to her, resting her

forearms on her knees and angling her body toward mine. Even after running the song through many times, she still smells amazing, that scent of hers hitting my senses with each of her shifting movements.

"You know, you don't have to always pretend to be an asshole. People might like you more if you didn't pretend to be such a dick," she says.

Her eyes roam over my face as she waits for my response. My brain sifts through the different answers I could give. Some of them sugar-coated, some of them fucking depressing.

"In this world, people form opinions on you no matter what you do. I could be the fucking pope and they'd still fault me for something. It's easier to just not give a shit."

"Do you, though? Not give a shit?"

I look away from her, staring instead across the empty floor in front of us. The small window at the top of one of the walls show that we've been here long enough for the sun to fully set. The fluorescent lights create a reflection against the polished hardwood.

"After so long, it's hard *to* care. Some days you care too much and the need to please every person who supports you is suffocating. So suffocating that I feel like every expectation of me is pushing into my windpipe, cutting off any hope of me getting air. And then other days you realize the expectations of you are smothering you, and your only option is to not give a shit. I often try to opt for the latter."

She's quiet as she mulls over my words. "How do you deal with that?"

Usually when people ask me how I handle the fame, I pose the question to them: how would *you* handle it? That typically gets the interviewer, radio host, whoever, to pause. I then ask: how *should* I be handling it?

They always skirt around both questions, which is ironic. They can throw the most personal questions my way, even when my team puts them on the no-ask list beforehand, but not answer one of mine. It's a question I hate being asked. It feels invasive and redundant. They can pick up any magazine and see how I handle it, or how I want people to see me handling it.

"Easy," I answer, looking at her once again, finding her eyes already on me. "I get drunk. I have sex. I've done drugs. I go numb, I take my mind off it. Numbing out the expectations, the pressure, everything...it's how I cope."

My eyes trace the splatter of freckles on the tops of her cheeks. The way her nose upturns, the blush on her face. "It's worked for me so far."

My fingers twitch in my lap, wanting to reach out and place a stray hair behind her ear. I want to have some kind of contact with her again. My hands were all over her body during the hours we were practicing. Now it feels odd not to be touching her.

I want to do all these things, but there needs to be a line drawn between us. I might not have to be as big of a dick to her as I have been, but I also don't want to let her in. She can't see the shell of a man behind the Nash Pierce persona. No one should.

My phone starts vibrating next to me, the sound ricocheting off the walls. The text message reminds me I have plans tonight—plans that were completely forgotten until now.

"Well, I've got to get going. Places to be." I stand up, stretching my arms over my head before pulling my shirt on once again.

"Minds to numb?" she throws out, her eyes locking on my abdomen, before flicking up to meet my eyes.

I lean forward, lightly tapping her nose. "Exactly. You catch on quick, Rose. I'll catch you later."

Then I breeze out of there, sneaking out the back door. I find Sebastian thumbing through his phone on a bench in the hallway. As soon as I come out, he follows me out of the building, hot on my heels.

Somehow, my fans haven't found me at this studio yet. *Thank fuck*. I'm able to easily slide in the back of the SUV, no cameras flashing and no one yelling my name.

Later that night or early the next morning, I couldn't tell you thanks to how fuzzy my mind is, I find myself leaving a popular club with a girl whose name I can't even remember. I know she's the daughter of someone famous, but the name has slipped from my mind.

The paparazzi might be yelling her name, in fact I think they are, but I can't make out what they're saying. There's too much alcohol in my blood stream.

I do know when we climb into the back of the waiting car, and the car door slams and hides us from the world, the feeling of her hand snaking under my shirt doesn't feel remotely the same as the touch I felt hours ago.

It feels gross and unwelcome. And that pisses me off more than anything else.

12
NORA

The next month flies by in a simple snap of my fingers.

One moment we're still learning all the dances at the studio, and the next we're going through a complete dress rehearsal.

We had a few weeks of twelve-hour days. Performing on the stage was almost like learning the dances from scratch all over again. We have the main stage, and then branching off from it are two catwalks. They are diagonal to each other, meeting at the tips to form an arrowhead.

The space between them will be the pit.

The catwalks are a lot longer than I thought they'd be, allowing Nash to be closer to his fans that don't have pit or front row tickets.

Since the main stages are so large, it's been an adjustment to make sure we're traveling the stage quickly enough. At times I feel like I'm all out sprinting to make it to my mark on time, but we've finally nailed down the whole show.

Which works out perfectly, because we fly out early

tomorrow to begin the first leg of the tour. We're starting here in the states, our first show all the way in New Jersey. It isn't until the day after tomorrow, allowing us a day to get settled before the madness begins. After that, we'll be traveling the country on private planes and tour buses.

Riley and Ziggy convinced me to do one last Mexican night at our favorite spot before Ziggy and I hit the road for the tour. I still need to finish packing, but I couldn't say no to my best friend. Luckily, most of my wardrobe for the tour is already packed away on one of the trucks making their way to the stadium, which means that's less for me to have to pack. It works out, seeing as I will have *very* limited space while on the bus.

After doing some research on what a tour bus even looks like, I think the other dancers and I will get to know one another pretty well with the small living quarters we'll be sharing.

After waiting fifteen minutes for a table inside the busy restaurant, we finally get seated in the back. Chips and salsa are placed in front of us once we sit, and before we dig in, I snap a picture to upload to Instagram. My followers haven't heard from me as much as usual because tour prep has overtaken my life, but I'm going to try and be better about it in the coming months.

Many of my followers have been with me for a big portion of my dancing journey here in LA, and I want to take them on the adventure of a lifetime with me. Above all, I hope my sister sees me living out what was at once her dream—wherever she is right now.

Once the picture has the filter I want on it, I tag the restaurant and post it with the caption: *One last time before leaving.*

I slide my phone into the pocket of my jeans then scoop some salsa on a chip and dig in, wanting to be fully present since this is my last night with Riley for the foreseeable future.

"I'm going to miss this place," Ziggy says, talking

through his own bite of food.

"Please, I'm going to miss you two! What the hell am I going to do here all alone?" Riley whines, too busy pouting to enjoy the food.

This will be the longest Riley and I have been apart, but we have some breaks in the tour where we'll be home on our off days. It's not like I won't see her the entire duration of the tour.

"I'm sure you'll get yourself into some kind of trouble." I laugh, before smiling at the waitress approaching us.

We give her our drink orders, asking to also start out with queso and guac for the table. Because if I won't be getting this food for a while, I'm going all out.

"The two of you are all badass, about to dance in front of *thousands* of people on a tour with Nash Pierce, and I'll just be here in LA, still trying to follow my dream but really just fetching coffees like a good little errand girl." Her bottom lips juts out dramatically as she dips her chip into the sauce.

"At least your boss is hot," Ziggy offers.

One night, after a few bottles of wine, Riley showed us her boss's Instagram. Ziggy's right; the guy is incredibly attractive.

Riley groans. "He's hot, but he's also such an ass. He's not hot enough to be that much of a dick. The other day he spilled his coffee on me on purpose because he said it was too sweet. That jackass ruined a brand-new dress of mine!"

My eyes travel over the menu as I try to decide what I want tonight. Usually I opt for the enchiladas because they're cheap and delicious, but tonight I want to go big or go home. *Oh, fajitas are twenty bucks? Sold. Guac is extra? Put it on my tab.*

"You don't need that kind of negativity in your life," Ziggy responds as the waitress sets his strawberry margarita in front of him.

Riley opens her straw and puts it in her own drink. "That negativity in my life is currently my only chance at having a job. I'll deal with it."

She then looks down at her menu, and it's quiet at our table as we each try to decide what we're having.

I finally settle on the chicken fajita platter, my mouth already watering at the thought of it. We give the waitress our orders when she returns, stuffing our faces with chips and dip in the interim while holding casual conversation.

The magical sound of sizzling fajitas breaks me from the current topic with my friends about what to pack for the tour. When I look up, I find our waitress nearing our table. She sets my food in front of me as I try not to drool. It smells divine, and I want to ravenously dive into it. Unfortunately, my mother raised me to have manners, so I don't. Slowly unwrapping the tortilla from the aluminum foil, I begin to concoct my perfect fajita.

"We're coming back here the second Nora and I are back for a bit." Ziggy moans, chewing a bite of his burrito.

Riley is busy looking down and mixing her taco salad. "Yeah, well, because I'm petty I'm going to order carryout from here once a week and send you pictures."

I gasp, a piece of my bite falling out of my mouth in the process. "You wouldn't!"

She stabs her fork into her bowl, looking up at me with a sinister smile. "You bet your ass I would. The two of you are going to be off jet setting around the world. This'll be my payback." She shovels a bite into her mouth.

"I'm going to forget you just said that," I say, while I fill my second tortilla. I polished off the first one so fast I'm not sure I breathed between bites. "Nothing can ruin this last supper of sorts for me tonight."

The restaurant around us gets louder and louder as I continue to pile on my toppings. When I look toward the front of the building, I find restaurant goers up and out of their seats, all staring at something—or someone. I can't see what everyone is staring at, but it must be something cool because half the people in the crowd are out of their seats and funneling to the front.

"What do you think they're looking at?" I ask, trying to

crane my neck to see what all the commotion is about.

Riley shrugs, her cheek puffing out with a large bite. "I don't know, but surely if it was a fire there'd be alarms, right?"

I nod, assuming she's right. Angling my second perfect fajita toward my face, I look at the bustling crowd once again. I try not to gape when I see the last person on this planet I was expecting.

Nash breezes through the restaurant, not paying any attention to the people gawking at him. People are pulling out their phones, snapping photos of him with their jaw practically hanging to the floor. He doesn't spare them a second glance, his gaze locked in on our table.

He looks oddly placed amid all the bright colors, his dark ripped jeans dull in comparison to the flags hanging from the ceiling and the red and blue walls of the restaurant.

My fajita stays in the air in front of me as he continues to make his way to *our* table.

What. The. Fuck.

"Oh, holy shit," Riley mutters through a mouthful of food. The words come out jumbled due to the mass amount of food stuffed in her mouth.

But same, girl.

"Let's go," Nash says as soon as he steps up to the table.

Awkwardly looking over my shoulder, I try to see if there's somebody behind me I'm not aware of.

His gray shirt bunches around his biceps when he crosses his arms over his chest. "*Nora,*" he drags out, an annoyed tone to his voice.

A lone piece of chicken falls from the back of my fajita. I narrowly avoid it landing in my lap. The fajita drops out of my hand in shock.

"Excuse me, what?" I ask, wondering if I've ended up in some parallel universe.

Why is Nash at this restaurant right now? And why is he looking at me as if I'm a child not listening to their parent?

He gestures behind him with a lazy lift of his arm. "If you can't tell, we're gathering quite the audience. Let's go."

Taking my napkin from my lap, I set it next to my plate. "Did we have plans?" I ask him.

I might die of embarrassment if I somehow missed the memo that I was supposed to be rehearsing with Nash and forgot.

He scratches his head awkwardly, his eyes bouncing around the room before landing back on me. "Uh no, but I'm here. I need to talk to you about something."

"What?" I blurt, wondering what we could possibly need to talk about. I look toward Riley and Ziggy, hoping they'll interject.

My friends are no help, however, because they both continue to chew haphazardly while watching me and Nash like we're a freaking two-person movie.

The fans behind him are inching closer and closer to our table—to him. I notice one of his bodyguards stepping out between the growing crowd and Nash.

The bodyguard, Sebastian if I remember correctly, aims a firm look at the people trying to close in on Nash. He folds his arms across his chest, becoming a large barrier between our table and the bustle of people trying to inch their way closer to Nash.

Riley kicks me from underneath the table. "Nora. You have to go." She looks at Nash from the corner of her eyes, doing an awful job at being sneaky. She aims a beaming smile his way, her foot knocking me in the shin for the second time.

I look down at my plate of half-eaten food. "But I haven't paid."

Nash reaches into his back pocket, pulling out a sleek black wallet. Thumbing through the bills in the wallet, he pulls out three hundred-dollar bills and places them on the table. "This should cover it."

Staring at the cash on the table, I think through my options. Monica would probably be chomping at the bit for me to go somewhere with Nash. It just feels incredibly random, and it's weird to see him out somewhere in my everyday life.

I stare down at my fajitas longingly. "But, I'm not done eating."

"Jesus Christ, Nora," Nash says through clenched teeth. He turns so his back is facing the growing crowd. "I'll get you whatever food you want when we leave."

"Go," Ziggy says loudly, looking up at Nash and giving him a big, forced smile.

Once I grab my purse from the floor, I slide my chair back. I look up nervously at Nash, unsure of where he plans to go now. The exit is blocked by a mob of people, all staring at us wide-eyed. Thankfully, one of the managerial staff walks up to us.

"Would you like to leave through the back?" he asks, pointing toward a small hallway.

"That would be great, thank you," Nash responds. For a moment, his hand hovers over the small of my back, but he thinks better of it and lets his hand fall to his side.

What on earth is happening?

His bodyguard walks close behind us, making sure no one follows us out of the building. As soon as the small door opens, a wave of cheers can be heard. When I look up, I see another group of people, all screaming Nash's name. Cameras flash, girls cry, and grown men rattle off questions in succession. It's absolute madness.

Nash steps in front of me, shielding me from the flashing cameras. I'm too confused to stop and ask questions.

Before I know it, I'm being pushed into the back of an SUV. I slide across the smooth leather seat, looking over to see Nash climbing in next to me. As soon as the door slams, the roaring crowd dulls.

I take a deep breath, buckling my seatbelt as the SUV pulls away from the building. Looking over at Nash, I find his eyes already on me. "Care to explain why you just kidnapped me from my going away dinner?"

A corner of his lip twitches. "That's your going away party? Two people? One of which is leaving with you."

"Oh, I'm sorry. I didn't realize you were going to steal me from my friends and also proceed to be an asshole." I lean forward as much as my seatbelt will allow, grabbing the headrest of the driver in front of me. "Excuse me, sir?"

The security guard looks at me through the rearview mirror.

"Could you possibly take me back to the restaurant? My friends are waiting, and I didn't leave them hanging to spend my time with a brooding popstar."

The same bodyguard that helped us out of the restaurant hides a laugh by coughing into his fist.

Nash reaches forward, thumping the laughing one on the back of the head. "Stop laughing, Sebastian."

"I'm sorry, sir." He clears his throat, looking away. "It's just, she kind of has a point."

"Oh yeah?" Nash stops looking at the back of Sebastian's head and looks at me. "And what point is that?"

"The point is," I begin, cutting Sebastian off before he can answer for me, "you swooped in out of nowhere and tore me from my friends *the night before we leave for months on end.* The least you could do is explain your reasoning and not be a prickly prick."

It's the driver's turn now to let out his own laugh. The ruckus from the two big men in the front have Nash sitting back in his seat with a scowl on his face.

"Any way we can turn around?" I repeat, trying to catch the eyes of the driver again.

"Keep driving, Matt," Nash says, smirking at me.

My arms cross over my chest. "Then where are we going?"

Nash smirks some more from where he sits beside me. "Would you let me make it a surprise?"

I laugh, leaning back in the seat. "Not a chance."

Shaking his head, he runs a hand over his mouth. The hair at the top of his head shifts around with the movement, the slight waves running in different directions. “Didn’t think so. We’re going to the Staples Center.”

I can’t hide the shock on my face, my jaw dropping enough to catch a fly or two. “The *Staples Center?* Why?”

“The next couple of weeks are going to be insanity. The start of a tour always is, in the best kind of way. I wanted to show you what an empty arena looks like. To give you an idea of what we’ll be performing in front of. Except, we’re doing only stadiums. So we’ll be performing in front of almost double the amount of people.”

I nod slowly, my mind attempting to play catch up. “And you want to show me, *why*?”

The look on his face is one I haven’t seen yet. It almost looks like he’s…*anxious*.

“I’m not sure,” he says. “I just wanted to see your face the first time you saw an empty arena I guess.”

I’m definitely in a parallel universe. Is this Nash being *nice*?

“Did you not have plans the night before going on tour? I feel like you would have plans.”

Over the last month, I’ve become more aware of Nash and his whereabouts, thanks to the media. I’ve told myself not to dive into what he’s up to in his free time, but once the apps were downloaded on my phone, I couldn’t *not* look.

In my deep dive of searching his name, I found out he loves to go out. With every passing night, he’s been seen leaving some kind of event with a gorgeous woman on his arm. I got lost in watching videos of him. In some of the videos, he’d be stumbling and slurring his words while answering various paparazzi questions.

He looks out the window, his voice lowering slightly when he says, “I could always have plans. Tonight I wanted these plans.”

I want to give him shit, tell him he’ll have way more fun somewhere else than with me, but I selfishly want to take this opportunity with him. Not because Nash’s team wants me to get close to him, but because *I* want to get to know him better. I want to get to know the man behind the persona.

I sit back, listening to Nash chat with the two men in the front seat, and he occasionally brings me into the conversation with them. It's odd seeing him so free with the people who work for him. The three of them joke around so easily. Nash definitely hasn't been a dick to the dancers and crew while we've been fine tuning the tour, but he wasn't joking with them in this manner either.

I didn't imagine I would spend the last night at home with Nash before we leave for tour, but despite the shock of it all, I'm looking forward to whatever tonight will bring.

Nash is an enigma, someone I never thought I'd get to know. Now that I have the chance, I want to learn everything I can about him.

13
NASH

I'm pulling a hesitant Nora through a side entrance when she stops in her tracks. She tucks a brunette piece of hair behind her ear as she takes in our surroundings.

"Nash, why is no one else here?"

The hallway we stand in is desolate. All the concession stands are closed, their menus dark and hard to read. During a basketball game or concert, this area would be completely packed. Not that I ever visit up here anyway. I'm always locked away in my dressing room until the last minute when performing anywhere. But I can imagine this place as bustling when the arena is hosting an event.

It just so happens that tonight, there's no event.

"No one else is here because I rented it."

Her Adidas stay planted on the floor as she looks at me with a skeptical look on her face. "You rented it?" The words come out slowly, her eyes still roaming over the empty booths and abandoned area.

I grab her by the wrist once again, continuing my walk to the court and pulling her with me. "Yep," I say matter-of-factly. "It doesn't hurt to have connections. Arenas, stadiums, theaters, they're all fucking epic when full of fans screaming your name, but there's something about them when they're empty that's special too."

We walk through one of the entrances, coming close to the empty court. I let go of her wrist, walking until I reach the center. From my vantage point, I can see every movement she makes as she looks at the arena, her mouth hanging open.

Bending at the waist, her hands come up to cup her mouth. "Oh my god, Nash. This is incredible."

The look on her face is intoxicating. It's pure joy—astonishment. I want to write a song about it.

It's thrilling to see the world through her eyes. To me, an arena is just another place I've sold out. But the look on her face? She still feels the magic from it, even when it's empty. She waltzes over to the sideline, running her hand over the folding chair.

I don't move, too busy watching her take in every detail while I take in everything about her. It's allowing me the chance to remember every single thing about this moment. I've always had a photographic memory; it's helped me immensely as a musician. And the next time I take my fame for granted, the next time I can't hear myself think because there's fifty-thousand people screaming my name and I get frustrated because I'm off-key, I'll remember this moment.

Nora's wearing a simple pair of jeans. I don't know if they're designer or thrift store or what the hell the brand is, but they fit every curve of her perfectly. She's lean and petite, but the muscles in her calves are noticeable even through the dark fabric. Her tank top hugs her figure just as much as the jeans do. It's a light color; I guess you would call it pink. It reminds me of the color of the ballet shoes I saw sticking out of her bag the first day I met her.

It's weird, this intense feeling of wanting to get to know her. I want to know how she got into dancing to begin with. I want to know her favorite color. I want to know her first impression of me.

On second thought, maybe I *don't* want to know that.

I have this odd need to know what she thinks about the music I write. Does she think I'm a sellout? Does she hear my lyrics and find them as lackluster as I do? I want to know all these things about her when I barely know her at all.

I guess what I want is a friend. A friend that isn't obsessed with the spotlight. A friend that will dish it to me straight. A friend that looks at the world I live in with awe.

I need to surround myself with someone who doesn't see the music industry as their own personal hell. I need to fall in love with music again. I need to look at this world through *her* eyes.

I just really need her. And I'm hoping she won't just brush me away when the allure of hanging out with someone famous wears off.

The truth is, my sanity is hanging on by a very small, thin thread. I hate myself most days. I hate the music I've put out recently even more. I just don't know who I am. I know who my team wants me to be, who the public thinks I am, but *I* don't really know myself anymore. The only things I know are the things I despise about myself.

I need someone like Nora to come into my life and show me the good side of this career—the good side of *me*.

"What are you thinking about?" She stops directly in front of me. When her eyes meet mine, she has the sweetest smile on her face. It's so genuine that it makes my pulse spike.

I'm so used to the fake smiles in this industry, but hers is anything but. I believe if I get enough of those aimed my way, my soul might slowly start to stitch itself back together. "I was thinking that it's refreshing to see your reaction to things."

She stuffs her hands into the back pockets of her jeans. "Why is that?"

I pick up the basketball resting close to our feet. As I

begin to dribble it, I think about how I want to answer her question. The thumping noise of the basketball echoes around us.

It's still going *thump, thump, thump* when I answer. "I've been in this business for years. It's actually hard for me to remember what being a normal guy is like."

I take a step, dribbling the ball closer to her. She quickly reaches out, trying to take the ball from me, but I was expecting her reaction.

She doesn't get the ball, and I continue to walk and dribble a circle around her while continuing to answer her question. "The people that I'm always surrounded with, they're in this business just as much as I am. Their faces might not be planted on billboards and magazines like mine is, but they're in it all the same."

I dribble the ball behind her, watching as her long hair falls down her back with her movement. "Because I'm always around people that are famous, I don't really feel the excitement of the industry anymore. It feels like a job, a job some days I don't like. And the people around me feel the same. But with you..."

Stepping back, I jog and dribble until I'm close enough to toss the ball into the net. The ball *swishes* through it easily. It bounces on the floor, each bounce getting smaller and smaller.

"But with me?" Nora asks, still standing at center-court, a thoughtful look on her face.

I stand under the basket, looking right at her, far away from her but still feeling incredibly close to her. "But with you, you're *excited* about everything that has to do with this." My finger reaches up and turns in the air, referring to the ability to rent out arenas—to the fame.

She takes small steps forward until she reaches the now resting basketball. Lifting it up, she begins to dribble it herself. "I'm from a small town. All of this," she gestures to the empty arena we stand in, "is exciting to me."

She dribbles closer to me, repeating my movements from earlier, circling me with a smile on her face.

"I need someone to show me the excitement for all this again. Because honestly? I don't see it anymore." It's the most honest and raw thing I've said in a while, and because of that, my heart is pounding in my chest. I'm usually only vulnerable in the words I write, not in the words I speak in conversation.

Nora pauses, swiftly stepping back and clutching it against her stomach. Her cheeks have gotten pinker since we first showed up, but whether they're flushing from the dribbling or excitement, I'm unsure.

"Have you ever thought that maybe it's not something you need to *see* again? Maybe it's something you need to feel," she says.

Sighing, I thread my fingers behind my head. "It's hard to even feel any kind of excitement like I used to. I sound like a dick saying it because I want to be my best for my fans. I *want* to feel it for them. But it's hard when everything feels the same. Same routine. Same pop songs. It's all the same and it's hard to feel anything for any of it anymore."

"I'm going to make you feel again, Nash Pierce. I'm going to make you feel it *all*." The words coming out of her mouth sound so sure. I'm happy she feels confident about it, because I'm a bit more hesitant.

I want to believe her. I need to believe her to keep my shit together. Because without this hope, I'm going to be headlining the tabloids for something awful, and I don't want to go there. I don't want to hit rock bottom.

Deep down, I can't help but think: *what if I've already jumped and it's bound to happen no matter what or who comes into my life?*

"That's a pretty lofty goal," I respond, stepping closer to her. We stand close enough that both of our bodies press against the basketball.

She has to crane her neck to look up at me, but she looks at me as if she meant every word she's uttered. "I've always been told I'm stubborn. When I put my mind to something, I won't stop until I get it done. You're my next mission, Nash. By the end of this tour, you're going to be so jazzed about what you do that you'll have no choice but to thank me when you win your next Grammy." She tosses the ball over her shoulder, no longer holding a barrier in place between us.

Alarms are going off in my head again, I shouldn't step closer to her. I don't want to make a move on her, so maybe I can have at least *one* normal friend. But damn, she's so fucking beautiful I just want to kiss her. I want to create a melody with our mouths. I want to thread my fingers in her hair and write a song about the way it feels. Shit, I want to do so many things.

Before I can wrap my mind around what I want to do or if I'll do it, she chooses for me. Nora catapults her body into mine, her arms snaking around my neck. She has to stand on her tiptoes to even make the position work, and for a moment my hands are stuck next to me as I process what in the hell she's doing.

"What are you doing?" I ask, my arms still hanging at my side like limp noodles.

Her breath is hot against my chest when she speaks. "I'm giving you a hug. My mom always told me and my sister there wasn't anything a hug couldn't fix." She tightens her hold around my neck even tighter.

I follow her lead, wrapping my arms around her middle, making sure they don't drift into dangerous territory. "I'm not sure a hug will fix me, Rose."

She laughs, pressing her cheek against my chest. "It's worth a try."

I pull her in a little closer, letting the feel sink in of someone touching me without expecting more. I have no clue when the last time was that I simply *hugged* someone. I know it's been a while.

Sometimes fans will want a hug at a meet-and-greet, or even when they run into me on the street. But it's never a hug like this. This isn't just a hug, it's an embrace. It feels different. And it feels good. She wraps her arms so tightly around me it seems like she's trying to keep me together by the iron grip of her arms.

We stand there for a few more moments before I feel her arms around my neck begin to loosen. Stepping away, she looks up at me with a gleam in her eye. “Want to play horse?”

I laugh, wondering where in the hell that question came from. “Sure?” I say hesitantly.

She skips over to the discarded basketball, picking it up and impressively balancing it and twirling it with her index finger. “Great, but we’re going to make it interesting. Every time you miss, you have to tell me a completely random fact about yourself.”

My arms cross over my chest. “Is that so?”

“Yep. It has to be *so* random, like something cheesy or silly or something. Deal?”

“How do I know you won’t sell my random facts to the highest bidder?”

She dribbles the ball as she walks over to take her starting place for the game. “I wouldn’t dare. C’mon.”

I decide I’ve already confided enough in her that she could make the cover story of any gossip magazine if she wanted, so this childish game couldn’t do any more damage.

I step behind her, waiting for her to decide on the spot she wants to shoot from.

And then, I hope this is just the first step in feeling again.

14
NORA

"I absolutely hate mac n' cheese," Nash admits.

The ball is still bouncing behind the basketball goal after he missed it by a hair. I'm smart enough to realize he could've easily made it if he wanted to, but we've had so much fun playing the game at this point it's become more about sharing random facts about ourselves and not about making baskets.

I stand in my spot, my mouth agape. "Did I hear you right? You *hate* mac n' cheese?!"

He laughs, scratching the tattoo on his hand. "Yep, I think it's disgusting actually."

A gasp leaves my mouth, the air making a wheezing sound as I suck in a breath. "That is the most un-American thing I've ever heard!"

Shaking his head, he lazily shrugs at me. "It's a personal preference. Half the time that shit is a weird unnatural color. My younger brother used to ask for it for *every fucking meal* growing up. And since he was the favorite, that's all we ate."

I walk over to grab the basketball from the ground. I hold it against me as I try to decide where I want to shoot from next. Part of me wants to ask him more about this brother, but I'm trying to keep this game lighthearted. "Your personal preference sucks."

His hand goes to his chest, acting as though my words physically hurt him. "Ouch, Nora."

I laugh, brushing his comment off as I plant my feet to get ready to shoot the ball. "I think half of the girls that have your underwear ad as their screensaver would probably change it if they knew that fact about you. You're a monster."

My arms stretch out when I propel the ball out into the air. It just *barely* misses, making my competitive heart angry. I was around basketball a lot in high school; it's something I'm pretty good at. Tonight though, Nash and I both kind of suck. Or, are pretending to suck.

"Your turn," he says, with a mischievous grin on his face.

"One time when I was a kid, I stole a live bunny rabbit from the pet store," I confess.

I can still see the look of horror on my mom's face when she went to grab my jacket from my lap and realized there was a rabbit sitting there. I think she almost dropped my little sister in shock when she saw a furry bunny chilling in my lap.

Nash looks at me with bewilderment. "I think I'm going to need more details about this."

I awkwardly laugh, the memory clear as day in my head. "We used to go to the local pet store to look at animals. It was one of my favorite things to do. One time, the worker gave me a rabbit to hold, then got distracted in a conversation with my mom. She had me placed in the child part of the cart, so when she finally said we had to go grab dog food from another aisle, I hid the rabbit under my jacket. After we paid, she was unloading me and my sister into the car when she noticed the gray bunny perched in my lap."

He picks up the ball, his long fingers holding it in one hand. "Did you get to keep it?"

My nose scrunches while I watch him pick a spot to shoot from. "No, I'm allergic."

Shaking his head, he barks out a laugh. "What a tragedy."

"Yeah, it was kind of awkward explaining to the employee that I stole the rabbit. I bawled the whole time, but my mom didn't show any mercy. She still made me go in there to return it and apologize."

Standing in place, he looks at me thoughtfully. "Your mom sounds great."

I smile wistfully. I try not to think about how much I miss her. Or any of them—my family. We all moved away as soon as I graduated high school. I don't like to talk about why. In fact, I avoid even thinking about it most times. It's too painful.

"Yeah, she's pretty wonderful," I agree, wishing I could talk to her more. And my sister Lenny, too. Especially Lenny...

"My brother had a rabbit growing up," he throws out randomly. "He named her after Britney Spears. I think I was about ten, which must've made him around five at the time. He took that rabbit everywhere. The kid was obsessed."

I can't help but laugh. "That is the best name I've ever heard."

Nash's lips turn up in a smile. "Yeah, well that rabbit chewed through countless pairs of my shoes. I swear Aiden trained her to do it or some shit."

This makes me laugh even harder. "That's the most epic trick."

"Aiden's a pain in my ass that way," he says, shaking his head with a smile.

Turning toward the basket, the muscles of his arm ripple under his tattoos as he sets up his shot. The ball leaves his hands gracefully, arching in the air and easily slipping through the net of the hoop.

"I win," he declares, his arms stretched wide in celebration.

I want to take a picture of the smile on his face and keep it in my memory forever. He looks so carefree. It doesn't look forced or strained. He looks *happy*.

I lift my shoulders, accepting defeat. "I guess you did. I put up a good fight though."

The ball rolls from its place below us, bouncing off the wall and coming to a stop behind him. "I hate it when people touch my elbows. I absolutely despise it," he tells me.

I offer a timid laugh, pulling my tank top that had been riding up down. "Nash, who is touching your elbows?"

His hand runs through the shaggy strands at the top of his head. The bright lighting of the arena makes the brown strands appear lighter than normal.

"I know it sounds fucking crazy, but you have no idea how many people try to hold you by the elbow." After taking a few long strides toward me, he's suddenly standing right in front of me. Without warning, his warm grip wraps around my elbow. "See what I mean?"

"You're holding my elbow..." I slowly point out, looking up at him with a curious look.

Sighing, he tightens his grip on my elbow a bit more. "Just wait, it gets awkward." He continues to stare down at me with an expectant look, his fingers splayed out on my elbow and coming up to wrap around my forearm.

Finally, I begin to understand what he means. "I think it's awkward because you're making it awkward."

He lets go, stuffing his hands into the front pockets of his dark jeans. Shaking his head, he gives me a small smirk. "No, Nora, you have no idea. Reporters all the time grab me right there while interviewing me. *So* many people do it. It weirds me out."

I look up at him, a grin on my face. "Next time you piss me off I'm just going to grab you by the elbows."

Our bodies are still close. Neither one of us have

stepped back from the other, even though he's gotten his point across.

His eyes flick down to the small space between us. He's close enough that I could reach out and touch the soft fabric of his T-shirt. I can feel the warmth of his breath when he lets out a long sigh. "I'm not sure I'd hate it coming from you."

Before I get the chance to ask him what he means by that, he steps away and races across the floor. His long legs take him across the court quickly, and before I know it, he's skipping stairs, racing through the auditorium seats.

"Where are you going?" I yell, watching the way his T-shirt stretches perfectly over his back as he goes, his arms pumping at his sides, the muscles rippling underneath it.

"Come join me!" he shouts back, not bothering to look over his shoulder.

I shake my head at him and do just as he instructs. My legs take me up the absurd number of stairs until I finally reach a grinning Nash, who's chilling in an auditorium seat like he didn't just essentially put me through a workout.

I grab the railing in the aisle next to him, dramatically gulping for air. "Are you trying to kill me with those stairs?"

He swats at the air, leaning further back in his seat. He's got his legs propped up on the seat in front of him, his arms resting on his thighs. "Oh, please. I know firsthand how conditioned your body is. That was nothing."

Giving him a pouty face, I straighten my body, returning to my normal breathing. I fall into the chair next to his, looking ahead at the empty court below us. "Maybe I didn't want to get a workout in tonight," I say.

I can feel his eyes against my cheek, but I still focus on the arena in front of us. "You're not even breathing heavy," he says.

Looking in his direction, I narrow my eyes at him in

disapproval. "Fine, you're right. I'm being dramatic. But, why are we up here?"

He reaches up, placing his hands behind his head. His position seems so relaxed. I take the cue from him, scooting forward in my seat and leaning back until I'm in an almost identical position.

"I think it's important to see the view from the audience. To know what the experience looks like from their vantage point." His tone is serious, and as I slowly start to shave away at the layers of him, I realize he's deeper than I expected him to be.

For someone who claims to hate his fame, he sure does try to understand and relate to his fans a lot.

"But you're not performing here." I take in his face, the face that's graced an unfathomable number of magazines, billboards, album covers, so many things.

It isn't fair for a face to be so perfect. His high cheekbones, the focal point. His sharp jawline and straight eyebrows also make the girls swoon. His lips are plump, a shade that women pay good money for, to have that same color of nude on their lips.

"No, you're right. When I first started touring with Anticipation Rising, I would sit in the audience before every show. I'd wonder how the hell I got to be one of the guys on stage instead of someone in the audience."

"Do you still do that?"

His lips thin. "No, I don't."

I bump him gently with my shoulder. "Maybe you should start again."

He bites down on his lip briefly, nodding his head. "Maybe I will."

It's silent, the both of us trapped in our own thoughts.

I still can't fully wrap my head around the life Nash has lived. He's been famous for most of his life. I can't imagine never having privacy, waking up in a different city every day, sitting in a place like this knowing that soon all the seats would be filled and the reason they were filled was because of you.

I don't have stage fright. I've loved the attention from a stage for as long as I can remember. But I've also never had the pressure of solely entertaining thousands of people.

As a backup dancer, we enhance the show no doubt, but fans aren't paying money to see us. We're there to make Nash look good—to put on a show. We don't feel the pressure like a headliner would.

I start to wonder what kind of toll that pressure can take on one single person.

"Tell me another random fact." His voice is quiet, but sure.

We both stare at the space around us instead of at each other. It's crazy to look around us and think about what this building looks like when it's at capacity.

"I miss my sister." The air is quiet as I wonder where she is in this world. After a sigh, I add, "I'll never go back to my hometown."

He doesn't know how much those two statements coincide, a raw truth of my past I'm still trying to come to terms with.

After graduating high school, I packed up everything I owned and left the town I grew up in. The town that went from my safe haven to a personal hell all in one night. I tried to take my sister with me, but she wouldn't leave. After the night that changed everything, our relationship changed drastically, and now we're practically strangers.

"Why is that?" he asks cautiously, his seat groaning underneath him as he adjusts his position.

I run my hands down my thighs nervously, not ready to divulge the past to him—to *anyone,* really. After it happened, I said my piece the only way I knew how—through dance, and then I left that shitty town and the human beings that live in it.

I don't want to say too much, but I also feel like Nash has told me things in the short time we've known each other that he doesn't tell others, so I feel like I need to give him *something*.

"I spent years in a place that felt safe. Then my safety net was pulled out from underneath me and somebody I loved in a matter of minutes. I left as soon as I could, flipping the whole damn town off through my rearview mirror as I left."

Nash shocks me when he reaches between us, his hand gently grasping my cheek. His thumb rests along my jawline. I don't resist when he guides my face to look at him. "Good for you for getting out of there, and I like the special touch of saying '*fuck you*' on the way out. You're so incredibly talented, and here in California, going on this tour, soon the world will really see that. To hell with the assholes that didn't."

I give him a sad smile, wishing it could be that simple.

Unfortunately, a small moment in time has left a part of me black and empty. And worse, it hurt one of the people I love most in this world.

I desperately try to fill the void by chasing my goals, hoping that the closer I get to my dream the more the black hole gets painted over. But apparently trauma works in different ways, and you don't just wake up one day and heal from it; you just make the effort to not let that trauma define you.

A shaky breath leaves me. "It's getting late. We should probably both try to sleep tonight before traveling tomorrow."

He keeps his hand on my cheek for a little while longer, his eyes searching my face like he's looking for some kind of answer.

I don't move away from his touch, allowing the small moment with him before our world gets crazy.

An uneasy feeling cascades over me. This night has been so simple with him. He's shown me a side to him I hadn't expected, and I'm finding myself wanting to get to know that side of him more and more.

But in the back of my mind, I know why I'm here.

I was hired to break his heart. Now that I'm getting to know him, I'm scared that his heart is already broken, and they're just wanting me to come in and break it more.

I don't want to do it. I want to fess up to it, but if I do, he won't look at me the way he's looking at me right now. He'd probably fire me, which is the least of my worries and also what I deserve, but worse, he'd hate me.

And I can't have him hating me. I was honest when I told him I wanted to help him fall in love with entertaining again. I meant it with every fiber of my being.

So now I'm left in the biggest catastrophe.

I promised his team I'd try my best to break him; I promised him I'd do my best to try to fix him. Only time will tell on which promise I keep—and which promise I break.

15
NORA

Euphoric.

The only way to describe the feeling of getting ready to walk out onto a stage surrounded by screaming fans, is *euphoric.*

When we boarded the private jet yesterday morning, it finally hit me that I was about to go on tour with an international phenomenon. As I stepped onto the jet, I realized how crazy my new reality was.

We were spoiled the entire flight, and it shocked me how huge the plane actually was. I didn't expect Nash's band and entire professional team—dancers included—to all fit on one jet, but we did.

It was mania as soon as we landed. I thought I'd have the day to explore New Jersey, but we had plenty of things to do in preparation of the first show. All the dancers had final fittings with wardrobe to make sure our costumes were perfect for opening night.

Looking down at my costume, I find it perfectly hemmed to custom fit my body. The dark, black jeans are skintight, a pair of thigh-high boots looping all the way up my leg. A red button-down shirt covers the top half of my body. It's expertly tied above my belly button, a black bra peeking out from between the undone buttons.

As I move in the outfit, the shirt rides up over the high-waisted jeans to show off my stomach. All the girls will wear the same outfit, the guys in something similar. They'll be in red button-downs, unbuttoned with no shirt underneath, and a pair of black fitted joggers.

I haven't seen Nash yet. He gave us all a pep talk before the first opener went out, but he hasn't been to wardrobe yet. Now that both openers have performed, the hyped crowd is cheering for the montage playing on the screen. It's only minutes before Nash is set to go out there, and we'll be following him soon after.

I'm standing with some of the dancers, waiting for our cue to take our places, when a warm body comes up behind me. I startle, getting ready to dart until I look over my shoulder and find Nash standing there.

Oh, holy fuck. He looks hot—majorly hot. He shouldn't be allowed to be famous and still be *that hot*. The first thing I notice is the red bandana that's tied around his head. It holds back the unruly curls at the top of his head.

I let my gaze travel down the rest of his body, to the simple white T-shirt and pair of black jeans that are ripped all the way down both legs. His feet are covered in a pair of stark white sneakers.

"Excited?" he asks, those perfectly hued lips enveloping a perfect smile.

"Nash!" a stage member shrieks, running up next to us. They're decked out in all black, a headset attached to their head. "You're supposed to be under the stage right now. You go on in two minutes."

"I'll be there," Nash assures the man, then focuses his attention back on me. "Are you excited, Rose?" Reaching out, he wraps a piece of my chestnut hair around his finger. He lets the strand fall, watching me until I answer.

"Yes. But, Nash, you've got to go." I point to the stairs

that lead below the stage. Down there is a network of small tunnels that allow the performers to get around quickly. Toward the middle of the show, I have to run through one of the tunnels before Nash and I perform our duet together.

He adjusts the bandana on his head, turning to show off a microphone on the other side of his face. It's almost the exact shade of his skin, something I wouldn't have noticed unless I was up close with him. "Yeah, I better get down there before the whole stage crew comes after me. Break a leg, Nora." He walks backward, grinning at me before turning around and disappearing into the tunnel entrance.

Hello, butterflies. You shouldn't be here.

I take a deep breath, trying not to think too deeply of why he went out of his way to say good luck to me before the show. I wish I would've yelled it back at him, my mind too preoccupied with why he wasn't where he was supposed to be to give him a proper response. He probably doesn't even need good luck; performing in front of thousands is just a typical day for him.

The stage in front of us goes dark, smoke starting to billow out of the cannons that surround the stage. Nash's voice comes over the speakers, to which the screams get even louder. A minute in, lights drench the stage in red as Nash's words appear on the screens behind the stage.

Then...it's time for Nash.

He pops out from the bottom of the stage, the crowd going absolutely insane.

"What's up, New Jersey?" he asks confidently, the band picking up the music until it's our cue to go out there.

"Let's do this," Ziggy says excitedly next to me. He takes the earpieces from around his neck and puts one in each ear.

I do the same, afraid the screams from the crowd might drown out the music.

When it's our cue to go on stage, the rest of the world

fades to black. There's nothing on my mind except the present. The feeling up on stage is like a drug. I haven't been on stage for a whole track before I'm completely in love with being up there. The feeling is unlike any other in this world. The way the screams from the crowd shake the entire stage, making me want to give every ounce of my soul to each move of my body...

As much as Nash has confided in me that he doesn't feel the same performing like he used to, I would never know by the way he lights up the stage. He griped a lot about having the dancers on tour and having to dance with them, but that's just another thing the crowd wouldn't be able to tell right now.

He moves as gracefully as the rest of us, giving just as much energy.

It's the most incredible feeling, watching him perform for thousands and thousands of people. He has small conversations with them throughout the show while we change backstage, allowing time for everyone involved to prepare for whatever is set to start next.

Nash makes sure to walk up and down the stage, getting close to as many fans as possible. His shirt gets thrown into the crowd halfway through the show, leaving only a thin tank top on his upper half. It shows off every sculpted ab along with the intricate artwork etched permanently on his skin.

It's halfway through the show when it's finally time for me and Nash to perform *Preach*. Suddenly I'm anxious, nervous to witness how the fans will react. It's different than him just standing up there with his guitar or sitting at the piano when performing his slower songs.

Another video montage plays on the screen while we get ready backstage. I'm running underneath the stage, a stage assistant walking fast behind me as I strip out of my top layer of clothes. She hands me the flowy piece of fabric I have to wear for this song.

I pause for a moment, pulling the gossamer fabric over my head and letting it fall down my body. It's a sheer red color. You can still see the black bra and high-waisted underwear I have on underneath it. It isn't too see-through, but it also isn't thick enough to fully hide the dark color that shields the most intimate parts of me from the world.

The fabric falls all the way down to my mid-calf. Two slits run up my legs, the opening going all the way up to my hip bone. As soon as I have the dress on properly, I pull my hair out from under the fabric. My hair cascades down my back, falling all the way down to the small of my waist. Next I slide off the pair of heels I have on, trading them for a pair of nude dancing shoes.

As soon as I'm fully dressed, I'm racing through the tunnel to make it to my mark on time—which I do, *thank god*. I find Nash already waiting on the rig that will lift us onto stage.

A stage crew member helps adjust his microphone pack on his pants, while having a small conversation with him. "How's that?" the stage member asks.

"Great," Nash responds, fiddling with his guitar strap. "I want to take one of my earpieces out to be there with the fans but fuck, I forgot how loud they were."

The stage member laughs, finishing messing with Nash's equipment and looking over at me. "You good to go?"

I nod, running my hands down my legs to help ease some of the nerves, the anticipation of this performance eating away at me.

Nash looks up from adjusting his guitar, giving me a smirk. "You ready to make all those girls out there jealous for three minutes and forty-six seconds?"

"If I say no, will it make a difference?"

He shakes his head, reaching up to fix a piece of hair that's still managed to fall over his eye. There's a sheen of sweat coating his body as I step closer to him on the rig. The tattoos running up both of his arms seem even more defined under the harsh lights from the stage.

"Nope. You're stuck with me at this point. Deal with

it." His eyes make a slow cascading motion down my body, and it feels like he's undressing me with them.

There's a handful of people underneath this stage with us, but they all disappear with Nash's eyes on me like that.

"You look hot, Rose." He says the words nonchalantly, a mischievous gleam in his eye as he waits for my reaction, totally unaware that he's sending my mind—and heart—into overdrive.

Meanwhile, my heart is thumping against my chest, trying to compete with the bass of the music playing above us. He *can't* be saying those words to me. He's *supposed* to be saying those words to me. I'm *supposed* to flirt back. I *want* to flirt back. I also want to run far away from this stage and not start this *thing* with Nash that can only end with at least one broken heart.

"One-minute countdown," a stage crew member shouts next to us.

The words return me to my senses, even though Nash's eyes are still roaming all over me as if he's imagining what I look like without any of this on.

I step closer to him, turning my body around until our backs touch. Between his thin tank top and my bare shoulders from the dress, our skin is pressed against the other's. Both of our bodies are warm, but I find goosebumps starting to raise on my arms.

Nash's breath is hot on my neck when he turns to speak over his shoulder. "Let's go show them what they're missing."

"Let's do this," I respond, taking a deep breath.

Above us, the music from the video goes silent, and for a brief moment, so does the crowd. Then, it erupts in madness. I imagine the band coming back onto the stage above us, the lights shading them in black. The focus is supposed to be on Nash and me up there, the band only there to enhance the experience.

My body shifts as the rig begins to raise. As soon as Nash's body is visible to the crowd, the screams become deafening. His shoulders press into mine as he shifts the guitar, his body leaning forward over the instrument.

It's his cue to start the song, the band waiting for him to start before they ease into the song as well. I stand there, pressed against Nash as he strums the opening chords. His voice fills the stadium when he begins to sing.

I take my cue, turning around and running my hands over him as the words captivate the crowd.

One November night, you stumbled into my life
I didn't want you
I barely even saw you
But two weeks later, you were the only thing that felt like mine
You told me you loved me
I told you I hated me
My words didn't faze you
You just kissed me and lit me
On fire, on fire, on fire
On fire, and preach

The words to the song continue to leave his mouth in an addictive and repetitive raspy tone. I can't make out faces in the crowd, but I can see the countless lights in the crowd, swaying in rhythm to the music.

We make it to the chorus. Once the guitar is handed off to someone on the side of the stage, I resume my position before him. His voice is sexily serenading the crowd when I drop down to my knees. The cheers get louder and louder when Nash spins me, my body falling back against him and dipping down.

I can't hear myself think for the rest of the song. The crowd is just as loud now as when Nash had first appeared at the beginning of the concert. The red lighting washes over his face, the vein on the side of his neck visible from the strain of singing.

My legs wrap around his firm middle, and he sings the last bit of the lyrics looking into my eyes before I flip backward onto the floor.

Oh baby, could you practice what you preach?
You lit the match then stepped out of reach
Oh baby, won't you practice what you preach?
You lit the match that's still burning here at your feet

The spotlight shines hot against my back as I slide down Nash's body as he sings the haunting closing lines. His fingertips making a searing brand through the thin fabric of my costume. Without a doubt, I know he can feel the racing beat of my heart underneath his burning touch. Now that the song is over, I feel incredibly vulnerable, his small touch sending heat throughout my whole body. We stand there, locked in an embrace as the world around us erupts in booming screams.

After a few beats, I attempt to step back, but Nash doesn't let me go. He tucks me underneath his arm, spinning me to face the crowd.

We stand there, waiting for the crowd to get quieter. As soon as the noise is manageable, Nash begins to speak over the people still cheering.

"Everyone, please give it up for this incredibly fucking talented dancer—a good friend of mine, Nora." He steps aside, holding onto one of my hands as the other one lifts up to get the crowd yelling once more.

Nash unexpectedly spins me, pulling me into a tight hug. As the crowd around us loses their damn minds, he kisses the top of my head, turning to face the crowd again.

I take it as my cue to leave and run off stage. I lean against a speaker as soon as I'm out of sight.

Holy shit. That feeling was insane.

It was so unlike the first chunk of the setlist, when all eyes were mostly on Nash. It was still fun and nerve-wracking to be out there on stage with him, regardless. But just now, with me and Nash performing *Preach*, so many more eyes were on *me*.

I'm jealous of *myself* for the chemistry Nash and I have

out there. I've performed with other dancers before. It's not the first time I've had to fake emotion on stage, or be intimate with someone to make the performance better. But it felt so different out there.

When he looked at me like that at the end, I wanted it to be real. I didn't want to put on a show for the fans, I wanted to be looked at like that and have it be real.

The thought is terrifying, and as I grip the extra speaker for dear life, trying to get my head on straight, I realize this task is going to be a lot harder than I expected.

I gave my word to try to get Nash to fall in love with me.

I didn't give any thought to what would happen if I started to unintentionally fall for *him* in the process.

16
NASH

I'm hungover as fuck.

As my mind starts to piece last night together, I feel a body press up against mine.

"Morning," the girl behind me whispers, cozying up to my neck.

"Who are you?" I ask, wiping at my eyes. *What the hell did I drink last night?* All I remember is walking to my room backstage and diving right into the chilled vodka that'd been set out on the table. The band slowly poured in not long after that.

I think back, trying to recall the details. We were a few drinks in when Monica came stomping in. The vein on her head was protruding, a sure sign she was pissed.

"Oh fuck," Troy drunkenly exclaimed next to me, a shit-eating grin on his face. "Monica's pissed at you."

"Actually, I'm pissed at all of you. You're supposed to be at the meet-and-greet in five minutes. Sober the hell up and get going!" She swiped the vodka out of my hand, putting it on the glass table of my dressing room with a loud *clank*.

"Totally remembered that," I whispered, standing up and stretching my back, steadying myself on an end table before almost toppling over. I could feel the alcohol dripping through my veins, making things slightly fuzzy.

Though, I probably could have tripled the amount of alcohol I had by then and still been functional.

Monica stepped around all of us then, walking over to the clothing rack. "Nash, you need to change." Her back was straight as a board in her suit jacket as she angrily flipped through the clothes on the rack.

She pulled out a few shirts, turning up her nose and aggressively hanging them back up. She finally found a shirt that appeased her, because she quickly tore it off the hanger and threw it at me.

"Catch," she muttered, a little too late, because I had already basically caught it by the time she decided to warn me.

I remember not being in the mood to argue with her. The high from the crowd had already worn off, and I was busy trying to catch a new high before I felt the lows when she rudely stomped in and started getting snippy with us.

I pulled the sweaty tank top off me and threw it onto the couch. Then I pulled the other shirt on, smiling wide at her once it was on. "I'm ready, boss."

She let out an annoyed grunt. Walking over to the mini fridge, she pulled out a glass bottle of water. Shoving it against my chest, she instructed me to drink it. "Chug this. Now."

I unscrewed the cap and washed down the lingering taste of vodka in my mouth. Once the bottle was empty, I looked at her with my eyebrows raised. "Anything else?"

Monica held one finger in the air, and then quickly walked over to the dressing room table. She grabbed a bottle of cologne from the counter, spraying it over each and every one of my bandmates before she made her way back to me. "Yeah," she demanded. "Spray this. You smell like a frat house."

"What the fuck, Monica," Troy whined, swiping at the air in front of him.

"I'm a grown-ass man," Poe added. "I've had one drink and smell nothing like a *frat house*." He held his fingers up in mock quotations with the last words.

Landon didn't say anything, he just stood up and took one last swig of his drink.

After Monica bathed me in my cologne, she snapped her fingers at us—our cue to follow her out.

The meet-and-greet went well, the small moments with my fans something I hadn't realized I'd missed. What I could go without, however, were the million questions directed my way about Nora.

Who is Nora?

Is she an old friend of yours?

Are the two of you dating?

How do I sign up to be one of your dancers?

The same questions were asked over and over.

I don't know when people will understand that I don't want to share my personal life with the world. Nora and I aren't dating. We're both just doing as instructed, and apparently doing it well if their sudden fascination with her is any indication.

My cheeks were starting to go numb from all the smiling when the last fans from the meet-and-greet were ushered out the door by Sebastian.

I was so exhausted from the excitement of the day that at one point, I just wanted to go back to the hotel room and sleep for five days straight. I was getting ready to do just that as we walked back to my dressing room when Troy came up behind me.

"Party in your dressing room?" he suggested. "I invited a few friends."

A few friends in Troy's world could only mean *a few girls*. I shrugged, too tired to even protest. But Troy wasn't even looking for my permission. He already had a handful of women waiting eagerly in my dressing room.

One thing led to another, and somehow, I ended up back at my hotel room with the horny woman that's currently next to me.

Her hand slides down my naked torso now, creeping down to find me still without pants on from the night before.

I push her hand away, not even fully awake enough to *think* about having sex. Plus, the pounding in my head is doing nothing to help turn me on.

"Who are you again?" I ask gruffly, pushing up and resting my back against the headboard.

"Samantha." She bites her lip, running a hand through her blonde hair.

"Well, Samantha, I think the party is over. Can I call you a cab?"

Her face falls, a whine coming from the back of her throat. "I have my own *driver*, thank you very much."

My phone vibrates from somewhere on the floor, but I can't even muster the energy to try to look for it

Jesus Christ, my head hurts.

Rubbing at my temples, I don't even look at her. If she wants to prove that she's somehow famous in her own right and has a driver, be my guest. I just want her out of my damn hotel room. "Perfect. Then leave."

She slaps at the down comforter. "You're a dick."

I chuckle, my fingers still digging deep into my temples to try and relieve the pressure. "You're not the first person to call me a dick, honey. You sure as hell won't be the last."

There are loud noises as she picks up her belongings. I expect to hear the slamming of the door, but it looks like my morning is only going to get shittier.

"Monica, I'm not in the mood." Sighing, I look up to find her at the foot of my bed, her phone inches away from her face.

She reads from the phone in front of her. "It turns out Nash Pierce hasn't changed one bit. His bad boy tendencies picked right up after giving the crowd of New Jersey a spectacular show. Fans speculated if one of the dancers on his tour, Nora Mason, was a new love interest, but Nash quickly put that rumor to rest. Sources say Nash was seen leaving the venue with an heiress to one of the biggest tech companies in the Garden State. Sources said Nash looked like he'd had a few drinks to celebrate the start of his tour. He and Samantha were all smiles as they got into a waiting car. Nash's dancer, Nora, was not spotted."

Every now and then, Monica paused to look up from her phone to give me a frown before continuing to read the article from some stupid gossip magazine.

"What's your point, Monica? I'm allowed to have fun." I stretch my legs under the comforter, waiting for her to leave so I can get up and shower. All I can smell is vodka and the scent of Samantha's overly sweet perfume.

Monica stuffs the phone into her purse. I don't know if I've ever seen the woman use the same purse, but she always has some new, fancy one with her. It wouldn't shock me if she had a full meal, a survival kit, and her laptop all in that bag. I'll give her one thing: she's always ready for anything.

Well, except me, because I still manage to get on her nerves, all these years later.

The feeling is mutual, but she's the best in the business. She and I were both nobodies when we first made our partnership. I owe a lot of what I've achieved to her. She's like a big sister to me, the one that always annoys the fuck out of me.

She lets out a shrill laugh. "My *problem,* Nash, is that your team is working tirelessly to clean up your image. You're getting older. This whole rebellious teenager phase has got to go. Would it kill you to be seen with the same woman twice? And not stumble out of the bar, alerting everyone you've been over-served?" Her thin arms cross over her chest, the fabric of her jacket bunching at the shoulders.

"I've told you guys this already. I don't want a relationship. Not since my last one." My thumbs twirl around each other in my lap as I watch her carefully. I'm confident that here in a second, I might see steam shoot out from Monica's ears like in the cartoons.

"Fuck, Nash, at this point I'd be happy with you having a consistent fuck buddy. A friends-with-benefits thing. Anything to let the media know that your dick is not an amusement park, free for anyone to ride. I get it. Taylor was a shitty girlfriend to you. She broke your heart. We all get our heart broken, Nash."

Like Monica has ever let anyone in her heart to break it. For twenty-six years old, she has her heart locked up like Fort Knox.

"Why does it matter who I stick my dick in? I'm clean. They sign NDAs. What's the issue here?"

She takes a deep breath, counting back from ten under her breath. "The *issue* is that you're making a point of being seen with these different girls. Honestly, if you could just hide that you're planning to screw your way through this tour, I'd be good with that. But when you let the paps capture you with each new girl, it doesn't look great."

I don't see what the huge problem is here. I'm not in a committed relationship. I'm allowed to fuck whoever I want. Just because I'm famous I'm supposed to pretend I don't like getting my dick sucked.

Yeah, no.

I have needs. Everyone has needs. These damn gossip columns need to stop acting like it's a big ass deal. Everyone fucks. I'd like to get ahold of the people who write these articles and ask if they're celibate. With the way they patronize me, they sure as hell better be. If they're getting their rocks off just like me and calling me out for it, that would be some shady shit. But let's be honest, most of these people behind computer screens think it's okay to openly judge celebrities just because we're famous, when they're probably doing the same things we are.

"Why don't you start going out with Nora?" Monica offers, slowly, as if she's talking to a caged animal.

"*Nora?*" I ask sarcastically, wondering where in the hell she's going with this.

I'm drawn to Nora in a way I've never been to a woman. But I'm not going to use her to appease Monica. If I take Nora on a public date, which I don't know if I even want to go down that road, it's not going to be because Monica told me to.

"Yes, Nora, the girl on your dance team that the fans are already loving. The one who hasn't been a part of some scandal or was caught last weekend crashing her daddy's lambo, high as a kite."

"Shit, Samantha?" I ask, not one to ever stay in touch with the tabloids, even when they don't include me.

Monica points toward me, then goes to sit in a chair by the hotel window. "Bingo."

"She didn't mention it," I respond truthfully. Or if she did, I was too drunk to remember her admission.

Monica pulls her phone out of her bag. Her fingers zip across the touch screen until she smiles up at me. "Everyone is *loving* Nora on social media, Nash. They're eating up that dance like candy. She's the good kind of publicity you need."

Figuring that Monica is here for the long haul, I get out of bed, using the pillow to shield my dick from her. I strut into the bathroom, turning the water on as hot as it will go. I grab the navy robe from the hook by the shower and wrap my body in the soft material.

I find Monica in the same spot I left her, her nose inches away from her phone.

"I'm not using Nora for publicity." The words are sharp as they leave my mouth, sharp enough to have Monica quirk her brow.

"And why not?" she asks, clearly unaware that I'm no longer interested in this conversation.

Propping myself in the doorway, I stare across the

space at her. I don't owe Monica any kind of explanation. If I say I don't want to use Nora for publicity, then that's my fucking decision. "Because I don't fucking want to, Monica. End of conversation."

Not caring what else she has to say on the matter, I leave her staring at me as I walk back into the large penthouse bathroom.

This bathroom is as big as my childhood bedroom, the shower probably large enough to fit a queen-sized bed. There are two shower heads on opposite sides of the wall. The water that falls out of each head steams as it meets the air. Stepping onto the cold black stone of the shower, I walk all the way in until I'm under both streams.

The water is blistering hot, but it's exactly what my body needs. I wash the night before off me, using the hotel issued loofah to scrub away at my skin.

Once my skin feels clean, Samantha washed clear off it, I lean against the shower wall. The water falls directly on my head, cascading down my face. I close my eyes, leaning forward and taking a moment for myself.

These days, showers are about the only time I'm completely alone. Most nights there's a woman sleeping next to me, and during the day my schedule is planned out for me. I go where they tell me to go—well, most of the time.

I've always hated mornings, using the excuse of a hot shower to try and cleanse myself of the night before. Unfortunately, no amount of hot water can rid me of my sins. You'd think I'd learn that the alcohol, the drugs, the money, the girls, all does nothing to make me feel better about myself.

Underneath the face that everyone loves, and all the money and fame, is a man that can't even tolerate himself.

I haven't always been this way. I used to be able to look at myself in the mirror. Somewhere along the way, I got lost. I lost sight in who the hell I am and what the fuck I want. Now? I have no fucking clue. I have so many other opinions running my life, that I don't know what mine are anymore.

I do know some things.

The feeling on stage, when I'm connecting with my fans, it's the best high I could ever chase. But as soon as I perform the encore songs, after the confetti has fallen to the ground and the crowd ushers out, the self-loathing snaps back into place like a leash firm around my neck, choking me. Then I'm gasping for air until I can take my first drink of alcohol. My first hit of a drug. The moment I enter a woman. These are all ways I *think* I'm chasing that high again. It's always just out of reach, coming close but never enough.

Recently there've been times—even when I'm not on stage—where the voice in my head has finally quieted down. The voice that usually tells me I'll never be good enough. And, it's only when I'm with Nora.

Something about her puts me at ease—all of me, even the bruised and ugly parts. Because of that, I don't want to use her just so the media thinks I'm growing up. I don't want to taint the friendship we've created with the schemes of the industry.

When I'm around her, I want to *forget* about the schemes and schemers of the world I live in. I want to be present in the moment with her. In the way she hums under her breath while dancing. In the way she's always pushing her hair out of her face, unable to tame that thick blanket of hair on her head. I want to be present in the way that, when she looks at me, I don't hate myself.

I'm a natural cynic. I'd admit it to anyone, but when she told me she'd help me fall in love with my career again—I wholeheartedly believed her.

Trusting her is easy as playing a song on the piano to me. It just comes naturally.

I'm trying to be wary of her, to not become obsessed with her. I have an obsessive personality. My ex constantly pointed it out to me, telling me I'd go from being obsessed with her to being obsessed with music, never being able to balance the in-between.

She also used that as an excuse to fuck one of my bandmates.

I can't let that happen with Nora. I can't want her the way I'm beginning to. We're in an industry that dooms relationships from the get-go, and I can't lose her. I'd rather be her friend forever, keep her positive attitude in my life, rather than lose it because my lifeless heart decided it wanted her.

But, that's easier said than done. Even though I can't remember most of last night, I can remember the way Nora's face kept popping into my head. I couldn't rid her from it, no matter how hard I tried.

As the hot water turns lukewarm, I discover that I might not have any say in the matter. Whether I want it to happen or not, Nora is quickly becoming someone important in my life.

And what I'm most terrified of?

In my life, the people that I've become closest to are the people that have broken me the most.

17
NORA

The first five stops of the tour go by in a blur. The feeling on stage every night has become intoxicating; I don't think I'll ever get enough of it. I'm slowly becoming better friends with the other dancers. Even though I miss Riley deeply, I'm loving my life right now.

And things with Nash? They're getting more intense.

It's become our ritual to sit in the empty stadiums each afternoon, the two of us sipping on coffee as we soak in the pre-concert silence. The contrast between our afternoons and evenings is stark. Nash told me an empty stadium is powerful in its own way—and he was right. There's something to be said in knowing that the silence of the space around you will be erupting in cheers in a matter of hours. It's the calm before the storm—and it's beautiful.

My calves are burning as I climb the concrete stairs. We're in Atlanta tonight and tomorrow, doing a double header. The sun is hot against my cheeks, my sunglasses not doing enough to shield my face from the Georgia heat. When I find a row that'll work, I shimmy through the seats until I'm right in the center. I plop down into the faded seat, taking in the sight before me.

The crew is working tirelessly at getting the final touches together for the night. I'll never get over how efficient the people that work on this tour are. They take a football field and completely transform it into a set that makes the crowd go wild each night we have a show. The fans love when the screens move behind Nash as he performs. They move into four different transfigurations, each one more spectacular than the last.

Behind the stage, I'm sure the pyrotechnicians are busy setting up whatever is needed to have all the flashy fireworks and smoke ready for the night. Three crew members wheel out the instruments for Nash's opening act. I'm watching them pull on different cords when movement catches my attention from the corner of my eye.

My stomach dips when I see it's Nash climbing the steps in my direction. The large gold aviators on his face cover his eyes, but there's no mistaking that his sights are pinned on me. I don't look away—I can't. Day by day, night by night, I'm falling further into the trap that has caught thousands—millions—of girls' attention. I can't help it. There's something magnetic about being in Nash's presence. I thought I'd be immune to it, but I was very wrong. He's got on a backwards ballcap to cover his caramel locks, no doubt a mess from whatever he did last night. The closer he gets, the more I think that hat may be one that was thrown onto the stage by a fan.

I've learned more and more about Nash from the few tour stops we've had so far. I've learned that he takes the time to learn the names of each person at his meet-and-greets, even if he's drunk. I've learned that he chants something to the sky before taking the stage to perform. I've also learned that he'll take items fans give him, and not only that but he'll wear them. He sports a few different bracelets that made their way onto the stage, the hat he's wearing now, and at times I've seen him wear other items from them.

I blushed the first time a fan threw their bra onto the stage, not realizing it was something that happened often.

"Good morning," Nash says gruffly, making his way through the aisle of stadium seats.

"Morning," I respond, looking up at him with a smile.

He reaches out, handing me my coffee. I told him my order once and since then he's somehow remembered exactly how I drink it. That small fact hasn't been lost on me. I'm trying to take him off this pedestal the world has him on, but it seems I'm falling victim just like everyone else.

Nash sits down in the seat next to me, his tan arm brushing against mine as he shifts to get comfortable. "I need a fucking IV of coffee today," he states before gulping down his black coffee.

The corner of my lip pulls up as I look over at him. "Rough night?"

I already know all about his night. It was all over my feed when I woke up this morning. I stayed in my bunk, scrolling for way longer than I'd care to admit, finding out *exactly* what Nash was up to last night.

He groans, using his free hand to adjust the black hat on his head. "Remind me to never fucking drink again." His voice is raspy, making me wonder what he'll have to do to get it ready to perform tonight.

Before the third show, he caught a cold that made him go through extra work to be able to sing. I had never thought about everything singers have to go through to put on a show, least of all how bad it could be for them to sing through a sore throat. Nash's team had two separate doctors clear him to perform, to ensure he wouldn't mess up his vocal cords in the process.

I take a long sip of my coffee, letting the bitterness wash down my throat. "I feel like even if I did remind you not to drink, it wouldn't do much. I don't think people would know what to do with a constantly sober Nash."

"You implying I'm drunk all the time, Rose?" There's a slight edge to his voice, a tone I wasn't expecting. I don't know if it's from the hangover he's fighting or if I truly offended him.

Planning my words out carefully, I take a moment before speaking. "I'm saying you're certainly not sober all the time."

His gaze is hotter than the sun against my skin. I'm itching to fill the awkward silence between us, not wanting him to be angry with me. When I first agreed to take part in this tour, I didn't think I'd give a damn about what Nash thought of me, but now I'm in a place where it would eat at me if I knew he was upset with me.

"Yeah...well," he pauses, slowly letting out a breath, "I don't know how else to cope. I have to be numb to be able to exist. If I wasn't numb..."

His words break off while he thinks about something, his head facing down as he stares at the people below us.

"If you weren't numb, you'd have to live with the pain, and that's not something you're equipped to handle. Not now, anyway."

His head snaps in my direction. I'm glad I too have on a pair of large sunglasses. He has a way of making me feel like he can read my every thought—without me having to say a word—and right now, I don't want him to know what's crossing my mind. I want to hide behind the glasses, cower away from his inquisitive gaze.

"What do you know about being numb, Nora?"

I don't answer him. Not because I don't trust him, I don't want him to know how truly numb I feel deep down. The numbness I've had to battle for years. It's still something I struggle with.

Shaking my head, I lift my straw to my lips, buying myself some time. Apparently, that's not good enough for Nash, because without warning, he sets his hand on my thigh.

He's touched me many times. His hands have skirted

around almost every inch of my body, but right now, it's different. In this moment, it's not for show. It's real, and it's causing my pulse to pick up.

His fingers tighten around my thigh, a supportive touch I'll never forget. "Nora?"

I swallow, turning my head to face him. "You're not the only one with demons, Nash. Yours just look different than mine."

He barely lets me finish my sentence before throwing his next words out between us. "Go out with me."

My chest pulls in with a deep breath when I register what exactly he's saying.

"Excuse me, what? I just told you I'm also equally fucked up, and you ask me out?" I stumble on my words, almost dropping my coffee in the process.

He cocks an eyebrow. "So, is that a no?"

"Yes."

Nash leans in closer to me. "Yes as in yes you will, or yes as in *hell* yes you will?"

"Yes as in no. No, I won't." Monica is probably screaming from somewhere in the distance, upset with me for not taking this opportunity. But I can't do it.

The way Nash is grinning at me, it makes him seem so different from the man in the magazines. It makes him seem real—*human*. It felt easy when he seemed like this rude, famous, unattainable guy. Now that he's next to me, slowly letting his guard down, I can't bring myself to hurt him.

Even though I want to say yes.

"You're telling me no?" he asks, confused, sitting straighter in the seat as he tilts toward me. "Can you at least tell me why?"

"Because you're..." my free hand waves around in front of him, "*you*. You're Nash Pierce. You go on dates with models and actresses."

"I can go out with whoever I please," he throws back, a bit of a bite to his tone.

"Nash, you don't know me," I point out, ready to beg

him not to start down this road.

"I'm trying to know you." His voice is softer then, and chipping away at my resolve.

The voice in my head telling me this is the worst idea, that this will set us down a path I can't come back from, is getting quieter by the second.

"It's a bad idea," I state, my thighs sticking to the plastic stadium seat as I adjust my position. I look down at the people we work with. I still don't know if anyone else on tour was propositioned by Nash's team just as I was. It feels like it doesn't matter, because right now it's looking like *I* might be the one with the measly shot at breaking his heart. Except now I don't want it.

I anxiously peek over at him, finding a sly smirk on his face.

"Some of my favorite memories stem from bad ideas," he says.

Sighing, I adjust my grip on my coffee. "You might hate me when you get to know me."

"Doubtful."

"Yeah, well," I let out a long breath, "don't say that yet. There's still a lot you have to learn, Nash Pierce."

He uses his index finger to slide his sunglasses back up the straight bridge of his nose. "*Nash*. Just Nash to you."

"Honestly, it's hard to look at you and not think of the man that's on every magazine cover. I think I have that underwear campaign you did forever ago branded in my brain."

His white teeth bite at the straw of his coffee, his lips smirking around it. "It was that good, huh?"

Using the hand not holding my coffee, I push his shoulder. "Not what I meant."

"Mhm," he hums, shrugging my push off. He turns his gaze back to the shuffle of bodies in front of us. "You just admitted you can't forget me in all my naked glory. Don't worry, Rose, any time you want to see the real thing, you just let me know."

Shaking my head, I can't help but smile. "You're so

freaking arrogant."

"So? Monica told me that a certain *someone* is building quite the fanbase for themselves."

I lift both my legs until my feet rest on the seats in front of me, my stomach dropping at the mention of Monica's name. "And who would that be?"

Looking over at him, I find him looking at me from over the top of his sunglasses. "*You*. Obviously."

I shrug, not knowing what else to do. I haven't had notifications on to my socials for a long time. Once my freestyles started gaining more momentum, I had to turn them off or my phone would never stop alerting me to things. I still check my socials regularly, and it wasn't hard to miss how much my numbers had climbed since opening night. It turns out people really do love the dance Nash and I do—it's gained me half a million followers in a few short weeks. I still can't entirely wrap my mind around it.

"They love you," Nash continues, the ice in his cup rattling as he adjusts his body into the same position as mine. His legs are much longer than mine, and in this new position they encroach on my space. Our knees brush against the other's, my bare knee against his.

I ponder his words, hearing the eruption of cheers from the fans in my head. "They love *us,*" I correct. "The act we're putting on."

He's quiet for a moment, taking the time to put his coffee down on the concrete next to him. "The line isn't always black and white for them with what's an act and what's not. Soon you'll find out just how often those lines blur."

I can feel a crease develop on my forehead as I think his words through. "How do you handle that?"

He laughs, a deep, throaty laugh that sends chills down my spine. "I don't fucking handle it, Nora. I'm a god damn mess. People just choose to ignore it. They think it's an act."

"Is it? An act?"

He steeples his index fingers, resting his chin between his index fingers and his thumbs. "Unfortunately, I think the fact that I'm a train wreck is the only real thing about me."

His words tumble around in my head, making me sad. He clearly isn't in a good place. "Why do you think people ignore it?"

I should stop asking him personal questions. It's really none of my business. I shouldn't get to know his demons, because the more demons of his I unearth, the more I want to get to know them. The more I get to know him, the more I hate myself for the inevitable of what'll happen between us.

He gives another dry, sarcastic laugh. "Why wouldn't they? I'm Nash Pierce. The bad boy. I'm everything they've made me out to be. A playboy. An alcoholic. A hot head. Why would anyone give a fuck that these are all problems, huge red flags, when it's feeding into the very image they have of me?"

"You're also talented. An artist. A singer. A lyrical genius."

He cuts me off by putting his hand on my thigh once again, his fingertips burning hot against my bare skin. "I don't need you to try and justify who I've become, Nora. What I *do* need you to do is be ready tomorrow for our date."

His fingertips dig deeper into my thigh for a few split seconds before he pulls his hand away. I watch him carefully as he bends down to grab the coffee he'd placed on the ground. The seat makes a loud snapping noise as he stands up.

I watch him twist his body as he stretches out his torso. He lets out a loud groan, fixing the hat on his head right after.

"What if I don't want to go?" I ask sarcastically.

"Then you don't go. I'll be waiting outside the dancer bus tomorrow at one. If you don't come, I'll take it as a no." He reaches out in front of me, his outstretched fingers wiggling.

I take the hint, putting the hand that isn't holding my coffee in his. His grip is firm as he pulls me out of my own stadium seat, which now reverberates behind me.

"Let's go blow their minds again, Rose."

He doesn't let go of my hand as he walks the two of us down the stadium stairs. His grip is firm the whole way down, no matter how many stares land on us.

And I begin to wonder...*is this the start of the fall?*

18
NASH

As it turns out, there's a fuck ton of people wandering around the stadium parking lot in the afternoon, a detail I wasn't privy to because typically I'm still sleeping off a hangover at this time. Or begrudgingly doing some kind of press work.

Shockingly, I don't have anything planned for the day—except for this date with Nora. We traveled through the night before arriving at our next tour stop. Today is an off day for the tour. The crew has begun to set up the stage for tomorrow, but for those of us performing, we have the day off.

A few crew members try to catch my attention as I weave through all the buses parked in the lot. I give them small waves, too focused on trying to find the bus for the dancers. Adjusting the beanie on my head, I stop a tiny girl pacing in front of a random golf cart. She's got a clipboard clutched to her chest like her life depends on it, while she whisper-shouts to someone on the other line of her phone.

"Excuse me?" I begin, taking a step closer to her. My words catch her attention, and she looks up at me, her eyes getting as wide as saucers when she realizes who's bothering her. "Do you know where I could find the dancer bus?" I give her an apologetic smile.

She's silent for a few beats, lifting her arm and pointing somewhere in the distance. I follow the line of her arm, trying to distinguish where exactly she's pointing to. I can feel my eyebrows pull together on my forehead underneath my sunglasses. I have no fucking clue where she's pointing to other than the mass of buses sitting in the parking lot.

"Could you, uh, maybe give me more details? A number?"

"Forty-two," she answers robotically, her jaw hanging open while she openly gawks at me. I can hear someone yelling through the earpiece of her phone.

"Thank you," I tell her quickly, nodding to the phone in her hand. "Might want to get back to that." I give her a small wave as my legs take me in the direction she pointed to.

I'm dodging members of my crew left and right as I weave in and out of the buses. I never realized how many buses even travel with us on tour but am quickly realizing it's a lot of them. I'm scanning all the numbers until I finally spot the one I'm looking for.

Keeping my head down, I pick up my pace as I walk to the bus. Luckily, there's no one else around to spot me. I'm sure the people who've already noticed me hanging out around the lot were confused. I must admit, I don't spend much time wandering around venues on my off days. Typically, I'm nursing a hangover right into the evening, just in time to rinse, repeat, and get drunk all over again.

I stop in front of the narrow door of the bus, my knuckles rapping against the cold steel a few times. As I wait for someone to answer, I swear I see one of the curtains toward the back of the bus open and close quickly.

The door squeaks open to a smiling Ziggy. “Well, look who it is.” He props his shoulder in the doorway, giving me a shit-eating grin.

“Hi, Zig.” My eyes wander to the empty space over his shoulder. I don’t find any sign of Nora, just stairs and an empty passenger chair. “I’m here for Nora.”

Ziggy chuckles, smoothing down the crease of his lime green jersey. “Oh, we know.” He straightens up off the wall, a whole head taller than me thanks to the lift of the bus. “Now, Nora’s daddy isn’t here so I feel like it’s my job to give you a few words. Our girl Nora here is something special, and while your team of dancers all respect the hell out of you, your rapport with women isn’t great. If you hurt our girl, well, you’ll have one pissed off dance crew.”

“Ziggy!” Nora shouts as she rushes up behind him, peeking over him, her face as red as the lipstick she wears each night we perform.

“What? We were all thinking it, I was just the one with the balls to say it.” He completely fills the space of the doorway, blocking her way out.

She stuffs something into the small purse on her shoulder. Once she catches onto the fact that he isn’t moving, she looks up at him expectantly.

Ziggy dramatically sighs, pulling his body to one side enough that her small frame can fit through the gap. “You two have fun.”

Nora stops right in front of me, a hesitant smile on her face. I return her smile, suddenly excited about the day ahead, relieved she isn’t standing me up. Briefly looking over the top of her head, I find Ziggy carefully watching us. His eyes meet mine and I can tell by the look on his face that he meant that warning of his.

Little does he know I have no intention of hurting Nora. I don’t even know what the hell I’m doing here in the first place. I’m not someone who casually goes on a day-date with a woman, even if this is *exactly* what Monica wants me to be doing.

I wanted a day with Nora, just the two of us. For once, I didn't want to deal with the pressure of being *Nash: the famous popstar*. I wanted to leave the pressure of all that behind and focus on getting to know a great girl instead. Hell, I just wanted to *pretend* I could be a normal guy for a day.

"Ready?" I ask, looking down to find her big eyes staring up at me.

"Yep," she replies, pulling the strap of her purse higher on her shoulder.

The door to the bus behind us makes a loud creak as Ziggy disappears behind it. It leaves us completely alone in the small alleyway between buses.

"Let's go," I tell her, reaching down to wrap her hand in mine. I do it without even thinking about it. Holding her hand seems like second nature at this point. We weave in and out of the buses until we reach the parked SUV, where Sebastian and Matt are both waiting for us.

"Where are we going?" Nora asks softly, giving them a small wave.

"Somewhere Nash shouldn't be going," Matt mumbles under his breath, eyes on Sebastian.

Sebastian lets out a small laugh. "Like we could tell Nash what to do," he says sarcastically. He turns around and opens the back door of the SUV, reaching his hand out to take Nora's.

She gives him the sweetest smile, pulling her hand out of mine and placing it in his. He winks at me over her shoulder as he goes to help her into the car.

Matt huffs from where he's perched against the driver's side door, and Sebastian halts to listen. "Yeah, it's not like he *pays us*—very nicely I might add—to make sure he's safe," he says.

I take this time to step in front of Sebastian, silently letting him know I'll get Nora's door as we've found ourselves in some kind of pissing match over this for no real reason. He steps back, allowing me in.

"You'll find out where we're going," I tell her, answering the question she'd asked before my bodyguards decided to go all mom—or worse, *Monica*—on me.

Nora reaches around herself, giving me a nod as she clicks her seatbelt into place.

I shut the door softly, ignoring Sebastian as he makes overexaggerated kissing noises next to me. *This idiot*. He knows I'm in new territory with Nora. I don't typically fuss over taking girls on a date, but today I've spent hours trying to figure out the perfect first date for the two of us. Even if Matt thinks it's unsafe for me to do it at all.

"Matt's right, I pay the both of you very generously," I remind Sebastian. "So stop annoying me."

This only amuses Sebastian more. "Retract the claws, Nash." He meows, putting his hand in the air to mimic a cat paw swiping at the air.

I ignore him, muttering "*asshole*" under my breath as I round the SUV to the driver's side.

Matt waits, holding the rear door open for me. He doesn't make eye contact with me, clearly still not on board with my plans for the day.

I slide onto the dark leather seat, finding Nora watching me inquisitively. My gaze skates over to her, finally taking in her outfit. And fuck, if it doesn't get my blood pumping south. She's got on a black-and-white checkered skirt, and it's riding up while she sits there, showing off a dangerous amount of her thighs. I've seen her in less during concerts. Now, she's wearing a simple black, long sleeve shirt. It hugs the top half of her body and stretches right under her ribcage, leaving a small gap of exposed skin between her shirt and skirt.

Matt's door slams a little louder than necessary once he settles in the driver's seat. I'm still too busy staring at Nora to pay attention to whatever conversation the guys are having up front.

She crosses her legs next to me, alerting me to the pair

of black chucks on her feet. Damn she looks fucking *hot* in a pair of chucks. The grungy, angsty, pre-fame middle schooler that is still buried deep inside me fucking digs it. My eyes snap to the stark white pair of chucks on my own feet. We look like a damn ad from the nineties. I'm into it.

"Right, Nash?" Sebastian pipes up from the front seat.

I look up from my feet to find Sebastian looking at me through the rearview mirror. Judging by the look on his face, he knows damn well I wasn't listening to a word he was saying.

"Hmm?" I ask, reaching across the space between our two bucket seats to grab Nora's hand. She doesn't protest as my fingers cover hers, our intertwined hands resting against her thigh.

"I was *saying*," Sebastian starts, "that you would be *happy* to wear the wig out to avoid being recognized—you know, to make Matt feel better and all."

"Wig?" Nora questions from my right.

"Oh yeahhhh," Sebastian drawls in exaggeration. "The team—well, Matt really—prefers for Nash here to wear a wig whenever he decides to go out in public without much security. A big, fat, curly, red wig."

"Fuck. That," I decide aloud, leaning back in my seat. There is *no* way in hell I'm wearing that god-awful wig. I've done it before and it's itchy as fuck. I'd rather be recognized than wear that thing that looks like it's part of a damn clown costume.

"Where are we going that you even need a wig?" Nora questions.

I sigh, pinching the bridge of my nose. "Well, now that my team has successfully ruined the surprise, we're going to a music festival."

"Sorry, Nash," Sebastian says proudly, somehow not catching on that he needs to shut his damn mouth already. "I just really suck at surprises."

Nora laughs as an inaudible sound of annoyance rumbles in my throat. "It's okay, I'm not big on surprises anyway," she offers.

I make a note to ask her about that later. *Who doesn't like surprises?*

"What kind of festival?" Her body turns toward me in the seat. With the shift of her body, our hands now rest on her bare skin. For a brief moment, that subtle contact is the only thing on my mind.

"It's kind of a mix of different genres," I eventually say. "Folk, alternative, bluegrass, it has it all. It's made up of smaller talent, but that's the reason I've always wanted to go. A lot of the time, the ones who have the most talent aren't the ones winning awards at shows. They're just out there doing what they love without the pressure of everything that comes with topping the charts. It's a big deal. I'm amped to go."

I proceed to list off some of the talent that'll be playing the festival. Then, I take in the confused look on her face. "You don't recognize any of those names, do you?"

She grimaces what looks like an apology and squeezes my hand at the same time. "Absolutely no clue who any of those people are, but I'm excited to find out."

"We'll be good as long as you tell me you don't listen to country radio."

Nora bites her lip, a hint of a smile on her face. "And what's wrong with country?"

I groan, leaning my head against the headrest behind me. "To each their own I guess, Rose. The twang and singing about a tractor, it just isn't my style."

"A little judgmental, are we?" Nora says. Her eyes find Sebastian's through the mirror. He's got a shit eating grin on his face again, a look of surprise now with it.

He slaps the dashboard in agreement. "I've been telling him the same exact thing for years!"

Proceeding to gang up on me with Sebastian, Nora looks back to me. "Not all country songs are about tractors, you know. Some of the best love songs are by country artists."

"Some of the most tragic love songs," Matt adds.

He flicks the blinker, trying to merge past a car going twenty under the speed limit in the fast lane.

"All genres have good, tragic love songs. They're called breakup songs," I counter. "Genre doesn't matter when writing from a broken heart."

I think of the album I wrote when my heart was shattered in pieces. There's nothing like your first broken heart. It hurts like a bitch. But writing about the girl that broke my heart did bring me a platinum album, so at least I've got that going for me.

Nora hums as she thinks my words over, otherwise silent until she smirks and finally says, "So, tell me more about this wig you'll be wearing."

19
NORA

“Are you sure you’re allowed to do this?” I ask Nash, my eyes flicking over to a scowling Matt.

He’s standing in front of the car, arms crossed over his chest, a disapproving stare directed at Nash’s back.

Both Nash and I stand just outside the rear of the car, the door of the SUV still hanging open, my purse on the seat I’ve just vacated. The discarded clown wig sits on the floorboards, the artificial strands of hair reaching in every direction.

Nash throws a dirty look over his shoulder, taking a step to the left to block my view of Matt. Dirt swirls in the air around us as a Jeep full of teenagers blows past us. “I’m allowed to do whatever the hell I want,” he says.

Matt huffs loudly, causing Sebastian to snicker. Nash shakes his head and reaches into the car, pulling out a black ballcap with a bright red stitched rose on the front.

“Do you have a thing for roses or something?” I ask, my finger tapping the rose tattoo taking up his hand. Both of his hands have the same tattoo spanning nearly all the skin there.

His lips pull up in a cocky smile as he as he places the hat atop my head, adjusting it till he sees fit. He pulls the brim down, obstructing my view of the world so I can only see him. Nash's eyes briefly drop to my lips before he meets my eyes once again.

Leaning in close, so close that his temple rests against the brim of the hat he's just put on me, he opens his mouth to speak. "Looks like it, *Rose.*"

The emphasis on his nickname for me has me involuntarily pulling in a deep breath. I feel the double entendre in his words all the way to my core. Even though all I'd meant was that it's apparent he likes roses—between the roses on his hands and the roses all over his fan merchandise. I hadn't meant...*me.*

"I'm starting to like 'em more and more." His teasing smile is confident.

We stand under the beating sun for one, two, three—I don't know how many seconds—locked in a stare with each other.

This man.

I'm falling into the trap of his charisma, fast. I feel like one of those girls that scream his name each night on tour. I can't look away from him. He's pulling me in and I'm not quick enough to stop the rollercoaster of emotions soaring through me.

All I know is I'm standing in front of him, in the middle of a random festival parking lot, the sun scorching hot on my back, and all I can think about is how I want to know every single detail of Nash Pierce.

I want to know what you can't discover from the tabloids.

I want to see that heart he guards so tightly.

I want to run away from the look he's giving me right now. I want to run and find a time machine so I can tell Monica there's no way I'd ever agree to any plan that includes breaking his beautiful heart.

His fingers move from where they'd been resting on the brim of the hat. He slides his hand down the side of my face, caressing my cheek softly. His eyes stay pinned on mine. I'm scared he can read every single one of my thoughts.

You'll hate me one day, I chant in my head, hoping he can't see my panic from the obtrusive thought.

His thumb brushes my cheek before he slides his hand around to the back of my neck. I'm too aware of Sebastian and Matt, standing only a few feet away, nothing but Nash's back shielding us from their view.

Nash's hand is warm on the back of my neck, and just before I give in to the feelings brewing inside me, I brace my hands against his stomach. My fingers twist around the fabric of his shirt. "Nash," I say his name, a beg on my lips, breaking our eye contact. "We should get going."

His head falls forward, our foreheads now resting against the other's. He sighs, applying more pressure on my neck for a moment before stepping away.

My arms fall to my side. I find both Matt and Sebastian pretending to be in a deep conversation by the hood of the car. I try to eavesdrop when Nash's voice breaks my attention.

"Here," he says loudly, his hand holding out my purse.

"Thanks," I say, taking it. I give him a timid smile, hoping he isn't too disappointed that I'd just stopped whatever was about to happen between the two of us.

Nash reaches back into the SUV, pulling a large pair of sunglasses on his face. He's now hidden under that beanie and a pair of wayfarer sunglasses. He looks like he could be stepping onto the set of a Ray Bans commercial. "Do you have a pair?" he asks, his pointer finger aimed toward his own.

I nod, unzipping my purse and pulling out mine. "Is this how we hide? No clown wigs?" I tease, hoping to ease some of this tension between us.

His lips twitch as he pulls his beanie down further. He looks sexy as hell. I'm not sure I'd recognize him if I didn't know it was him under the beanie and sunglasses.

Nash grabs the top of the SUV door, slamming it loudly and stepping closer to me. His feet kick up dirt as he steps closer to me. “Ready?” he asks, holding his hand out, a silent invitation.

I take it, not wanting to ruin the vibe for the day. Even if I’m still cautious about what I could allow to happen between us, I still crave this quality time with him. I want to see him just being Nash, and today seems like the perfect opportunity to do so.

The two of us stop near Matt and Sebastian. Sebastian has a grin on his face, one I’m quickly learning almost never leaves his face. Matt on the other hand, looks like he desperately wishes he could force Nash back into the car.

“Nash,” Matt begins, his hands tucked into the pockets of his dark jeans.

“Don’t start with me, Matt. Please,” Nash asks of him. A moment of eye contact passes between them, some sort of silent understanding, and then Nash pulls me along with him.

“Monica is going to kill me,” Matt notes, following hot on our heels.

“She’ll kill us all,” Sebastian jokes.

Nash stops abruptly. My hand falls from his grip as he quickly closes the distance between him and the two men. “The two of you need to pull your panties out of your ass and let me live a little. Shit, I just want to go to a festival with a girl without a ton of people following me around. Is that so much to ask? *Really*?” His chest rises and falls in frustration as he stares down both Matt and Sebastian.

Sebastian is the first one to raise his white flag. He lifts his arms in surrender. “We’re just trying to do our job, boss.”

Nash barely seems to register what Sebastian has said, he’s too busy staring at Matt. The four of us stand silently in the middle of the desert, waiting for someone to make a move.

People mill around us from all directions, making their way exactly where we're trying to.

"You aren't a normal guy anymore, Nash," Matt says softly. "If anyone catches wind that you're here, there'll be a crazy mob of fans within five minutes. It's just me and Bash here," he nods to Sebastian, adding, "and it's up to us to keep the two of you safe, because *you* decided you didn't want anyone else to know about this little excursion. I'm not going to apologize for wanting to keep you safe. You just better stay incognito."

It looks like Matt wants to say something else, but after thinking on it, his jaw snaps shut. He turns around and starts to walk toward the large mass of people lining up at the front gates.

As the four of us head in that direction, I peek over at Nash. Most of his face is hidden behind the beanie and sunglasses, but the tight clench of his jaw is still visible. Between the tic of his jaw and the way he's gripping my hand, I assume he's still on edge about it all.

I use my hand that isn't holding his to reach across and wrap around his bicep. I let my body drift even closer to his, leaning my head against his shoulder as our steps fall in line together.

By the time we make it through the gates, the tension with Matt seems forgotten. Both Matt and Sebastian have backed off a bit, giving us the illusion it's just the two of us here at the festival.

"Want something to drink?" Nash asks as we walk past a vendor selling drinks out of a retro looking bus. The back half of it has a large window cut into it. There are tiki lights framing the window and inside works a girl with bright green hair. She bends over the counter, handing a guy two large beer cans.

"I'm good," I tell Nash, looking up at him. "But if you want something..." I lift my hand and point toward the booth, silently letting him know he can get whatever he wants.

He swivels his head from me to the booth, then back at

me. I would bet underneath the sunglasses his eyebrows are furrowed in concentration. "I actually don't want anything," he mumbles, more to himself than me.

I stop in front of the booth, having to speak loudly over the booming speakers, the voice of the artist on stage spilling loudly from them. "Are you sure?"

"Yes, I'm fucking sure. Christ, what is wrong with people treating me like a child today? I already got patronized from Matt, I didn't think I'd get it from you, too." His T-shirt bunches around his biceps as he crosses his arms over his chest, my hand he was holding now laying limply at my side.

"Woah," I begin, throwing my hands up defensively. "I didn't mean anything wrong by that. I just figured you may actually want a drink and were being nice denying one because I didn't want one." I awkwardly look down at my shoes, noticing the soles of them turning from white to brown from the dust on the ground.

"What, because I can't go an afternoon without a drink?" Nash pulls the sunglasses off his face, pinching his nose and rubbing his cheeks. He must register it was the wrong move at the same time I do, because a few seconds later he quickly whips the sunglasses back to cover his face, muttering "*shit*" in the process. The two of us scan the people around us, wondering if anyone recognized him in that short time.

I make eye contact with the girl with the green hair working the liquor booth. She stares intently at the both of us for a few moments too long, making me second-guess if Nash went unrecognized with that mishap. The customer at her booth must say something to get her attention, because she blinks a few times and looks away from us, toward them.

I look around us one more time before looking back at him. I find him already facing me, waiting for an answer. Sighing, I run my hands over the pleats of my skirt. "I didn't mean it that way, it's just—"

"It's just you think I'm an alcoholic?" A girl with a cup

that's half her size bumps into Nash. She barely glances his way as she haphazardly throws an apology over her shoulder and continues on.

My hands find my hips. "Stop putting words in my mouth. It isn't a secret you like to drink. We've talked about it. I was just trying to be nice. Don't be a dick."

His lips pull into an apologetic smile. "You're right, I was a dick. I'm just on edge, I guess."

I close the distance, bumping his shoulder with mine, trying to resume normalcy. "Let's go watch someone play."

He nods, taking my hand once again and pulling me toward the sound of music and screaming fans. Keeping up with his long stride, I take one last glance over my shoulder. There's a pit in my stomach when I see the woman working the alcohol booth with her eyes pinned on us, and worse, her phone in our direction.

I try to shake the worry off, hoping she didn't recognize Nash like I think she may have. I want to enjoy the day with him, and I don't want to worry him about that if I could be wrong. Pushing the anxiety to the back of my head, I become fully immersed in the day with Nash.

Before I know it, the sun has fully set, and the day has flown by.

Tugging on Nash's hand, I guide us through a throng of spectators. My hand is clammy in his, the other wrapped tight around the base of cotton candy on a stick. Flashing lights illuminate the people around us sporadically. Finally finding an open area on the far-left side of the stage, I stop, turning to face Nash.

The person on stage talks to the crowd while the stage crew moves things around behind him. The large screen behind the band has a large, artistic sugar skull on the banner. By the song they start to play, it seems like some kind of indie band. Nash's finger absentmindedly taps to the beat against the top of my hand.

Watching the mirage of colors from the stage lights illuminate his face, I realize I want to relive this day over and over. It's been everything I could have wanted in a date and more. The realization hits me like a ton of bricks.

Today was a date. A date I enjoyed more than any other date I've previously been on. And the small feelings I was harboring for Nash this morning have multiplied tenfold.

Every time his blue-green gaze falls on me, I feel it all the way down my body. I've learned so many insignificant things about him that now they've piled up and transformed into something *very* significant. Something that feels a whole hell of a lot like developing feelings—real, deep feelings that lead to falling.

I try to shake the gnawing feeling of that—and what it could mean for me, him, and the impossibility of an *us*.

Nash is the perfect distraction from my intrusive thoughts. I'm snacking on the cotton candy when his hands lock around my waist. Pulling me in close, he fuses our bodies together.

"How is it?" he asks, eyeing the pink and blue swirls of sugar in my hand.

"Delicious," I say, pulling at a chunk of the cotton candy. Raising my hand, I hold the treat in front of his lips, a silent offering.

He responds instantly, his lips parting. He maintains direct eye contact as he leans forward.

I place the cotton candy on his waiting tongue, tingles running down my spine when the wetness of his mouth rubs against my knuckles. The look on his face as he swallows makes it seem like maybe it wasn't an accident at all.

My sticky fingers rub together at my side as Nash reaches in and grabs his own piece of the cotton candy. I stay zoned in on his every move as he guides the pastel strings my way. My mouth opens with zero hesitation, letting him place it directly on my tongue. I close my mouth, letting it disintegrate on my tongue as Nash watches in fascination.

"Nora?" he says, his voice raised to cover the crowd around us that's singing along to the music.

"Yes?"

"Ask me to tell you something random." His eyes dart down to my lips before making eye contact once again.

I can't help but pause, wondering where this is leading. Unable to resist, I do just that, waiting on pins and needles for his response.

He wastes no time answering me. One second, I'm still living in my own fantasyland where Nash and I are just friends and my own personal feelings haven't gotten involved. In this moment, I'm still able to pretend I'm not falling for Nash, ignoring the fact that one day I'll have to break both our hearts by breaking his.

I'm no longer toeing the line between my heart and my head. My heart has taken the lead and said, *to hell with the wreckage guaranteed to happen*.

Because in the next moment, the lips that serenade countless fans every night are uttering the words that ignite fireworks in my stomach.

"I'm going to kiss the hell out of you, Rose," he tells me.

And I let him.

His lips, that sing the sweetest melodies, are on mine. And as our lips finally collide, the last thought in my mind before I lose myself in him is wondering how I've waited so long to feel his lips on mine.

20

NASH

I don't hesitate for a second longer. I've been wanting to kiss Nora's pouty lips all damn day. Watching her stick that cotton candy in her mouth, her lips wrapping around her fingers, has been sending my head spinning. I can't wait any longer. All the reasons I shouldn't kiss her just disappear, and the only thing left on my mind is if I can taste that cotton candy on her lips.

So I try. Our lips crash together then. It's slow at first. A beat that builds and builds until we hit the crescendo. Then the beat drops and we're all lips and tongues and not holding back. My forehead knocks against the ballcap on her head, blocking me from being as close to her as possible.

I momentarily pull away from the sweet taste of her, twisting the hat until the brim is out of my way. She smiles, a blue tint to the lips that have probably left my balls the same color all day. Now that her hat's been adjusted, I pull her in close again, my body folding into hers until I'm damn near lifting her tiny body off the ground to be as close to her as possible.

My one hand stays on the small of her waist, a place my hand has been many nights on tour, but never like *this*. My other hand leaves her neck to brush her long hair off her shoulder. Now that I have free access to her pale skin, I lean in, anxious to memorize the taste of it.

The feeling of my lips against her skin is something I want to write songs about. The lyrics fly around in my head as I kiss a trail from the shell of her ear all the way down to her collarbone. Her skin tastes salty from the day in the desert heat. I can feel the thrum of her pulse beneath my mouth. I nip at the soft skin at the base of her throat, reveling in the way her heartbeat creates its own rhythm against my lips.

"Nash," she says breathlessly. The cotton candy falls at our feet, long forgotten as Nora's hands wrap around my neck. She applies pressure to the spot where my hair meets my neck, coaxing my head even further down. "Oh my god." Her fingers tighten around my neck. Anxious to taste her once again, I make my way back to those cotton candy stained lips.

Her mouth anxiously awaits mine, and as soon as my lips are in the vicinity of hers, she's opening hers, letting me in instantly.

Her fingers are hot against my neck as she plays with the stray strands of hair peeking out under my beanie. I'm semi-aware of the concert going on around us, the bass of the speakers bumping erratically like the beat of my heart.

I don't know if our mouths stay fused for one song or five. All I can say is, now that I've felt Nora's mouth on mine, I can't go back to what we were before. I won't be able to look at her without wanting my lips on hers.

I've kissed more women than I could ever begin to keep track of. And none of them kissed me like Nora is right now. And none of them were Nora. And I wish they all *had* been Nora.

She's standing here, pulling emotions from my cold black heart that I haven't felt in years.

Part of me loves it.

Part of me hates it.

As I pull away, resting my forehead against hers, I can't help but wonder what we've started.

I want her. I want her so fucking *bad.* But I'm very aware of the promise I made myself the last time I developed feelings for a woman. I vowed I would never let someone take an axe to my heart like Taylor did. I didn't want to become obsessive again.

Peering at Nora, I hope she's different than Taylor. Part of me wonders if she is even capable of doing the awful things Taylor did to me. Looking at her now, I can't see her doing any of the things that led to the demise of me and Taylor—the fallout leaving me with a broken, shattered heart.

Nora's chest rises and falls quickly as she greedily takes in air. My own body does the same, my eyes examining her. I want to keep her lips on mine. Anger bubbles inside me at the thought of someone else's lips on her. Jealousy is not a feeling I've been familiar with lately. I lean down, giving her one more peck on the lips before throwing my arm over her shoulder and tucking her into my side.

Nora's tiny hand lands on my stomach, her head coming to rest against my chest. The two of us stare at the performers on stage, getting lost in the talent of the band before us. For a long period of time, we don't speak. I love that she looks just as lost in the music as I am, not trying to fill the space between us with idle conversation.

Tonight, I won't overthink whatever the hell we're doing. I'm having a good time without the use of substances for the first time in—well, I don't know how long. I want to keep her close to me without thinking of what happens next.

If I could pause time and live in this moment where neither of us are asking for more, I would.

And maybe I can.

It's later in the evening when the last band is finishing up their encore on stage. My arms are wrapped around Nora, her arms the same around me. Her face is pressed against my chest, her breath hot against the thin fabric. We've been swaying with the wind as the band performed their last few songs. My chin is perched on her ballcap.

"Nash?" Nora says, her doe eyes looking up at me. When I look, I swear I see something like worry in them.

"Hm?" I ask, my arms tightening slightly around her. The people around us start to make their way away from the stage, the stage now filling with crew members to pack up the band's equipment.

Nora busies her fingers, toying with the waistband of my jeans. "Can you promise me something?" she asks.

Anything. Nothing. Everything, I tell myself. *Only time will tell.*

"What?" I answer, my heartbeat picking up with fear of what she'll ask of me.

Ask for anything but my heart, I want to tell her, my heart far too jaded to fit in her hands.

"Promise me you'll always remember this moment and how you felt when you think of me." Her words are slow, and well thought out.

My eyebrows pull together, wondering where that comment even came from. It seems random, but I don't question her. The look on her face makes me think twice of saying something sarcastic.

"There's so many moments I could remember you by, Rose," I finally answer. Which is true.

There's the moment that she first got that nickname from me, the color of her cheeks in that small studio office a shade that reminded me of a rose.

Or the first rehearsal we had for the tour, the way her breaths would turn shaky as my hands roamed across her body.

The time I took her to an empty arena, the two of us sharing random confessions, the night becoming one of my best nights in a while.

I can't wipe the memory of the first time we performed together in front of tons of people. Or the smile on her face as the mass of screaming fans in the audience shouted her name.

And then tonight—a night I'll never forget. I'm not sure I'll ever look at cotton candy again without my dick stirring, the memory of her cotton candy lips on mine now branded on *my* brain.

"But no matter what happens," she begins, her hands twisting around my shirt, "I want you to remember me this way. *I* want to remember us this way, the way we are *tonight*."

"What do you think will happen?" I glance down at her curiously.

By now, the crowd has thinned out substantially. Looking over her shoulder, I can see the vendors packing up their booths and people making their way back to the parking lot. I try to avoid eye contact with both Sebastian and Matt, not wanting to explain myself about what transpired tonight.

"You're you," she finally answers, slightly pulling away as she talks. "Something is bound to happen," she says, a faraway look in her eyes.

"You can't predict the future," I remind her, wondering why I even want to argue the subject. Letting it go, I give her what she wants.

I wrap her hand in mine and give her a quick kiss on the top of her head before pulling her toward the parking lot. We're having idle chatter when the first camera flashes.

My stomach drops, the blinding flashes all too familiar to me.

"Nash! Nora! Are the two of you dating?"

Pulling Nora to my chest, I try to shield her from the

storm of people with cameras racing our way. I yank the ballcap off her head, quickly positioning it so the brim covers her face as much as possible.

"Nora! What is it like being with Nash?"

"Nash, look this way."

"Is this the first date?"

"Nash! Nash! Over here."

"Nora, can you tell us more about your relationship with Nash?"

Nora turns her head, looking toward the throng of paparazzi following our every move.

"Don't answer them," I demand, looking over my shoulder to find Matt herding a person away from us. Sebastian flanks Nora's side, making sure no one can get close to her.

"Nora, honey, care to answer some of my questions?"

A man with a T-shirt two sizes too small for him tries to inch his way toward Nora.

Sebastian stops the dude in his tracks instantly, but it isn't good enough for me. I've made it a point not to talk with paparazzi for years, let alone look directly at them. But this guy asking Nora intrusive questions and trying to get close to her doesn't sit well with me.

"Back the hell off," I warn him, staring the guy dead in the eye.

I instantly regret lashing out, because his eyes light up like a fucking Christmas tree. "Territorial, I see," he shouts, Sebastian's large body now blocking him from view.

It takes us five times as long to get to our car as it should, navigating the thirty-or-so cameras flashing in our eyes. The whole time, the paparazzi yell questions at the two of us. My blood begins to boil, pissed that Nora is having to learn about the paps the hard way. Some of the questions they ask her make me want to turn around and punch them square in the nose.

They've pissed me off numerous times throughout the years, asking things they've had no business asking me.

But now that they're aiming that shit toward her, it's not okay with me.

I should've paid more attention to our surroundings, making sure we weren't put in this situation in the first place. I was too lost in spending time with her to even worry about the paparazzi. I let my guard down, and I'm pissed at myself for it.

Matt has the door open for us in no time. I don't hesitate to gently push Nora into the backseat. I quickly follow behind her, sliding into the seat while still trying to shield her from the cameras now pressing against the car windows. The door slams behind us, and Matt and Sebastian get in the car only moments later. Matt has the car started with his next breath, then he quickly revs the engine and drives us away from the flashing lights.

It takes longer than desired to get out of the parking lot, the paparazzi blocking the car from the dirt road that'll lead us out. Once we've made it to the road, Matt weaves in and out of side streets and various highways, finding the quickest path back to the stadium.

No one in the car speaks the whole ride home. I'm still pissed at myself for not being more observant of my surroundings, wondering how or when we were even recognized. Matt is silent in the front, probably biting his tongue to so he can't say he told me so.

Nora must be thinking the same thing I am, because as the car slows down and stops, she looks at me. "There was a girl at the alcohol booth when we first got there. I noticed her looking at us weird, but I didn't think she recognized you. Do you think she told someone? I should've—"

I stop her from continuing by squeezing her thigh, her skin butter soft against my fingertips. "There's no use in playing what-ifs. Those fuckers can find me anywhere."

Matt laughs from the front seat, turning the keys to stop the engine. I'm already fully aware that I will get a lecture from my whole team as soon as I'm back on my bus. I hate that they're probably right. Today was a bad idea. But damn was it a perfect day—until it wasn't.

Sebastian and Matt both exit the car, most likely making their way to debrief the rest of the team on the shitshow that just happened. I'm sure pictures of me and Nora are already plastered all over the gossip sites.

"Well…" Nora breathes out, her hand landing on mine.

"That was a clusterfuck," I respond, finishing her thought.

She laughs, her head falling back against the headrest. "Definitely a clusterfuck. I can't believe that's what you deal with every time you go somewhere."

I angle my body toward her, brushing my thumb against the soft skin of her wrist. "You get used to it."

Her free hand finds my cheek, and even in the darkness of the car, I can see her eyes studying my face. "No, you don't," she finally answers, indirectly calling me out on my bullshit.

Leaning into her hand, I utter words that I hope don't scare her away. "They'll follow you now. They're vultures, and you're their newest fascination. You'll have to be careful wherever you go. If they think there's the smallest chance we *might* be dating, they'll go nuts. It's odd, why people have such a sick fascination with who I spend my time with."

"But we aren't dating," she says, her voice low but direct.

Her words catch me off guard. Not because I necessarily think we're dating either, but because I've lived in the reality where the women I spend time with would do anything to be dating me. Hell, dating me is a one-way ticket to fame.

I've already been used once by Taylor, and I'm sure countless other women but that was mutual. Now I'm bitter and expect to be used. It's why I *let* women use me. They use me for a photo op as we leave whatever club I got drunk at that night, I use them for a release. It's a symbiotic relationship that's been at work since the messy breakup with my ex.

"I don't know what we're doing," I answer her truthfully. I don't do feelings. I've sworn them off, but here I am, definitely fucking feeling.

A heart as broken and jaded as mine has no business feeling again.

Nora said she'd make me feel again, would get me to fall back in love with what I do. What I didn't expect was to fall for her, too.

"We're having fun. But you're *you* and I'm *me* and I don't know how an *us* could possibly work. We're just having fun, right?" she says.

"Fun," I repeat, missing the warmth as soon as she pulls her hand from my face.

Her smile is relieved when she looks up at me. Leaning in quickly, she plants a kiss against my lips. Not wanting to miss an opportunity for a different kind of relief, I deepen the kiss. Circling my hand around her waist, I pull her across the seat until she's pressed up against me.

We make out in the backseat of a car like a pair of teenagers at a drive-in movie, and it feels fucking great. I could get addicted to the taste of her, obsessed with the moans that fall from her mouth as my hand slips under her skirt.

I'm getting dangerously close to the warmth between her legs when her hand finds my chest, gently pushing me away. "I think we've had enough fun for one night."

I lean back and laugh, deciding right then that I want to have all the fun with her.

Not waiting for an answer, she grabs her purse and opens the car door. She steps out of the car, shutting the door without looking back at me. Before I follow her lead, I adjust myself in my pants, the hardness pretty obvious in my jeans.

The two of us fall in step together as we make our way toward her bus. The conversation is easy, the stress of the paps finding us feeling like a distant memory.

We stop in front of her bus, and she rests her shoulder against it.

"I had fun tonight, Nash," Nora says, a smile on her face.

"I did too," I tell her truthfully. Grabbing her by her waist, I pull her in for a hug. "Was it the best first date you've ever had?" I tease, already pissed off if she gives me any other answer but yes.

She shakes her head against my chest and laughs. "It was an amazing first date."

"And you almost said no," I remind her, my hands finding both sides of her face.

I lean down, stealing the words from her mouth with my tongue. She doesn't object, her lips moving effortlessly against mine.

"What a mistake that would've been," she jokes once we finally break apart.

It takes five more minutes for us to finally say goodbye, the both of us getting distracted by each other's mouth to properly say goodbye.

Finally, Ziggy opens the door, the smile on his face almost splitting his face in half. "Nash, I'm going to need to interrogate our sweet Nora now. Goodbye!" He grabs her by the arm, almost tripping her in the process as he tugs her up the few steps.

"Goodbye, Nash," Nora says sweetly, steadying herself by grabbing the railing.

"Goodnight, Rose," I respond, backing away while getting one last look at her for the night.

I'm almost to my own tour bus, lost in thought about Nora, when it hits me.

I had fun with her tonight—pure, sober fun. It's not something I'm used to, and the realization is jarring. My time with her was fun, carefree, until the paps showed up at least.

I felt like myself again, whoever the hell I am underneath all the pressure and expectations of whatever everyone else wants me to be. It's a great feeling to feel this way again, clear headed and excited. It's as terrifying as it is exciting.

I know I have an addictive personality. It's something everyone has probably learned about me by now. And I'm scared I could easily trade in my current addictions—booze, sex—for her. An addiction to love is something that has scarred me in the past.

Now I'm left wondering what happens to me when I trade my current vices in for Nora. Or when this thing, whatever the hell it is, blows up in both of our faces.

21
NORA

Two days later, I'm attempting to take advantage of the late start to my day by sleeping in. However, it isn't my lucky day because apparently Monica has other plans for me. After fielding three calls from her, I finally answer the fourth time.

"Hello?" Clearing the frog in my throat, I pull the phone away from my ear to see that it's only seven AM. I inwardly groan. *So much for sleeping in.*

"Were you asleep?" Monica asks, and if I'm not mistaken there's a judgmental tone to it.

"I have the day off," I whisper, trying not to wake up the five other dancers in the bunks nearby. Propping myself up on one elbow, I shift the phone against my ear. These bunks aren't the most spacious quarters. The ceiling above me is too low to allow me to fully sit up without bumping my head.

"No, you don't. I want to meet with you. I'll be outside your bus in fifteen minutes. Be ready." The phone line goes dead before I can even string together a response.

Groaning, I throw my phone on the mattress next to me. I rub the heels of my hands over my eyes as dread settles in my stomach. I was naïve to think Monica wouldn't say anything about the leaked photos of me and Nash. The pictures of us at the festival were apparently the most interesting thing in the tabloids for the last two days. My follower count on Instagram has been skyrocketing. Anytime I check my tagged photos, I find photos of me and Nash at the festival all throughout my feed.

It turns out people were taking photos of us far before we left the venue. I woke up yesterday morning to a million texts from Riley, all of them screenshots of me and Nash throughout the day. She sent at least twenty different angles of the two of us making out before I threatened to block her.

If I never saw pictures of me kissing again it'd be too soon. I've found myself over-analyzing my hand placement and the angle of my head. If someone would've told me a year ago that my tongue in Nash Pierce's mouth would be front page on every gossip site, I would've checked them for a concussion. But in a wild twist of events, this is my life now.

Unfortunately, my life now also involves Monica Masters, and I've wasted three minutes dissecting the paparazzi photos from the other night for the thousandth time. If I don't get my ass out of this bed as soon as possible, I'm going to be talking to the ever so chic Monica in my fraying flannel pajama bottoms.

Pulling on the bunk curtain as quietly as possible, I climb out, trying my best not to disturb the curtain of the bed below mine. Once my bare feet land safely on the carpeted floor, I search for my suitcase and pull out the first outfit I find. Then, I tiptoe my way to the bathroom.

Once I'm inside, after grabbing my toiletry bag from the shelf to my left, I quickly brush my teeth. Now that I have about ten minutes until Monica gets here, I decide to get ballsy and pull out my mascara. I do a few coats on each side before throwing the tube back in my bag. I do a quick job of brushing my hair, and after realizing I don't have time to use an excessive amount of dry shampoo, I decide on putting it up in a messy bun. My fingers slide the ponytail holder off my wrist, quickly maneuvering my hair into a large mass on top of my head.

As fast as I can, I strip out of what I slept in and pull on the outfit I grabbed from my bag. I pull the leggings on, seeing then that I'd snagged a pair of my black moto tights, so the kneecaps and up the sides of my thighs are now covered in faux leather. Making sure my nipples aren't greeting Monica this morning as well, I throw on a strappy black sports bra.

Last on my body is a light pink long-sleeve T-shirt, the back of it completely open from my shoulders to the middle of my back.

I give myself one last once-over in the small bathroom mirror before deciding this is as good as it's going to get in the time Monica gave me. Opening the door, I flip the light switch off and then quietly pad down the narrow hallway. No one has left their bunks in the time it took me to get ready, which makes me let out a sigh of relief. The last thing I wanted to do this morning was explain to one of my peers why I was meeting with Nash's manager.

Taking a seat on the soft leather couch of our makeshift living room, I hastily pull on my socks and sneakers. My phone is in my hand as I leave the bus and head outside.

I find Monica standing a few feet away from the door with a look of annoyance on her face. A quick glance at my phone alerts me to the fact that I still had four minutes before I would've been categorized as late.

"Took you long enough." Monica sighs, her eyes slipping from my face and down my body. It dawns on me that she doesn't have her cell phone glued to her hand for once.

"I wasn't aware we had a meeting this morning," I tell

her, adding under my breath, "let alone a meeting before the sun has barely risen..."

She lets out a puff of air, which is the most of a laugh I've ever heard her give. "Oh, Nora, didn't you know the most productive people are up before the sun rises?" The bottom of her heel taps on the asphalt below her, her eyebrows raised as she waits for me to answer.

"I wasn't informed of that tidbit of information," I respond, taking in her immaculate appearance. She's got a full face of makeup on; and her hair is in perfectly straight pieces, landing just above her shoulders. She's dressed as if she could pop into a meeting at any second. All before 7:15AM.

"I read it in a book somewhere," she deadpans, starting to walk toward the epicenter of our parked buses.

"Guess I'll have to put it on my reading list," I say, seeing no choice other than scurrying after her. "Where are we going?"

She looks over her shoulder briefly, her steps not faltering to allow me to catch up. "We've got to talk. The team is very impressed with those paparazzi photos. Give me an update on where you are with Nash."

I have no idea where she is leading me right now, but I follow along, wanting to be done with this conversation as soon as humanly possible. "Uh, we're friends?" I try, desperately wanting to change the subject.

"How do you think he feels about you?" she pesters, actually gracing me with eye contact for a whole five seconds.

"We've been on one date. That's the same sort of timespan he gives every girl he hooks up with. Can't say I think he's feeling anything too deep."

"Yeah, well, he usually isn't caught on secret dates with girls—especially *sober*. By the way, next time Nash decides to take you somewhere, you tell me right away. I almost didn't have the paparazzi there in time to get those million-dollar shots of you two."

Please tell me those photos aren't actually worth a

freaking million bucks…

"It's a good thing we know we have to keep tabs on Nash at all times," Monica continues. "We've learned the hard way that he can disappear or wind up drunk in a random woman's bed one too many times. Usually both."

Stopping at a food service truck, she asks the man in the window for a latte. He looks to me, asking what I would like. I tell him my order, still processing all the information Monica has thrown at me in the last few minutes.

"You told the paparazzi where we were?" Chewing on my lip, I can't fathom why Nash's team would possibly put him through the circus of dealing with those people on purpose.

Monica smiles, and I don't know if it's in response to my question or to the man handing her the coffee she ordered. "Oh, sweetie," she begins condescendingly, "of course we did. Nash needs all the good publicity he can get. And *you,* my dear, are the exact kind of publicity he needs."

I thank the man for handing me my coffee. Then, popping the straw into the lid of the cup, I follow Monica to the small table seated a few feet away from the truck. We both take a seat followed by a sip, each of us taking a moment to let the caffeine run through us.

"Does Nash know this?" I finally question, already suspecting the answer but hoping I'm wrong.

She rolls her eyes as if that's ridiculous. "No, and he *won't* know. Just add it to the list of secrets you and everyone else are keeping from him."

The coffee I'm slurping on feels like a lead brick in my stomach at her words. The more I'm immersed in his world, the more I learn how manipulated he is by the people around him. *Me included.* The thought makes me feel uneasy. *I signed up to be one of those people.*

I don't want to do it anymore. I don't want to break his heart just so he can write a good song or two. I'm just scared I'm in too deep at this point to get out.

"What if I don't want to keep secrets from him?" I ask quietly, looking at anything but Monica. I'm too afraid to see the look on her face.

"What kind of question is that, Nora?"

Sighing, I shift my position, still not looking her in the eye. "I mean, the more I get to know him, the more I don't want to hurt him. I think he's a good guy underneath the persona he shows the world."

"I never told you he was a bad guy when you *signed up for this*." She emphasizes the last few words, just furthering the upset feeling in my stomach.

"Yeah, well..." I try to think of what I'm even trying to say here. Staring at the light brown color of my coffee, I finally spit *something* out. "I didn't think he'd be who I've learned he is, okay? I don't want to be the person to hurt him."

It's silent. And after the silence bleeds on for way too long, I finally get the nerve to look at Monica. The look on her face can only be described as unamused.

Finally, her perfectly lined lips open. "It's a little late to decide that, don't you think? The only reason you're on this tour is because you said you would do this. If you need to, frame it in your head as...not hurting him, but *helping* him."

A sarcastic laugh falls from my lips before I can stop it. "How would I be helping him?"

She takes the time to take another sip of her drink before answering me. "Because if he writes another album like his first, he'll solidify himself as a songwriter with staying power—not someone who occasionally pushes out mediocre albums every few years. He'll prove he has the kind of talent we all know he has deep down but haven't been seeing lately. If you can pull this off, one day down the road, he'll thank you. Trust me."

It's my turn to roll my eyes now, because I think her words are such bullshit. For starters, we've only been on one date. I know I'm not even *near* the position to break his heart. But I do know he's started to trust me. He's let his guard down for me, and if he found out today about what *really* got me on this tour, I know it wouldn't break his heart. But, it would break his trust in me, and that's something I know I don't want.

Long story short: I'm screwed.

Monica spends the next ten minutes droning on about what I've promised. I've spent the whole time already thinking up an apology to Nash when he finds out I began our friendship with ulterior motives. Those motives are out the window now, though. I want to get to know him just because I enjoy spending time with him. Not like it matters.

The fact is, I started this tour with him because I wanted to follow my dream of dancing in front of crowds—at all costs. And I got that chance. I've been living my dream night after night. I thought it would be the best ticket to achieving my dreams. It seemed like an easy decision at the time, because I thought he'd be a dick and not even give me a second glance. I didn't think he'd be a decent human after reading what the media says about him. I *really* didn't think I'd ever have so much as an actual conversation with him.

No matter what I thought in the beginning, the truth now is that I've become friends with Nash. I know he's started to trust me—a trust I do not deserve at all.

I leave the meeting with Monica, only feeling shittier about myself as a human. I even make it as far as rushing to Nash's trailer, where I anxiously beat on the door of it for a few minutes until it hits me that he isn't in there.
I go back to my own bus feeling defeated, losing my nerve to come clean to him, the fear of losing him starting to overtake me.

22
NORA

I find myself in an empty dance studio hours later, still trying to rid myself of the memory of the conversation with Monica this morning. There's a pit in my stomach the size of Texas when I think of how giddy she seemed about me and Nash getting close in the way that we have.

I felt physically ill all morning, the donuts Ziggy pilfered from food service not helping the anxiety coursing through my veins. Thankfully, we have access to a gym with a studio a block away from the stadium we're performing at tonight. I was able to call the gym ahead of time and book the room for myself.

Getting back to my roots, I film a few freestyles for my Instagram account while I'm here. I realize most the people who follow me *now* may not be here for my dancing videos, but I want to stay true to my OG followers. Plus, it feels good to let my body take the lead for the first time in a while. I'm so used to the same routines for tour that letting loose is just what I need to take my mind away from the stress of my personal life.

I lose complete track of time. My body stays moving freely to the songs on shuffle through the speakers. It's well into the afternoon, the evening creeping in when I finally stop for the day. My legs feel like jelly, and while I begin to stretch out my muscles, all I can think about is how I wish I had access to a warm bathtub.

My leg is propped up on the ballet barre when a squeak on the floor has me looking toward the door. Much to my surprise, I find a smirking Nash walking toward me.

"Don't stop on my account," he says with a smartass tone. He doesn't bother to hide it when he clearly checks out my ass.

I roll my eyes, going deeper into the stretch so I can feel the tension all the way up my calf. "How'd you find me here?"

We make eye contact through the large mirror in front of me. He stops a few paces behind me, his eyes unabashedly running down my body.

Pulling out his phone, he pulls up the Instagram app and shows it still open to my profile. The video I posted an hour or so ago starts, the studio in view behind me. "I saw this," he says. "It wasn't hard to find out where you were after that, I just had to ask a few different people."

Trying to hide the growing smile on my face, I switch legs. "I wasn't aware that you followed me. Or that you were invested in my whereabouts."

Stepping closer, his large hands find the small of my waist. He slides his fingers through the open part of my shirt, grazing the bare skin there until it feels like it's burning. The feel of his fingers digging into my skin has my stomach muscles tight, anticipation building with his touch.

We spent nearly all of yesterday stealing small moments together, but somehow, I'd still forgotten what it felt like to have his hands on me. I continue to stretch my legs, my eyes carefully watching him in the mirror.

Nuzzling against my neck, I can feel every one of his words against my skin when he says, "I followed you the night of the festival. If I gave a shit about social media, I might be offended you didn't notice."

He applies pressure through his fingertips, sending tingles all the way to my core.

Once he realizes I'm not going to humor him about the follow, he presses on—literally, as his pinky drifts into the waistband of my leggings.

I watch him touch me in the mirror, trying my best to ignore it. "I need to make sure I finish stretching," I tell him.

He hums, his other hand slowly drifting down the leg that is placed on the barre. His long fingers glide against the fabric. At the touch, a shiver goes down my body, making my toes curl. "I didn't say you had to stop," he counters.

My head falls back, hitting his hard warm chest. I can feel the denim of his jacket scratch against the bare skin of my neck. "You're distracting me," I point out, no longer feeling the deep stretch in the back of my calf, but not wanting to put my leg down in fear of losing his touch.

"Am I?" he teases, his teeth nipping at my ear.

I'm just about to answer him when another finger slips into the fabric of my leggings. Part of me is screaming to stop him, knowing exactly where this could lead. However, the larger part of me is melting against him, anxious to see what his next move will be.

"I missed you today," he states, his whole hand now in my pants. So achingly slow, his hand is nearing the point where he'll find out I have nothing on underneath these leggings.

"That's good," I answer breathlessly, barely registering his admission. I'm too caught up in the way his hand is getting closer and closer to—

A long breath leaves his lips when he's met with bare skin. "No, it isn't good," he breathes, his voice scratching. A narrow digit hits my folds and the movement has us both breathing hard. "I don't like missing people, Rose." His finger goes all the way in, causing my body to start to go limp. Luckily, he supports the extra weight, the finger inside me overtaking my senses.

"You don't?" I ask, finding his eyes through the mirror in front of us. I find his blue gazed pinned on me. His tongue comes out to lick his lips and it's one of the hottest things I've ever seen.

"No," he says. "To miss someone means to care. And to care means to let someone in. I'm done letting people in, Rose."

His finger hooks inside me, making me arch my back against him. The new position pushes the hardness of him against my ass. Letting out a moan, I balance myself by grabbing onto him.

"Why?" I question.

A low rumble leaves his chest moments before his lips start traveling down the hollow of my neck. Teeth scratch against my skin, the leg on the floor slowly turning into jelly. "That's a story for never."

I bask in the feeling of his lips against my neck and his finger inside me. I'm getting closer and closer to release, but it isn't good enough for me. The quick movement of letting my leg fall to the ground pushes Nash out of me. I take advantage of him being stunned, spinning my body so our fronts are now pressed against the other's. There's no mistaking the hard bulge that now rests against my stomach.

My eyes find his while my hand snakes underneath his shirt. I'm met with the warmth of his skin. Splaying my fingers across his chest, I let my hand drift lower and lower, getting desperately closer to the waistband of his briefs. "I missed you too," I admit, without thinking about the weight of my words. Slipping my fingers underneath the band, I watch in fascination as his eyes become hooded.

"You did?" The vulnerability in his tone sends an arrow straight to my heart.

I nod sincerely, my fingertips exploring his warm skin.

"I don't want to miss you," he admits to the space

between us.

"Then don't," I say, raising to my toes. My lips find his neck. His head tilts instantly, allowing me even more room to explore. I'm memorizing the curve of his Adam's apple when in one swift motion, he's lifting me by my hips, my back hitting the cold mirror. My weight rests on the barre attached to the wall. Not trusting the barre to hold me for long, I wrap my legs around his middle, pulling him in close to me and dispersing the weight.

Picking up where I left off earlier, I slide my fingers back underneath his waistband. Nash helps me balance while I quickly undo the button of his jeans. The fabric falls down his hips. Not wasting any time, my fingers move swiftly underneath his briefs, pulling at them until there is nothing in the way. I'm cascading down the exposed skin on the way to his hardness when he traps my lips in his.

The kiss is heated, burning a trail from the point our lips meet all the way down to my toes. His moan is lost in my mouth the moment my hand wraps around his length. I didn't know a kiss could be felt in so many different places.

One of his hands slaps down on the mirror next to my head, his mouth tearing away from mine.

My core tightens as he lifts my shirt off, pulling my hand off him in the process. The soft pink shirt lands softly on the floor. His eyes roam slowly over the swells of my breasts.

Frustrated by the clothes still separating us, I slide my hand underneath the denim of his jacket, coaxing it off. I'm seconds away from tugging his shirt off when he drops to his knees.

He places each one of my legs so they rest over his strong shoulders. Nash's hands grab at my leggings, pulling them down in one, swift tug. He traces a wet trail from the inside of my knee all the way up my thigh.

"That's the problem," Nash breathes, his breath hot against me as he continues the previous conversation.

I look down, trying not to clench my thighs when I see the sight of him looking up at me from between my legs.

"It's too late, I already miss you. And I don't know what the fuck I'm going to do with that information, Rose." He doesn't give me time to respond. He spreads my legs open with expertise, his mouth landing on my very center.

His tongue works against me instantly. My body reacting to every lap of his tongue as a small part of my heart becomes his with his admission. A moan echoes off the walls when a finger joins in. My hands twist in his hair, needing something of him to grab. Holding him against me, I feel my muscles begin to clench.

"Fuck, Nora." His breath tickles the inside of my thighs.

"So close," I pant, my back arching off the mirror as he hooks his finger.

It doesn't take long for me to reach a release. My body writhes against his mouth as I ride the waves of my orgasm.

"Holy shit," I whisper, my hand reaching toward him as he stands up.

His fingers wrap tightly around my wrist before I can get my hand down his pants. He groans, his lips pressing softly against my temple. "I have to go."

Our chests rise and fall in perfect sync. Nash sighs, bending down to hand me my discarded leggings. Holding them above the ground slightly, he gestures for me to step into them.

I've got one foot into the hole when he speaks again. "Monica is waiting in the car with Bash and Matt. I have an interview for a magazine I agreed to a year ago. I think Monica would wring my neck if we were late. It took me being a pain in the ass for a solid hour for her to let us stop here on the way to the interview."

Once both my feet are in, I steady myself by grabbing his shoulders as he pulls the black fabric up my legs. Shivers run down my spine as I feel his knuckles on the side of my leg, my body already craving his touch all over again.

“I’m shocked you’re listening to Monica,” I mutter.

Nash helps me back into my shirt. Giving me a sideways smirk before answering, “Yeah, it’s part of this whole new Nash. You’re helping me fall in love with my job again. I figured that would be a lot easier if I wasn’t constantly battling with my manager.”

Before I have a chance to say anything, Nash’s hands find my cheeks. I can smell myself on his fingers, something I thought would gross me out, but the warming in my belly proves exactly the opposite. “Thanks for the pick me up, Rose. Having my face between your thighs was exactly what I needed to get me through another god forsaken interview.”

His thumb brushing over my cheek, he lays one last, long kiss against my lips. Then, I watch in silence as he swaggers right back out of the room.

Stopping at the door with one hand on the handle, he turns around to face me. Grabbing at the tent of his jeans, he leaves me with a sentence that has me wanting a replay of what we just did. “We’ll finish this later, Rose. I’m not done with you.” He gives me a wink and then he’s out of sight.

I’m not sure how long I stay with my feet planted, eyes glued back on the door as if he would reappear. All I know is that singing is not the only wonderful thing he can do with his mouth.

I want to feel it again.

23
NASH

"Fuck no," I tell Poe, throwing the nearest thing to me (an empty water bottle) at him.

The fucker catches it easily, wagging his eyebrows at me. "Oh, just admit it, asshole. You have a thing for the dancer!" He looks over to Landon, bumping him on the shoulder. "Tell him, Land."

Landon shrugs, biting at his lip before answering. "I mean, you do seem to really like her, Nash."

Scrubbing at my eyes, I let out an audible groan, pissed off at them for calling me out like this. It's been a week since I had my first *real* taste of Nora, and apparently, it's fucking obvious that all I want is more. I've had a busy schedule on top of the tour the past week, so I haven't seen her as much as I would like to.

It's completely out of character for me, but I haven't let her finish me off yet. I can't fucking explain why, it's not like she hasn't tried—and tried she has. I haven't let her go further because deep down I know shit is different with her, and I'm absolutely terrified about what happens when—*if*—things go further between us. I'm not strong enough to be in control of my feelings for her, if I'm even doing that now.

When I told her in that dingy dance studio that I don't miss people, I was being completely honest. I don't want to fucking miss anyone. I don't want to be put in the place where another can take a bulldozer to my heart. Deep down, underneath the Nash Pierce the world sees, I'm just a broken guy who puts too much value in a relationship.

It's part of the reason Taylor and I broke up. I was too obsessed with either her or the music, unable to balance both. My self-worth was dependent on what kind of boyfriend I was to her and what kind of music I was putting out in the world. There was no in-between for me, and it wasn't the least bit healthy.

I'm not naïve enough to think the downfall of our relationship was completely her fault. Some of it was on me, for sure. I had trust issues a mile long, and they only got worse when we weren't together. Which, with my life, was a lot. But trust issues and self-esteem problems be damned, it didn't mean she had the right to fuck my best friend behind my back.

After walking in on her riding Collin's dick like it was a damn mechanical bull, I swore I would never put my self-worth in another's hands. And part of that promise was to never do another serious relationship at all.

Now I find myself wondering if I've healed enough since Taylor to be *able* to do a normal relationship. If I wanted to, that is.

Could I date Nora without becoming so obsessed with her that it drove us both crazy? Would my shitty self-esteem and trust issues get in the way?

I'd love to say I think I've healed since the betrayal. But I'm not completely sure I have. Now that I'm faced with the reality that I might *want* to let someone else in again, I'm wondering if I even can. I'm afraid all this time I may have just been putting band aids on my wounds in the form of alcohol and sex.

I know that eventually, maybe soon even, I'll either have to walk away from Nora or go all the way with her. I also know that either option could lead to my demise.

I'm running through the possibilities when something bounces off my head. Shaking away the thoughts, I look toward a wide-eyed Poe.

"Dreaming about Nora?" he teases, unknowingly right on the money with his assumption.

"We're just getting to know each other," I grumble, standing up and reaching for the ceiling of the bus. I stretch out my arms, the boxing workout from this morning leaving me sore.

Poe lets out a cackle, Landon quietly laughing next to him. I get annoyed enough to consider firing the two assholes and just finding new bandmates.

"Getting to know each other, my ass," Poe continues. "You look at her differently, Nash."

Rolling my eyes, I start to walk away from him. I'm about to walk off the bus altogether when my curiosity gets the best of me. "How do I look at her differently?" I ask, feeding right into the palm of his hand.

"It's hard to explain. You just have this *look* when you're truly happy. Sometimes it appears when you're on the phone with your little brother, sometimes in the midst of a songwriting session, and often when the crowd sings your song back to you. You look at her the same way. When you look at her, you look happy."

I stand there dumbfounded, still staring at him when a soft knock breaks my focus.

Slowly, the door opens, a mousy assistant on the other side. She has two coffees in her hand—one for me and one I ordered for Nora.

"Your coffees, sir," she says, hesitantly looking from me to the guys and back.

It isn't hard to miss the loud rumble of laughter coming from both Landon and Poe. "Case in point!" Landon jokes from behind me. "Nash Pierce is a *simp!*"

I don't spare either of them a second glance when I rip the coffees from the girl's hands.

"Thanks, Layla," I say, breezing past her before those two fuckers can get any more of a rise out of me.

"It's Lauren!" she yells behind me.

I turn around and smile, feeling a little guilty. "Thanks, *Lauren.*"

Weaving in and out of the parked buses, I make it to one of the stadium entrances. My eyes track the empty seats until I spot her. I find her pretty high up, her eyes glued to the crew members that are setting up for tonight. It's looking like it might be a rain show, which requires a few extra steps for setup.

Taking advantage of the moment, I watch her, trying to see the setup through her eyes. Stage members in black shirts are scattered around the different stages. The lighting crew is behind the stage pit, a pile of members fiddling with a spotlight. I remember the first time the boys and I had our first stadium concert. We were all amazed at the amount of work it took to get our stage set. Years later, my stage setup and production are way more complicated, meaning a lot more people are involved.

When my eyes find Nora again, I find her doe-eyed gaze already on me. My feet start to make their way to her of their own accord. As I get closer to her, I find a beaming smile on her face.

"I was starting to think you forgot about me," she says, greedily taking her coffee as I hand it to her. She grabs it so quickly that I almost drop my own. The moan that escapes her lips as she sucks on the straw makes the shit I got from my bandmates almost worth it.

I take the seat next to her. "And deal with you later with no caffeine in your veins? I'm not trying to torture the crew."

Her hand thumps me on the arm playfully. "You don't even know what I'm like without my coffee," she counters, proceeding to take another slurp of her iced coffee.

Running my hand over my mouth to hide my smile, I shake my head. “That’s false. During one of our rehearsals for our solo you had mentioned how you didn’t have time to grab coffee. You were crabby the whole damn day. I was close to having my assistant fetch you a coffee just to get you to stop criticizing my dancing.”

She narrows her bright eyes. “If I remember correctly, you weren’t exactly pleasant that day either.”

Thinking back on it, I remember the massive hangover I was nursing as well as the scratches I had down my back from the woman I slept with the night before. I don’t remember her name, despite her obvious attempt to mark me as if the gashes down my back would make me want to call her the next day. (It didn’t.)

Between the hangover and the sore back from the talon marks, the last place I wanted to be was at a dance rehearsal. Nora’s out of character attitude that day didn’t help the situation. Choosing not to bring attention to the reason why I acted like a prick that particular day, I throw my arm around her.

She easily leans into the crook of my arm, the silence between us comfortable as we take in the view below us. My fingers rub absentmindedly over the fabric of her shirt.

“They’re saying it’ll probably be a rain show,” she finally says, nestling her head into the crook of my neck.

“It’s looking like it.” The weather forecast is calling for a high chance of rain starting at five and going through the night. Our openers go on at seven and by the talks of my team, it’s a good chance all of us will be playing with heavy rain.

“Do you like rain shows?” she asks, setting her coffee in the cupholder to her left.

“They’re my favorite,” I answer honestly, recalling a vivid memory from my first rain show. It was the wildest experience. There’s something about the devotion of the fans, still there to watch you perform even in the pouring rain. Every rain show since I’ve made sure to give my all and then some, letting myself get soaked from the drops just like the fans.

“I’m excited. Except I hope I don’t fall.” Her second sentence is said as an afterthought, as if it only just occurred to her that was a possibility.

“They’ll put something on the bottom of your shoes for more grip,” I assure her.

One time I put on the wrong pair of shoes that wardrobe left out for me and completely ate shit while performing. The video of me busting my ass replayed on gossip sites for weeks. Of course, they questioned if it was because I was so hammered that I couldn’t even walk without biting it. Trying to sell the best story possible, they failed to leave out the details of the pouring rain and the soaking wet stage I was performing on.

Her fingers play with the threads of my ripped jeans, the occasional brush of her fingers against my exposed skin making my dick stir. “That’s good,” she says softly.

“I’m psyched for you to have your first rain show. There’s nothing like it.”

“Oh, I bet.”

Our conversation dies down then. People are constantly trying to get my attention, always needing me for something, so the comfortable silence we can fall into means more to me than I could put into words. I’m not used to silence. In fact, I used to be under the impression that I couldn’t handle silence, not wanting to be left alone with my thoughts for too long.

With Nora, I can be left with my thoughts and have them not be dangerous.

It’s a feeling I want to chase and run from all at once.

24
NASH

"Thank you, Nashville!" I shout, pushing wet strands of hair out of my face. My white T -shirt is completely plastered to my body. The soaked, white sleeves doing nothing to hide the string of tattoos going up both my arms.

The crowd erupts in cheers. There are screams and yelling coming from every direction. The show is coming to a close, the rain beating down on us for the duration of it.

In front of me I see thousands of drenched fans, all with smiles on their faces as they chant for an encore. Soggy poster boards wave in the air, the words bleeding down the boards from the rain. Through the chants and the cheers, one word starts to become more and more pronounced.

A smile tugs at my lips when their cheers clearly make out her name.

"Nora! Nora! Nora!"

Their screams are relentless, and after taking in what

it feels like to hear them say her name, I throw them a bone. Walking down the catwalk, I pull out both of my earpieces.

"Do you guys want Nora for an encore?" I tease, knowing exactly what they want. An encore of *Preach*. It isn't my normal encore song, the slow tempo not typically how I like to end a show, but these fans have really stuck it out in this weather. Who am I to deprive them of what they want?

"*Preach*!" they scream.

I make eye contact with some of the fans in the pit, their hair sticking wet to their faces as their hands thrash in the air with excitement. They're wearing merch from different phases of my life—clearly dedicated fans.

"Let me see what I can do," I hint, my voice lowering. I turn toward my band. "What do you guys say? Should we end the night with *Preach*?"

Troy answers immediately, hammering his drum set as a clear yes. Poe and Luke both nod in agreement. Landon is the last to respond, sliding his hand down the keyboard and giving me a thumbs up.

Turning from the band, I look back toward the audience. "We're getting warmer," I tell them, placing only one of my earpieces back in my ear. "Can somebody bring me my acoustic? And a headset?" I ask over the mic, knowing somebody from the stage crew will oblige.

Moments later, a tech runs out the guitar I use for *Preach*. Handing him the one I often use for the closing of the show, we trade. A sound engineer rushes out, hot on the heels of the stage tech. I let him fiddle with a headset for me while I continue to interact with the crowd.

Their cheers get even louder, Nora's name still clear as day.

Putting the guitar strap over my shoulder, I look down to make sure the guitar is tuned for this song. Slowly making my way back to where I left my mic stand, I address the crowd once again. "Even warmer," I say with a laugh, their screams almost shaking the stage.

"Oh yeah, could someone send Nora back out, please?" I add as an afterthought.

We've never performed *Preach* as an encore, so I know this is something completely unexpected for everyone involved. Nora just exited the stage, so I know she won't be in her typical costume for *Preach*, but I also want to give the fans what they want. A reward for sticking with us through the rain.

The public has only gotten more and more fascinated with Nora since we were first spotted together at the festival. We've had the occasional paparazzi steal photos of us on the outings we've been on since that night, only fueling the fire into the public's want to get to know her more. I haven't been seen with a woman this much since Taylor, and it's clearly piquing the interest of my fans. That fact is only made even more obvious as the stadium erupts into deafening cheers around me.

Turning toward left stage, I find Nora making her way out. She gives the crowd a wave, making them yell her name even louder.

As she makes her way toward me, I look out toward the crowd. "I don't know if you guys are here to see me or her at this point. It hasn't been this loud all night."

Everyone goes wild. "*We love you Nash!*" is heard, separating from the rest of the cheers.

Nora makes her way toward me at centerstage. "What is going on?" she says to me over the crowd so only I can hear.

Leaning away from the microphone, I put my lips close to her ear. "We're giving the crowd what they want." I pull her into the crook of my arm, her soaking wet body molding to my own.

"You'll have to forgive us," I say to the crowd. "We weren't prepared to perform this as the encore. You better like it. Right, Nora?"

Standing on her tiptoes, she leans toward my mic. "Oh, I'm sure they'll like it."

The audience eats out of the palm of her hand, going completely insane.

"Let's get to it then."

Nora takes her place behind me, giving my thigh a squeeze before we begin.

The energy from the crowd for the duration of the song is unbelievable. Everyone on stage gives this last song their all. Nora improvises some, allowing me to perform from further down on the catwalk, closer to my fans. She doesn't miss a beat, giving the crowd exactly what they want.

The music fades, barely audible with the deafening roar of the fans. Moving my guitar to my back, I take Nora's hand in mine. Both of our chests are heaving, the amount of energy we just exerted causing us to be short of breath.

"One last round of applause for my girl," I catch myself quickly, "my girl, Nora." Lifting her hand in the air, I pull on it until she lands a few steps ahead of me. The crowd eats it up, screaming in excitement for her.

She attempts to push her sopping wet hair out of her face, some strands still plastered to her forehead despite her best efforts. The hand that's not wrapped in mine comes to rest on her chest. Her mouth muttering a "*thank you*" to the crowd before us.

"And another round for the kickass guys behind me." Hitching a thumb over my shoulder, I step aside to give the crowd a view of the band and backup vocalists behind me. The fans give them a booming standing ovation.

Closing the distance between me and Nora once again, I pull her to my chest, embracing her in front of everyone here. "You killed that, Rose," I say into her ear. Unable to help myself, I place a kiss on her damp forehead. Her skin is cold from the rain, despite her cheeks being flushed from the dancing.

Facing the crowd one last time, Nora now tucked into my side, I tell them goodnight, giving a bow before escorting Nora off the stage as the lights go black.

Her hand splays against my chest as she beams up at me. "Holy shit, that was *amazing*." The look on her face stops me in my tracks.

We're standing just out of view from the concert goers. People bustle around us, all trying to get my attention, but I can't look anywhere but at her. The look of wonder on her face is something I never want to forget. In this moment she's doing exactly what she promised she'd do—she's making me fall in love with music again. Because there's no way I can't possibly love something that brings that much joy to her face.

Ignoring every single person trying to steal my attention from her, I tug on her hand, ignoring Tyson when he shouts my name for the third time.

Nora asks where we're going, but I don't even have the patience to stop and answer her. The only thing on my mind right now is getting her alone. I want to bask in the astonishment radiating off her in this moment, and I'm not willing to share it with another god damn soul.

We rush past what feels like a million people, and it isn't until we reach a dark hallway backstage that we aren't surrounded by others for the first time since the show ended.

"Nash?" she demands, her short legs trying to keep up with my stride.

Stopping without warning, I close the distance between us, pinning her up against the nearest door. Our bodies meet from chest to thigh, our body heat warming the other. "That was the best show of my fucking life," I exclaim, nipping at her jaw.

Her hands find the back pockets of my jeans, her fingers digging into my lower back. "Really?" she asks breathlessly as my lips wander over her collarbone.

"By fucking far," I admit. The atmosphere from the crowd, the rain, seeing how immersed she was in performing, her enjoyment at the end, *this* is the high I've desperately been chasing. The fame, the money, the girls...none of it has come close to the feeling after being on stage with Nora, seeing her love this world as much as I used to.

"Why can't every show be a rain show?" she asks.

I laugh at her question, my hand coming to rest on the back of her neck. "Then they wouldn't feel so damn amazing."

Stealing her next words from her lips, I crash against her. Our hands grab at whatever we can. My hands are in her hair, on her hips, fisting her shirt. I can't get her close enough, wishing our soaking wet clothes were littered on the floor.

"Let's go," I say, pulling away from her to catch my breath. Looking at her, I find her chest heaving up and down, the outline of each of her nipples through her shirt, sending my head into a tailspin.

As soon as she nods, taking my outstretched hand, I'm pulling us down the hallway like my ass is on fire.

Walking quickly, I guide us down the hallway and out a side door, forgetting about the pouring rain outside.

We both pause, staring out at the waterfall of rain before us. Shrugging, she says, "It's not like we aren't already soaked." Without warning, she takes off. She runs out into the pouring rain as if it's nothing, tugging on my hand to bring me with her.

We run around the side of the stadium, dodging golf carts and crew members hiding underneath umbrellas. Neither of us spare them a second glance, both too focused on what will happen when we're alone again.

Taking the lead, I guide us in the direction of the buses. We weave in and out of them, heading for my hopefully empty one. Nora laughs behind me as the rain pelts against us. After what seems like an eternity, we make it to my bus, and I'm so fucking thankful that no one is in it.

Opening the door, I pull her up the narrow stairway, making sure to lock the door behind us.

As soon as we make it inside, our bodies are pressed together once again. We kiss like we're running out of time, like someone could stop us at any moment. When her lips crash against mine, I coax hers open. My tongue meets hers, savoring the sweet taste of her. Time flies by as our hands explore each other.

Deciding I need more, I fist her wet hair, pulling her head back until she's looking at me. "I need you, Rose," I plead, tightening my hold on her hair while running the tip of my nose across her jaw.

"Ask for nicely," she says, gasping when I suck on her neck, no doubt leaving a mark—marking what's mine, at least for the moment.

"We've discussed this before," I tell her, adjusting myself in my jeans. "I don't typically have to ask, let alone nicely."

Stepping away from her, I back up until one hip rests against the small kitchenette counter.

A punishing smile lights up her face. She backs up until she hits the couch behind her. Taunting me, her small hand pushes her wet hair off her shoulder. It makes an achingly slow descent from the hollow of her throat, over her breasts. Her nipples are at full attention through the wet fabric of her shirt and bra. Continuing the path, her hand folds the fabric of her shirt in her hand, pulling it up to expose skin.

Time seems to stand still as I wait for her next move. I'm hard as a fucking rock, not expecting this side of her. Her eyes shine bright with defiance. Water is dripping off both our bodies, hitting the floor beneath our feet. The only sound to be heard is the rain against the bus and our racing breaths.

Her eyes stay fixated on mine while her hands start to pull at the sheer fabric of her shirt. Unabashedly, she lifts the shirt up and over her head, letting it fall to the ground with a *plop*. The sight of her standing in front of me in a black bra made of lace, makes me take a heaving breath in. Her stomach pulls in as I don't hide the way my eyes devour every exposed inch of her.

"I'm yours. All you have to do is ask for me, Nash."

Stuck in a battle of wits, I begin to lose my will to win when she reaches behind her, unclasping the bra in one easy swoop. Torturing me to no end, she keeps her hand draped over the cups of the bra, not exposing herself just yet. Her hips sway in a perfect rhythm, the straps of her bra falling from her shoulders with the movement.

I can't hide the tent of my jeans when her eyes fall to my obvious erection. I'm sticking to my guns, wanting her to admit she wants this just as bad as I do, when she does something that makes me lose my grip on the small amount of restraint I still had.

The bra drops to the floor as she licks her lips, her gaze still pinned on my dick. Losing the battle with my self-control, I fly across the room before I can even get a good look at her chest.

"For you I'll fucking beg," I exhale, claiming her mouth.

She's wrapped in my arms in the span of a single breath. Lifting her up, I support her body with one arm as the other reaches between us to caress the side of her exposed breast. As my hand palms her, I walk us all the way down the bus until I'm kicking open the door to my small bedroom.

A giggle escapes her lips as she lands on my bed with a soft thud. I cover her body with mine shortly after, marveling at all her exposed skin in view. I run a finger over the side of her ribcage, entranced with her milky white skin.

"We're going to get your bed all wet," she notes, her back arching as I take one of her peaked nipples in my mouth.

"Does it look like I give a damn?" I say, switching to the other side. My tongue works over the mound, a loud moan filling the silence when I nip at the soft flesh. Her wet hair fans out around her face, no doubt soaking through the comforter.

"Guess not," she says through an exhale, her hands pulling at my shirt. The air is warm against my chest as she pulls the shirt off, discarding it somewhere behind me.

The moonlight reflects in her eyes as they bounce over the tattoos that line my chest and abdomen.

Her finger traces a quote running down my ribcage. "I want to know the story of every one of these."

"Oh, Rose." I sigh, suddenly embarrassed by most of the stories behind my tattoos. "Half of these I got while drunk or high. I couldn't tell you about the meaning behind them." Trying to distract her, I start to move further down her body, licking each nipple before starting a wet trail down her stomach.

"Then tell me about the meaningful ones." Her hands grab at my hair as I bite the skin above her waistband.

As I peel off what little wet clothes she's got left from the waist down, I look up, not wanting to think about anything but this very moment. "Maybe one day." She stops questioning me long enough to discard what fabric was left. I take a step back, committing the sight of her completely naked and sprawled out on my bed to memory.

Pushing up on her elbows, she stares at me intently. "What if we don't have the luxury of maybe one day? What if we only have today?"

I find her question odd, but I'm over the talking. I want her mouth on mine and me buried inside her, the ache of her teasing me for weeks finally catching up to me. "Then let's not waste another fucking second of it with our bodies not connected in every damn possible way." Grabbing her by the ankle, I pull her across the bed until she's at the edge of it. Her eyes are wide, assessing my next move.

Dropping to my knees, I line my face up with her core. In an instant, my mouth is on her, greedily tasting the most intimate part of her. She pants and moans, her body writhing with pleasure.

"I'm so close," she pants minutes later, trying to pull me away from her by my hair. Her attempt is futile, only making me work her harder, sticking a finger inside her to join my tongue.

"Nash," she yelps, her body trying to scoot away from my mouth.

Pinning her down, I lap at her until she climaxes, my name falling from her mouth over and over.

I kiss my way up her body as she comes down from the orgasm. I'm caressing the spot behind her ear with my tongue when she gets up.

"My turn," she instructs, pushing me down onto the bed. Her small hand stays firm against my chest, making sure I don't try to move. There's a look of determination on her face when she begins to slide down my body, her hand hesitantly leaving my chest when she realizes I'm not trying to stop this.

Her tongue runs over her lips as she deftly undoes my fly, not hesitating to pull down both my jeans and briefs.

She doesn't waste any time pulling my dick free, and it stands at perfect attention for her. I don't know what I was expecting, but I wasn't ready for her eager lips to be on me in the next breath, her tongue swirling around the tip before taking as much of me in her throat as she can.

My fingers thread through the wet strands of her hair, guiding her head gently. She takes me deeper, causing me to throw my head back in pleasure.

With each work of her tongue, along with the look of determination on her face, I get a little more lost in the euphoria.

I'm falling, afraid the second our bodies become one that it'll be over for me. That somehow, despite all my best efforts, she will hold my jet-black heart in her hands. I've gotten to know her heart at an intimate level, and now that our bodies are about to get as intimate as two humans can get, I'm worried about what will happen when reality catches up with us.

She's too sweet for me. I'm too jaded for her. But damn will I enjoy her while I can.

Nora asked what would happen if we didn't get a *one*

day, and I couldn't give her a straight answer. What I do know, is that I'm going to drown myself in all the *todays* I have left with her.

25
NORA

Nash doesn't let me bring him to a release. After exploring him with my mouth for a few minutes, he abruptly pulls me off him and turns the both of us, caging me in with his body.

"I need to be inside you, Rose. At this point I'll fucking beg if I need to." He runs his hard length against me, eliciting a moan from my lips.

Grabbing his face by both sides, I look him dead in the eye, hoping he sees my heart with my next words. "I want this as bad as you do, Nash. Maybe even more."

My eyes travel over every slope and plane of his face. His straight nose, the cleft above his lip, the slant of his dark eyebrows. I try to capture every single detail of this moment. The vulnerability being my favorite part of it all, but also the part that hurts me the most. I want him to know that at the end of this, when he'll most likely hate me, that I really did end up wanting him just as bad, that the feelings he pulled from me were raw and real. And completely unexpected.

He sighs, the air tickling my neck. “I don’t see how it could possibly be more. I’ve never wanted something as bad as I want you.” It feels like he wants to say something else, but I’ll never know what that is because before he can say anything else, he sheathes himself into a condom before pushing inside me and then, we both get lost in the feeling.

“Fuuuuck,” he groans, his head falling against my shoulder. “You feel too damn good.”

My legs fall open, letting him even deeper inside me. Grabbing my hip, he thrusts in while his fingertips dig into my skin. I want him to leave marks, to wake up tomorrow and have a reminder of how real this moment was.

Picking up speed, Nash brings his body down, bringing his lips to mine. My hands trace over the tense muscles of his back, feeling the strain in them each time he pushes inside me. His hip bones get more and more punishing as he picks up speed. Water is still dripping from his hair, the cold droplets landing on my shoulder.

“Nash,” I breathe, my next words falling flat as he pulls his hips all the back before slowly sliding back in. The move is taunting, making my back arch. I try to swivel my hips to get him to pick up the pace, but it only ends up earning me a cocky smile from him.

“Patience, Nora,” he rasps. “I’m not done fucking you yet.”

A loud moan escapes my lips. He swallows my next one, our tongues moving in and out as our hips do the same. My senses are on overdrive—the feeling of him inside me and the pressure of his fingertips searing into my skin, branding me forever. When his lips leave mine, I’m disappointed until I feel his hot breath up against the shell of my ear. Nipping at my earlobe, a low growl leaves his chest.

My fingernails bite into his back as his teeth nip at the tender skin on my neck. He bites and then sucks, his tongue taking the pain from his teeth away. I know for a fact that tomorrow I will wake up with marks across my neck from him, but I don't care in the slightest. I *want* to wake up and have proof that tonight happened. That if only for a fleeting moment, I was Nash's—and he was mine.

Nash keeps the rhythm achingly slow, and no matter how hard I try to create more friction, he refuses to go any faster.

My eyes drift open, finding Nash's eyes already on me. The moonlight drifts in through the small windows, allowing just enough light in to see the shadows across his face. His eyelids lower as he slowly pushes all the way in.

"I love watching you come apart, Rose." His hand leaves its place on my hip, slowly traveling up my body until his fingers thread in the wet strands of my hair. He gently pulls at the hair, angling my face up so I stare at him once again.

All too quickly, I'm close to another orgasm. Nash increases the speed of his hips and it's too much. I can feel the pressure building in my abdomen.

"Come apart for me," Nash instructs. The muscles in his back begin to tighten as another orgasm rips through me. I'm still riding the waves from my climax when Nash has his own. His moan alone has me turned on all over again.

It's silent in the bus as we catch our breaths. Part of me is dreading the next part, expecting him to pull out and move on with the night. My preconceived notions of him get the best of me. I'm proven once again that Nash isn't who he's made out to be. He shocks me by pulling me to his chest seconds after he pulls out of me.

Burrowing his head into my neck, he takes a deep inhale. "Fuck, Rose. That was..." It's silent as I wait for him to finish his sentence. "That was everything," he finally says, making my heart skip a beat.

One of my hands comes up to find his head. Holding

him against my neck, I relish in the moment we're having. Sex with Nash is phenomenal, but it's the cuddling afterward that has me feeling things I have no right to feel.

For the next few hours, we have sex on and off, neither of us able to keep our hands off the other for very long. It's evident that Nash knows his way around the female body, bringing my body to more orgasms in a narrow timespan than I thought possible. The moments with him buried inside me make me feel a passion I didn't know existed. I've never felt so physically in sync with a person like I do with Nash. It's hard to put into words. It's hard to imagine that these moments might only be fleeting—temporary.

Cuddled against Nash, my head resting on his chest and my fingertips tracing his tattoos, it's hard to remind myself that one day he could hate me. With every breath I take, I hold in the desperate want to admit to the scheme that got me here in the first place. It's on the tip of my tongue, but I'm too scared.

I'm scared to lose the moment we're in. I'm scared to see him put a fence back around his heart and soul. I'm just now getting to really know him—fall for him—and I don't want to lose the look of affection in his eyes when they land on me.

My heart constricts when I think about all the lies I've told him. All the ways those closest to him have deceived him. I need to come clean to him, because I want the truth to come from my lips and nobody else's, but first I want more time with him.

"Tell me a secret, Rose." His lips move against my temple, his breath warm against my skin.

I'm going to break your heart is what comes to mind, but I push it away, not ready to admit my betrayal yet.

"You make me feel safe," I confess. Something I didn't realize I've been desperately chasing for years.

The finger that was playing with my hair stills briefly. "What does that mean?"

Unwanted memories flash through my mind, just as vivid as the day they happened. I try to clear my head by leaning in, giving him a soft kiss on the piano tattooed on his chest. "It means you make me feel safe," I repeat, apparently not ready to divulge *any* of my secrets to him tonight.

"What do I have to do to get inside that pretty head of yours?" Shifting in the bed, he brings us face to face, a finger tapping me on the temple.

"I don't remember that being part of our agreement when I told you I'd make you fall in love with music again," I tease, moving the hair off his forehead.

"Well, I'm making an amendment."

"Too late. Now you tell *me* a secret," I say, smiling when he rolls his eyes.

His gaze travels to where my hand is resting on his chest, the beat of his heart drumming against my palm. "It's working," he says quietly.

"What is?"

Grabbing me by the hips, he rolls us until he's placing me on top of him. My thighs rest on either side of his body in a straddle. Bracing myself, my hands fall to his chest.

He tucks my hair behind my ear. "*You*. You're working. You're making me see the magic in my life again."

Why does he have to go and say things to make me want him even more?

My throat begins to constrict. I try to swallow the emotion, not trying to tip him off to the sinking feeling in my chest. "Yeah?" I ask hoarsely, unable to come up with any other words.

"I haven't felt this content with life in a very long time," he admits, a shy smile on his face. "You know the other day I realized that I haven't been drunk in weeks? I've had drinks, sure, but I haven't been piss drunk for a while. And it's because of you."

Don't tell me that, I plead silently. *Don't stop your bad habits because of me, Nash.*

All I want is for him to stop feeling the need to get

drunk to survive his days, but I don't want to be the reason for it; there is fear when I remind myself our goodbye is inevitable.

"All I've done is show you how talented you are, and how valued you are by so many people. You haven't been drunk because *you* haven't wanted or needed to be. That's not because of me."

A crease forms on his forehead as he thinks my words through. "Maybe, but you've still helped me see what I've been taking for granted for too long. So, your promise to make me fall in love with music again? It's working."

Smiling, I lean down to kiss him. "Watch out, you're feeding my ego. I might get a little cocky."

"Absolutely not," he whispers, stealing my next breath with his lips.

Our bodies become intertwined once again, and each time I learn more and more about how talented he really is, those fingers that expertly work guitar strings each night plucking so much pleasure and emotion out of me.

I fall asleep next to Nash at an all-time high. I'm happy, my feelings growing tenfold for him overnight between the joining of our bodies and the hushed confessions of the night.

It's perfect.

26
NASH

Sweat drips down my back as I finish up the last of my reps. My muscles strain as I try and push my body a few more times.

"Keep pushing, Nash!" My trainer, Zach, says, clapping aggressively next to my ear until I'm done.

"Three...two...one...done!" he says, stepping back as I drop down from the pull-up bar.

Catching my breath, I walk toward the bench a few feet away from us. Grabbing the water bottle and a towel, I wipe at my face, removing the sweat from the workout.

"You psyched for the hometown show tomorrow?" he asks, taking a seat.

I follow his lead, falling onto one of the benches.

"Yes and no," I answer. The truth is, I get to perform at the stadium I grew up attending football games at with my dad and brother.

It's always a surreal moment when I'm standing on stage, on a field, remembering this is my life. But being in Colorado also reminds me of the rocky relationship I still have with my parents. They didn't ever really give a damn about me or my younger brother until I made it big.

My dad laughed in my face when I told him about the talent show that would go on to change the trajectory of my life. He called me names that would stick with me for years when I told him I wanted to go for it and join a boyband.

And then our first record went platinum. Our songs could be heard on every local radio station, our tour selling out instantly. After that, he started to play the role of a father who gave a damn. My mom was just a passive parent, never really showing affection but never disciplining either.

As soon as I had any sort of money, I would send it home to my younger brother, Aiden. Our family wasn't poor; there was always food on the table and a roof over our heads growing up, but he was a handful of years younger than me and I wanted him to have anything he wanted.

When I could, I would fly him out to travel with me, but he didn't love being on the road like I did. He liked being home. He had a better relationship with our parents than I did, which made me only see him occasionally.

I know he'll be there tomorrow. Despite the harboring resentment toward my parents, I still sent them two tickets to the show, just in case. Although deep down it wasn't out of the kindness of my heart, it was to remind my dad that the dream I had that amused him so much was still selling out arenas.

"Any plans tonight?" Zach lines the weights back up on their rack, keeping the gym we rented out for the day neat as always.

His question brings a smile to my face, thinking of the plans I have for Nora. "Actually, yes," I tell him. "Nora and I have plans."

He nods his head. Nora has come to a few workouts with Zach over the last two weeks, claiming she needs to stay in shape. The two of them have gotten along great, which doesn't come as a surprise. She gets along with everyone I'm close to. She's slowly started placing herself more and more in my life, and I have no desire to stop her.

"Right on. Enjoy them! I can't believe the North American leg of our tour is almost up."

"I can't either. Time has flown. But I'm also ready for a break before going overseas." My brain has been all over the place trying to think of what Nora and I will do with our days off together. I asked her if she was going to go home at all, and her answer was an immediate no.

She's been down about not being able to see Riley recently though, so tonight, as a surprise, I flew Riley out for the show. I rented us a cabin up in the mountains, a place that a few of the dancers, Sebastian, my brother, and Riley can all hang out with me and Nora. I thought it would be a fun way to get together the people that we're closest to before heading abroad for a few months.

Nora doesn't know it, and I've been amped all morning to surprise her with her best friend.

"Hope you get a few workouts in while on break." Zach smirks, giving me shit.

I roll my eyes at him. He knows I'll keep up with my workouts. They're a part of my daily routine.

I'm kept busy the rest of the day with meeting after meeting. My team has been pressuring me about the next album, asking about songs I've written so far. Truth is, I wasn't writing anything worth a damn for a while. But the more time I spend with Nora, the more I manage to throw together lyrics and some chords.

The song journal that was sitting empty for months is now starting to fill with ideas, with little snippets of lyrics or melodies for a song. She's made me feel inspired again. She's become my muse, but that doesn't mean I want to share my words with my team just yet. The label is breathing down all our necks for me to release an album after this tour ends, but I've been pushing back.

They're fine with me releasing songs I had no part in writing, but I put my foot down. I want this next album to be different. I want to go back to the way it was with my first album, where I had part in writing every single song. I assure my team that soon I'll get them a couple of songs to demo; I just need a bit more time. They surprisingly allow me the time, something I wasn't expecting them to concede to so easily.

"Has she landed?" Sebastian asks me from the driver's seat, turning into the private airport's parking lot.

Checking my phone, I see a text from the pilot from five minutes ago, stating that they've landed.

"Yes, they have," I tell Bash. Pulling out a pair of sunglasses from a holder, I place them on my nose.

"What about Aiden?" he asks, putting the SUV in park.

"Aiden's flight was earlier today when I had a meeting. I sent Monica to go pick him up."

Bash laughs, his hand running over his lips to cover his smile. "Sorry, boss, but I'm picturing Aiden driving her fucking nuts the whole entire ride."

I snicker, imagining the same thing. Aiden is only five years younger than me, but our personalities are vastly different. I would bet a lot of money that the fact that he *never stops talking* would drive Monica absolutely bat-shit-crazy.

"Why'd you have to pick Riley up? You have people for this, you know." His jet-black hair is freshly cut, the hair cropped short on his head. I stare at a hair that appears longer than the others, spacing out before he gets my attention again.

"Yeah, well I didn't know who to trust with Nora's best friend. Plus, it's not like I had anything going on," I joke, both of us knowing there's always something I should be doing.

"Is that her?" he asks, his eyes trained on a spot over

my shoulder.

Turning around, I find Riley making her way toward us, fully enamored in a conversation with the pilot. Jake, one of the pilots I use often, appears to be wheeling her suitcase for her, his eyes trained on her as she babbles on about something we can't hear. Whatever it is, it must be interesting, because he nearly walks right into a parked car, not paying attention to anything but her.

"Yep," I say with a smile, just now noticing the captain's hat that is perched on top of Riley's head.

"You didn't tell me Nora had a friend that looked like *that*," Bash hisses, looking at Nora's best friend.

Chuckling, I look toward Bash, my hand reaching for the door handle. "Put your tongue in your mouth, Sebastian. That's Nora's best friend. She'd probably kill you for looking at her friend like that."

"Oh, but she wouldn't have a problem with your pilot looking at her like *that?*" he argues, opening his own door.

I can't help the laugh that escapes my lips, suddenly incredibly fascinated with how Riley is ruffling Sebastian's feathers before ever even speaking to him. I've only met Riley in person once, the encounter brief when I sabotaged Nora's goodbye dinner with her. However, I've gotten to know Riley a little better through the video chats Nora has had with her lately. Even though I don't know her well, I can tell she has a huge personality, it's completely obvious when she stops in front of us, Jake still beside her.

"Nash!" she says, showing off her white smile. "Have you met my friend Jake here? He let me wear his hat." She pulls on the navy brim of the hat to show it off.

"Of course, he's met him; he signs his paychecks," Sebastian says from over the hood.

Riley's head swivels to Sebastian, her mouth agape before quickly gaining her composure. "And you are?"

Jake suddenly looks uncomfortable, as if it's just occurred to him that he's heavily flirting with someone I paid him to fly here.

I join in on the conversation before Sebastian can be even more of an asshole. “His name is Sebastian,” I tell her, looking over my shoulder to give him a dirty look. “Someone whose paycheck is *also* signed by me.”

Bash sighs, looking away from us, suddenly very interested with something on the hood of the vehicle.

“Anywayyyy,” Riley drawls, “now that I’ve flown private, I don’t know how I could go back to flying coach. You ruin me, Nash.” Pulling the hat off her head, she gives it back to Jake with a smile. He takes it quickly, his eyes hesitantly looking to me as if I give a damn that he let her wear it.

“So, the flight was good I presume?” I question, reaching to grab her suitcase from Jake.

Riley flips her hair over her shoulder, biting her lip to hide a smile. “Real good,” she snickers. “It was full service.”

Sebastian chokes on air just as Jake hurriedly excuses himself.

Riley steps up until she’s uncomfortably close to me. Pulling off my sunglasses without even asking, she looks me up and down. Her thin eyebrows pull together while she looks me over. “Nash Pierce in the flesh,” she muses, handing me back my sunglasses.

“Can I help you?” I laugh nervously.

Shrugging, she says, “Just had to get a good look at the famous popstar who’s fucking my best friend.”

Before I even have time to react, she pulls open the rear passenger door and climbs in. Sebastian and I both stare at each other dumbfounded as she slams the door. My fingers tighten around the handle of her suitcase, at a complete loss for words.

“Holy shit, I think I’m in love,” Sebastian announces, running a hand over his clean-shaven chin.

“Well, she’s *something*.” I walk to the trunk of the car, waiting for Sebastian to pop it. He takes the suitcase, then throws it in the back of the car.

Riley spins in her seat, her brown eyes assessing the two of us. “Can we stop for food? I’m famished.”

We manage to pull off the surprise for Nora. It takes her what felt like a full minute to process that her best friend was waiting on my bus. I’d texted Nora to come see me, telling her the door was unlocked and she could just come in.

Riley had been sitting in the driver’s seat, pretending she was driving the rig when Nora opened the door. Once Nora caught up to her best friend being here, she ran and tackled her, the two tiny girls falling to the floor in an embrace.

“I’ll leave ya to it,” Sebastian had said, patting me on the shoulder and escorting himself off the bus. He and Riley had spent the whole-time exchanging jabs on our way back from the airport. Neither one of them were bashful about their sudden attraction to the other.

It took a few hours to gather all the people coming up to the cabin with us. I had to spill the beans to Nora on the plan for the night when Riley basically ruined the surprise for her. Despite the surprise being spoiled before we even made it to the cabin, now that we’re standing in the doorway, it seems like it doesn’t faze Nora at all as she admires the vaulted ceiling of the log cabin.

“This is crazy cool,” she whispers, stepping deeper into the entryway.

“Yeah, I wouldn’t call this a *cozy* cabin like you said,” Riley points out from the other side of Nora. “Cozy means small and quaint. This thing is ten times the size of our apartment.”

“It’s fucking epic!” Aiden agrees, jumping over the back of one of the leather couches and falling onto it. “Shit, this is comfortable,” he says, his arms folding behind his head.

Kissing Nora’s temple, I try to read her face to see how

she likes it. For some reason I desperately want her to love the place, the surprise a week in the making. “Whatcha think, Rose?”

“I think it’s amazing,” she answers, her eyes finding mine. Standing up on her tiptoes, she lays a kiss on me. “Thank you.” Her fingers delicately play with the hair at the back of my neck, something I recently discovered I love.

“If you would’ve told me a year ago that Nash Pierce would be looking at my best friend like a lovesick puppy, I would’ve questioned your sanity.” Riley stares at me and Nora, her eyes drifting between the two of us. The look on her face is unreadable, but before I can question her on it, Aiden speaks up from the couch.

“Is there any food at this place? I’m starving.” He crosses his ankles on the couch, making himself at home.

Pointing to the kitchen, I look at my brother. “The pantry should be fully stocked.” I had my team hire someone to buy groceries for us for the night, knowing there wasn’t anywhere that’d deliver this far up the mountain.

Aiden shoots up from the couch. He’s beelining toward the kitchen in an instant. “Let’s see what I can cook up!” Aiden has always been a good cook, his ability to throw random ingredients together to make an incredible meal very useful when we were kids.

“I can help,” Ziggy offers.

Michael, another one of my dancers, follows closely behind him offering to help as well.

This leaves me, Sebastian, Riley, and Nora all standing in the foyer.

“Want to go check out our room?” I ask Nora, needing to get her alone for a few moments.

Riley has been attached to us all day, which is fine. I understand she wants to spend time with her friend. But now I need to get Nora alone, get reacquainted with her body.

Riley pulls a piece of candy out of her pocket, popping

it into her mouth. “Is that code meaning you guys are about to go bone?”

Sebastian clears his throat at the same time Nora punches Riley in the tit.

“Ow!” Riley shouts, rubbing at her chest. “What the hell, Nora Boo?”

I look at Nora curiously. “Nora Boo?”

“C’mon!” Nora groans, grabbing my hand and pulling me toward the stairs.

“How do you know our room is up here?” I ask, letting her pull me up the large staircase. Our feet thud against the cherry wood, laughter erupting from the kitchen below us.

She doesn’t bother to look over her shoulder as she continues to climb the stairs. “Just a guess.”

Taking the lead, I point her down a long hallway. Our room sits at the very end of it, the master suite of the house. Walking in, we find a large room with a large, wood four-poster bed. Cabin-themed bedding covers the bed, a stuffed animal bear sitting at the end.

“This *room* is bigger than my apartment,” Nora observes, referring back to Riley’s comment from a few minutes prior.

She scans the room, taking it in. There’s a large fireplace with two wingback chairs in front of it. To the left of the fireplace is a wall of windows, showcasing the beautiful mountain landscape. The bed sits across from the windows, allowing the breathtaking view to be seen from the bed.

Coming up behind Nora, I lean over her shoulder, kissing the spot behind her ear that gives her goosebumps. “Penny for your thoughts, Rose?”

Her body relaxes against mine. “I’m kind of speechless,” she whispers. “This is just too much. You didn’t have to do this.”

My arms wrap tighter around her. “I know I didn’t have to. I *wanted* to.”

Surprising me, she quickly turns around, her hands

finding either side of my face. Standing on her tiptoes, she pulls my face closer to hers. She pulls until our foreheads rest against each other. "I don't deserve this, but thank you." Her lips find the corner of my mouth, her kiss soft and gentle.

"You deserve it all, Rose. I'm just trying to be the guy to give it to you."

Her breath catches, her eyes frantically moving over my face. Before I can elaborate on the feelings bearing down on my chest, she's sealing her mouth against mine. Her tongue is eager, pushing into my mouth as soon as I allow her in. She wraps her arms around me, pulling me in closer.

I deepen the kiss and lift her off the ground. Her legs wrap around my middle, her back arching as my hands knead at her ass.

Walking across the room, I rest her against the first surface I find, an old cherry wood desk that sits in a corner by the large windows. A few books and a vase fall to the ground while I make room for her on the desk.

Nora laughs against my lips, reaching down to grab the hem of my hoodie. She pulls up, leaning away from me enough to remove it.

Following her lead, I remove her T-shirt and sweater. Her hands run up and down my back, her nails digging into the skin. My hand finds the cold window behind her, holding my weight as I lean in, kissing a path down her shoulder. Reaching the strap of her bra, I use a finger to move it out of my way, letting it slip down her arm.

Nora's fingers find the drawstring of my joggers, undoing the knot. Her fingers are cold against my skin as she slips a hand into my briefs. My head falls back when her fingers wrap around my length, pumping up and down in a tantalizing rhythm.

The urge to bury myself inside her is overwhelming. I'm stripping her out of her jeans and underwear as fast as I can. Not even bothering to completely remove my own pants, I sheathe myself in a condom as fast as I can.

I'm inside her in an instant, pushing her further across the desk and into the window. Her heels dig into my ass as our bodies sync to the same rhythm.

Her hands are everywhere at once—on my back, in my hair, holding my face as we get lost in each other. There are noises below us, but it doesn't deter us from stopping.

"Nash," Nora pants as I bite the tender skin around her nipple.

Her moans send tingles down my spine, making me pick up the pace. Our bodies slap together, both of us desperately chasing release. Nora gets louder and louder the closer she gets to an orgasm.

I trap her mouth in mine, swallowing her moans. "You're being loud," I say, my teeth scraping against the hollow of her throat.

"Sorry," she offers.

"Don't be sorry," I demand. "You can scream for all I care. Let them know how good this feels. How perfect it feels when I'm inside of you."

My words have her moaning even louder. Between the moans escaping her lips and the way she's rocking her hips back and forth to control the pace, I can't hold on for much longer. I've been thinking about fucking her all day, and now that I'm finally able to, I can't last forever.

She spasms around me. The way she tightens around my dick has me following her lead. My body hunches over her as I spill into the condom.

Cold air seeps in from the large window behind us. I pull out of her slowly, backing up so I can see the look on her face. Tendrils of brown hair have spilled out of her loose braid. I reach up and move a piece from her cheek. There's a surge of peace that runs through me as she effortlessly nuzzles into my hand on her cheek.

Looking at her now, I can't deny that I've fallen for her.

From the first day we met, there was something about her that had drawn me to her. It was refreshing to meet someone who didn't fall at my feet. She didn't seem to care about the fame or fortune. She was interested in the man underneath all the bullshit.

At first it infuriated me, the way she could see all the parts of me I didn't want to confront, but over time, I grew to love those things about her. She's the first real thing I've had in my life in a long time. Our friendship developed into something more, and it's easy for me to admit to myself that at this point, I'm deeply in love with her.

I swore I'd never love again. It was something I sang songs about but didn't intend to ever experience again. I should've known after we went to the arena together that eventually, my intentions didn't matter. My heart wanted her, *needed* her, more than I ever could have imagined.

I'm seconds away from telling her my feelings when a knock sounds at our door.

"Hey, lovebirds," Riley shouts from the opposite side. "Due to the silence, and Nora's moans no longer echoing off these walls, we all can tell you're done boning. Food's ready whenever you decide to get your dick back in your pants, Nash."

Just when I think she's retreated back downstairs, I'm proven wrong. Riley speaks from the other side of the closed door once again. "Nora, Nash gets you for the rest of the tour. Get out here and hang out with your best friend! I know you got off so it's time to join us."

Nora groans, her head falling against my shoulder in embarrassment. "I can't take her anywhere."

27
NORA

After one of the best evenings of my life, I lie in bed with Nash, the two of us completely naked. I'm sprawled across his chest, his fingers absentmindedly playing with my hair. The moonlight lights up our room, the wall of windows allowing some light into the otherwise dark room. We sit high up in the mountains, the view from our room spectacular. No matter what direction you look in from the windows, you're met with beautiful trees and snow-topped mountains.

"Thank you for all of this," I say, leaning up to peek at him. Looking at him makes my heart constrict inside my chest. These moments with him are more than perfect. As I take in his features, I'm still taken aback by how incredibly sexy he is. The same lips that have kissed every inch of my body pull up in a side smile.

"What?" I ask playfully.

"If you look at me like that again, Rose, I just might fucking fall in love with you," he hints, as if he didn't just throw out words that could change everything.

My mouth opens and closes awkwardly, trying to think of what to say back. I desperately want to tell him the truth—that I've already fallen in love with him. Somehow in the midst of scheming to get him to fall in love with me, I fell too. I've handed my heart right over to him, knowing deep down I could never keep his.

The truth of what brought me here begins to weigh heavy on my chest. It's pushing so hard against me that I can't think of anything but coming clean to him. I suddenly can't keep up the charade for a moment longer. I know there will be consequences, but I desperately need him to know I love him.

And...that I've also betrayed him.

How do you tell someone that you love them and betrayed them in the same moment?

"Nash, I need to tell you something," I whisper. Tucking my hair behind my ear, I look at him cautiously, hoping he sees the sincerity in my eyes. The hum of the heater is the only sound in the room for a few moments.

Reaching up, he runs his thumb over my bottom lip. "Not tonight," he says. "Tonight, let's just pretend that the world I live in won't try to tear us apart."

I look away regretfully. *If only you knew.*

"Whatever is weighing on you, can it wait until tomorrow? Tonight, I just want to pretend. I just want to be Nash and Nora."

The vulnerability in his eyes shatters me, but no matter how bad I want to confess every dirty secret I've kept, I want to give him what he wants. He deserves at least one more night of being happy. Tomorrow, once I tell him, he'll realize his world was bound to tear us apart from the start, and I knew it. And, not only did I know it...I took part in planning the demise.

Swallowing my emotion, I nod, fearful my voice would break if I spoke. Leaning down, I kiss each one of his cheeks, his forehead, his jaw, trying to mark each part of that beautiful face. "Just Nash and Nora," I repeat, hovering over his lips.

He pulls me against him, lazily slipping his tongue between my lips as if we have all the time in the world.

"You've made me a liar, Nora. I said I'd never fall in love again, but...I know with every part of me that I love you. And I know that I'm fucked up and have a shit ton of baggage, but I want to work through it because of you, Rose. I want to work through it *with* you. I desperately want us to work, to keep you forever. In loving you, I think I've finally found how to love myself as well."

A lone tear betrays me, slipping down my cheek. Nash wipes it away with the pad of his thumb, keeping his hand on my face.

"You don't have to say it back," he rushes. "I know it's soon and I'm probably fucking crazy. I'm impulsive and never think before I act, going full speed ahead always being my MO. But through songwriting, I've had to get very in touch with my feelings and because of that, I *know* I fucking love you. You're changing me, and I don't want it to ever stop."

My foot finds his under the covers, and I tangle my legs with his to get even closer to him. I don't tell him I love him even though I desperately want to. It isn't fair for him to know how I really feel until he knows the truth behind how we met.

Tomorrow. I'll tell him tomorrow after the show. He deserves to know the truth, even if means the end of us. Monica will probably have my head for coming clean, but it's the right thing to do. I don't see any other option here. I need him to know what I've done. It's going to blindside him, but he needs to hear it from me—that all along, the plan has been for me to break his heart.

I knew all along it was a bad idea, that it went against all my principles, and I did it anyway.

And now, I'll have to face the consequences.

I'm going to lose the man I love.

"You're changing me too, Nash," I say, desperate for him to know how true that is.

After high school, I thought my heart was tattered and bruised, unable to trust a man again. With Nash, it was different from early on. I trust him with everything that I am. He worships every inch of my body, embedding himself deep into my soul in the process.

I would do anything to keep him. To keep this feeling of being loved and cherished. I thought I'd known true love before, but one night was all it took to prove how wrong I was.

Nash's hand slides up my thigh, coming to rest on the curve of my hips. "The day we met, I was so pissed off about having dancers."

I laugh, remembering how grouchy he was. "You don't say?" I tease.

A smile lights up his face. "Hey, I'm trying to be romantic here." There's a playful glint to his eyes, one that has started to appear more and more in the time I've gotten to know him.

I gesture for him to proceed. "Then, by all means..."

"I was pissed off about having dancers," he repeats. "It wasn't as much the dancers as it was feeling like I didn't have control of anything in my life anymore. And I didn't know how I felt about that. I didn't want control, but I also needed to feel control over some aspect of my life. For some reason, I latched onto this idea that refusing to have dancers was one way to show I could take back some control of things."

His fingers trace along my collarbone as he continues. "After our encounter in the room, I left even more pissed off. You may not remember this but as you were walking out the door you asked—"

"If you were okay," I finish for him, remembering the moment clearly.

He swallows slowly, looking at me with such honesty in his eyes. "Yeah," he rasps. "When you left, I realized that was the first time someone had asked if I was okay in a long, long time."

"The way you stormed into the room, it was obvious

something was wrong."

"Well, people don't always like to ask if I'm okay. They're too afraid of me saying no and them actually having to do something about it."

There's a pang in my chest for him. The more I learn about him and his world, the more I want to shield him from every person that has ignored *every* one of his warning signs about how sad he truly feels. It's clear there aren't many people in his life that he trusts.

And now I'm one of them.

"I was so mad at you for asking if I was okay, for caring more about me than people I've known for years. And then..."

His voice trails off, leaving me wondering what he's going to say. When he doesn't answer, I prod him for more. "And then what?" I kiss the top of his hand, my lips feathering against one of the tattooed petals of the rose.

"And then I saw you dance. You moved so effortlessly out there; it was so damn clear how passionate you were about dancing. For a brief moment, I hated you for it. I hated that you so clearly loved dancing, because I was remembering the times I felt that same passion and love for singing."

"There was a time I hated dancing too," I say absentmindedly.

His eyebrows raise, my admission a shock to the both of us. When I stay silent, he goes on with his story. "When they told me we were going to dance to *Preach* together, I about lost my damn mind. I couldn't fathom sharing the stage while singing that song—something so personal to me. It's already so fucking personal to stand in front of thousands of people, singing about having your heart broken. I couldn't wrap my head around having someone else up there with me, sharing in the moment."

"I didn't know..."

His shoulder moves in a slight shrug. "How could you have? All I did was throw a fit, not giving anyone a reason for not wanting to do it except that I didn't want to share the stage. I'm glad it happened, though. Without *Preach*, I don't know if we would've become...this."

I smile, trying not to make it look as sad as I feel. He has no idea how right he is. His team convinced him to do *Preach* to throw us together.

It's all been planned. And here he is, thinking our love story happened on its own.

"You didn't think we'd end up cuddling in a cabin in the mountains? Damn, that's the first thing I envisioned when we met," I joke.

He shakes his head, pulling me against his body in one fell swoop. "You're a smartass."

"Just telling the truth." I try and turn to face him, but he locks me against him.

"Yeah, I don't fucking cuddle." He rests his jaw on my shoulder, adjusting my body so my back presses against his chest.

"What would you call this?" I question, interlocking my fingers with his.

His lips gently press against the base of my neck. The feeling of his fingers gently pushing my hair to the side has my arms breaking out in goosebumps. "Fuck." He laughs. "This is cuddling. Landon and Poe were right, I'm a simp. I didn't *used* to cuddle—thought it was utter bullshit and unnecessary—but I could get used to this."

"Me too." Looking over my shoulder, I find his eyes. The reflecting moonlight makes his eyes appear darker than they are in the daylight.

"Stay with me," he whispers, his hand stroking my hairline. "Stay with me when I piss you off. Stay with me when this gets hard. Stay with me through it all, Nora. Please."

His grip on me loosens, allowing me to turn and bury my face in his chest. It's the only way I'm able to hide the tears welling in my eyes. Each one of his words felt like a punch to the gut.

It's sometime early in the morning.

Nash is finally asleep after we spent countless hours exploring each other, and I'm standing in the large bathroom, staring back at my reflection.

It's hard to look at myself. His earlier plea is running through my mind on rewind. I know it was hard for him to ask for me to stay, to be vulnerable like that. That knowledge makes this situation so much worse. He wants me to stay, and I want to stay, but I know after I confess all our ugly truths, he will want me as far away from him as possible. And I can't even blame him.

I hate myself for what this is going to do to him.

I wanted to be the one to save him. The irony isn't lost on me. Because the truth is, I was sent to ruin him.

When I was eighteen, something happened that made it hard for me to look at myself in the mirror. So I feel that pain. I've buried that pain, that loathing, deep down inside of me, trying to push past the experience.

My therapist told me I was also a victim for what happened that night, but I didn't believe her for a long time. What happened to my sister...it felt like it was my fault, and it took me a long time to even *look* at myself in a mirror. I'd finally gotten to a spot where I could look at myself again when this opportunity was dropped in my lap. But here I am for the second time, hating what I see staring back at me.

Looking away from my reflection, I glance down and see Nash's song journal sitting on the counter. I stare at it for a while, my eyes boring a hole into the rich leather cover. I know it's a huge invasion of privacy to open it, to look deep into the inner workings of Nash's mind, but I can't help it. Taking a seat in the chair perched in front of the vanity, I open the journal.

Not wanting to wake Nash, I use the early light to help read the lyrics he's poured onto every page. Tears spill from my eyes, and I have to be careful to make sure they don't fall onto the pages. With every lyric, poem, note he's jotted down, I feel more and more guilty. Reading through these pages is like experiencing our love story all over again, from Nash's point of view, start to…near finish.

It's the most achingly beautiful thing.

I don't know how long I sit in the dark, committing every single stroke of his pen to memory. When our love story comes to an end, ending in guaranteed heartbreak, I want to remember these words.

Once I reach the end of the journal, I get an idea. I know when I come clean to Nash, there's a good chance I won't get to explain myself, to give him a good apology. He'll probably want nothing to do with me or my excuses, and I'll respect that.

But I need him to know how sorry I am, so I write it down, pouring my heart out just like he's done in his own words.

Nash,

If you're reading this, there's a good chance our story has come to its impending end. I wish I had a good explanation of why I did what I did, but in reality, I don't. There will never be words that can justify why I agreed to hurt you. I couldn't let us end without telling you my story.

This is the last time I'll be selfish when it comes to you. I write these words knowing it'll probably be easier for you to not know these things, but I can't help it. You must know how deeply I've fallen in love with you. I know I told you lies, deceived you, but I also fell for you. You're an amazing person, Nash. You didn't deserve what we did to you.

When I first got the offer, I debated on taking it. It felt like a perfect opportunity for me to chase my dreams. When I told Monica yes, I honestly didn't think you and I would ever speak. I mean that. I didn't think I'd ever get the chance to hurt you. It was the perfect opportunity…or so I thought.

Every moment we spent together I wanted to come clean to you, but I couldn't do it. I told myself it was because I didn't want to hurt you, but it was mostly because I didn't want to lose you. It probably makes me the worst person, because I'd like to say I'd go back and tell Monica no. That's what I keep telling myself, but now, as I confess my truth, I'm not sure that is the truth.

It's incredibly selfish, because I know you're hurt and I don't want you to be hurt, but I also don't know if I would change knowing what it is to be loved by you. To be loved by you, Nash Pierce, is like performing in a rain show. It's beautiful, exhilarating, epic.

You once said if all shows were rain shows, they wouldn't feel so special, and I now understand what you meant. If all love was like your love, the world would be a lot better of a place.

I'm not asking you to forgive me. I know what I've done is wrong, and that it's something we can't come back from.

The only thing I ask of you is to know it was real for me. It was the rain show of my life. My epic love.

Everything you felt, I also felt.

I love you, Nash. I love you so much.

I'm so fucking sorry.

Always yours,
Rose

28
NASH

The night at the cabin flies by all too quickly. I could've stayed trapped in that bedroom with Nora for weeks, maybe forever, living off whatever we could find in the pantry. The feeling of her leg draped over me in the morning, her hair sprawled out around us, was a wakeup call I could get used to every day. The two of us watched the sun rise over the mountains from the large bed, our limbs tangled together. It was one of the most peaceful moments of my life. I didn't feel pressure to be anyone but myself.

I was deliriously happy listening to Nora recall a high school spring break trip she took with Riley's family to go skiing. Apparently, she fell face first when getting on the ski lift, too busy trying to flirt with the lift attendant to realize the chair was right behind her. Her cheeks were that perfect shade of rose as she recounted Riley's tears freezing on her cheeks from laughing so hard.

We were lying in bed watching the sunrise when I realized I'd left my phone in the car the night before.

Crawling out of bed, I kiss Nora on the cheek and head toward the door. I'm sure I have an abundance of missed messages from Monica and Tyson, and whoever else from the team who needs something, but if they really needed me, they knew they could reach Sebastian.

Speaking of Sebastian...my eyes go wide when I step out into the hallway and find both him and Riley tiptoeing in the opposite direction toward a room. Sebastian's only got on a pair of boxer briefs, which is more than Riley. She has a big sheet draped around her shoulders, and it appears she doesn't have anything on underneath.

"Nash, can you grab us some—" Nora stops in her tracks behind me, her eyes stuck on the two bodies on the other end of the hallway.

Nora's words catch their attention. After a few awkward moments, it occurs to me that Sebastian looks more embarrassed than Riley.

Finally breaking the silence, Riley speaks. "Oh, don't look surprised. Surely you saw it coming." She tugs on the sheet, making it fly in the air like a cape. She struts back to one of the bedrooms, not bothering to look back at us.

Sebastian is still standing in the hallway, his mouth hanging open. He watches Riley disappear behind the door before looking toward me. "Yeah, I'm just going to," he hooks a thumb over his shoulder, "see y'all later." Putting a hand over his junk, he walks back to the bedroom, throwing one last anxious glance over his shoulder before closing the door.

"Well, that was..." Nora says behind me.

"Interesting," I finish, shaking my head with a smile. Riley is right, I can't say I'm exactly shocked the two of them hooked up; they were flirting all night last night. I think I'm more taken aback by how unapologetic Riley was about it. I can't wait to get the details from Bash later. It appears he's met his match in Riley, and it's quite possible that she might eat him alive.

The rest of the morning went by quickly. We made breakfast together as a group, all of us piling around the table and shooting the shit. Eventually, the time came where we had to head out, those of us having to perform tonight needing to get to the stadium.

Now I'm sitting in hair and makeup, letting my hairstylist, Toni, fuss with my hair when my phone rings. Looking down, I find Taylor's caller ID blinking on the screen. She's been calling and texting for a while now. She's probably trying to weasel her way back into my life so she can be in the spotlight once again; too bad for her I want none of it. I decline the call, wondering if I should just go ahead and block her.

"How's this?" Toni asks, looking at me through the large mirror in front of us.

Looking up at my hair, I find the same tousled locks that have been my signature look for years now. The long curls on the top of my head fall in different directions. A look that is supposed to look messy, as if I didn't try at all, but a look that Toni has expertly fussed with. I honestly feel like I can achieve the same look by myself, just messing with it a little straight out of the shower, but I don't tell Toni that. She's been with me since I went solo, and I enjoy the time in the chair with her before a show. It calms me, hearing stories about her kids; and hearing her gripe about her husband is something I've grown accustomed to over the years.

I fix a piece of hair that's hanging directly over my eyes. "It looks great," I tell her, knowing a few songs into the setlist it'll take up a mind of its own.

Callie, my makeup artist, takes the spot Toni just vacated. Rubbing her hands together, she gives me a smile before lathering something on my cheeks. Twenty minutes later, I'm done with hair and makeup and have picked one of my options for wardrobe.

"Knock, knock," Nora says in the doorway of my dressing room. She's already dressed and ready for the show. Her hair falls down her shoulders in loose curls. I want to run my hands through it, mess it up a little before the show, but I know she won't allow it.

"There you are," I say, pulling her to my chest. As I breathe in her familiar scent, I relax. I haven't had a real home in a long time, but without permission, she's slowly becoming mine. My hand rests on the back of her head, holding her against my chest. Her breath hits my skin through my T-shirt, comforting me even more.

Nora is quiet against me, her heart hammering against my body. Her arms wrap tightly around my middle, her hands fisting the leather of my jacket. We stand like that until I finally pull away, my hands going to cup both her soft cheeks.

"What's going on in that mind of yours, Rose?"

Her long eyelashes reach her brow bone when she looks up at me. The crimson red of her lips is making me have dirty thoughts, memories flooding my mind of when those same painted lips have been wrapped around me after a show.

"I'm just really, *really* happy," she answers, a sad tone to her voice. She takes a deep sigh, loosening her grip around me.

"Then why does it sound like there's a *but* coming?"

My mind travels back to last night when I told her I'd fallen for her. It wasn't something I was expecting to blurt like that. I hadn't really even put an official label on the feelings I was having for her in my own head. I just knew she was slowly becoming my favorite person. Every moment I saw her was easily becoming my favorite part of my day, and she'd become my home. I didn't need to go lose myself in another woman or in a bottle, because when I was with her, I didn't hate who I was. Better yet, I knew who I was.

Before I'd met her, I was slowly drowning in my fame. Each day had run into the others. I was surviving, and some days I was barely doing that. The media would have a field day if they knew the number of times my security team had found me faded at the bottom of a bottle. My "*relaxing weekend retreats*" were code word for rehab. I wasn't in a good place. I hated myself but didn't have any desire to change. Now, Nora has made me realize that I want to get my shit together. For her, for my fans, but most of all for me. I needed her to remind me of everything I've taken for granted recently, and she did just that.

I've thought this many times before and I'll think it again a million more times I'm sure, *but…*

Nora made me fall in love with music again, and in the process, she made me fall in love with her, too. Falling for her was effortless. It was as easy as coming up with the lyrics she's now inspired.

Getting lost in my thoughts for a moment, I forget that I even asked her a question until she answers it.

"There's no *but*. I'm just excited for your hometown show tonight." She rocks back and forth on her heels with a smile. I can tell something is bothering her by her demeanor.

"What were you going to say?" I push. My thumb flicks over her cheek, removing a fleck of glitter that had fallen from her eyelids.

She leans into my hand, kissing my palm gently. "We'll talk about it after the show, okay?"

Taking a step back, I examine her, trying to find any clue as to what's wrong. Unfortunately, I come up short. Part of me begins to worry that she's freaked out about what I confessed last night—about falling for her. In hindsight, I shouldn't have said anything. We haven't been together a long amount of time, and I know that having a relationship with me comes with a whole lot of baggage, but the moment felt right. Up in the mountains with her, away from the expectations, and eyes, of society, I felt completely at peace. I was so at ease that my feelings fell from my lips before I could think about the repercussions.

"Talk to me, Rose. If this is about last night—"

She cuts me off instantly, standing on her toes to reach

my face. "Last night was perfect, Nash. Totally perfect."

Leaning in, she brushes her lips against mine. I'm sure I'm about to ruin her lipstick, but I can't help it, I deepen the kiss, needing to feel the intimacy with her. Needing to reassure myself that I didn't mess things up last night.

To my relief, she meets my tongue with hers. Biting down, I pull on her bottom lip, testing it between my teeth before letting go.

Three taps against the doorframe has us breaking apart. A crew member clad in all black stands in the doorway, a timid smile on their face. Waving awkwardly in the air, she looks down at her shoes and says, "They're ready for you, Nash."

"Better get to it, superstar." Nora pushes on my shoulder, guiding me toward the door.

Planting my feet, I turn around, my hands coming to rest on her hips. "We'll finish this after the show. Okay?"

Nora nods, giving me a fake smile.

I follow the crew member out, looking over my shoulder before we step into the hallway. "Hey, Rose?"

"Hm?" she says, standing in the middle of my dressing room. One arm stretches over her middle, her eyes looking at me questioningly.

"What I said last night...I meant it."

I don't wait to see her reaction. Instead, I catch up with the crew member, exchanging pleasantries with her as we make our way toward the stage.

I'm listening to her rattle on about her new cat, Mittens, when a familiar face stops me in my tracks. Standing right next to the entryway to below stage, I find my ex-girlfriend, Taylor.

Taylor's smile is predatory. One of her bony shoulders leans against a speaker box. Stopping in front of her, I let my eyes rake over her. The fake blonde strands of her hair twist around her shoulders, the curls reminding me of snakes, matching her venomous personality perfectly.

"I don't remember inviting you. Tell me, did you get tired of riding my best friend's dick?"

Throwing her hair over her shoulder, Taylor steps closer to me. One of her long nails begins to drag across my chest. "Aww, baby, are you jealous?" she purrs, looking at me like she's plotting something.

"Maybe if it was a few years ago. Now? Looking at you makes my skin itch. I mean really, Taylor, lay off the lip fillers."

Her puffy lips part in frustration, a hurt look overtaking her face. The old Nash would've felt bad for the low blow, but the Nash that saw my best friend buried balls deep inside her doesn't give a shit.

A hot pink nail runs over her lips. "They're natural," she spits out, regaining the feisty personality that attracted me to her in the first place.

I laugh, knowing damn well she's paid a pretty penny to make her lips that huge.

"What are you doing here, Taylor?" I ask with a sigh. I know I'm supposed to be below the stage right now, getting mic'd up. They won't start the montage or send the dancers out until I'm ready, but that doesn't mean I won't have multiple people pissed off at me if I don't make it down there quick.

My question seems to perk her up. She goes from frowning to smiling once again. Biting her lip, she takes a step closer to me, causing me to take one large step back to keep my distance.

"I've been calling and texting you," she states, her eyes roaming over me. "You look good, Nash."

I ignore the second part of her answer, focusing instead on the first. "And I've been ignoring you. Funny how that works, isn't it?"

"I have some information I think you'd want to know." She shifts her weight on the pair of heels she's wearing.

"Not interested," I bark, moving to side-step around her. Her hand juts out, landing on my chest and pinning me to my spot. Looking down, I swat her hand away. "Don't fucking touch me."

"You're going to want to know about this, baby. It

involves your shiny new plaything." She pauses. "Nora, is it?"

This comment catches my attention, although I play it off like it doesn't. "There's nothing you could tell me that'll make me change my mind about her. Which is why you're really here, isn't it? You want me to pine after you forever. Been there, done that, now I'm fucking over it. Deal with it."

Her lips widen in the most sinister smile. It catches me off guard, because clearly Taylor thinks she knows something that'll change things. "Spit it out," I finally say. "Tell me whatever the hell you think you know so we can get this show on the road."

I'm actually shocked that we've made it this long without someone coming to find us. Taylor's eyes light up like a damn kid in a candy store when she spots Nora heading toward the stage.

"Perfect!" Taylor yells clapping, getting Nora's attention.

I can't help but feel uneasy when I see Nora's eyes widen in horror when she spots Taylor. She looks from me to Taylor, and back; her gaze glued on Taylor's.

"Just the girl we were talking about," Taylor taunts. "Nora, nice to meet you, hon."

Hon. As if Nora and Taylor aren't the exact same age.

"What's going on?" Nora asks hesitantly.

The crowd outside begins to go wild. My guess is that they've dimmed the lights, preparing for my arrival on stage.

"I'm so happy you asked," Taylor says, clapping her hands together. "I was just telling Nash here the real reason why you're on this tour."

The color drains from Nora's face. "No," she breathes, looking at me with a stricken look on her face. "Nash..." she begins, but Taylor begins to speak over her.

"Nora here, isn't as sweet as the tabloids make her out to be. Turns out she isn't just a dancer on your tour..."

"What the fuck are you talking about?" I ask, my head

beginning to spin with questions.

"You were played, Nash. Your team wanted a better album out of you. Your writing has been shitty recently. The last album you wrote, the one about me, was phenomenal. Because you were broken. They wanted that again."

"Your point?" I ask, cutting her off. My eyes find Nora, but she looks like she's seen a ghost.

"My point being they wanted you to get hurt again. They asked me to do the job, but things got murky when they realized they couldn't come up with a valid excuse for me to be on the tour with you. Insert Nora here."

"Nash, I can explain." Nora's eyes are pleading when she looks at me, stepping in front of Taylor.

"Explain what?" I demand.

Taylor laughs sarcastically. "She needs to explain that she isn't just a dancer on your tour. Your team found her, hired her to weasel her way in. The real reason she's here is to break your heart, Nash. Your broken heart means better songs, which means more money for everyone in on it."

The world around me starts to go blurry. All I can see is the devilish smile on Taylor's face and the devastation on Nora's. My chest suddenly feels heavy, and I can't help but take a few steps back from Taylor's words. Memories flood my head, every single one of them involving Nora.

It can't be true.

Taylor is spewing bullshit.

I'm about to tell her to go fuck herself, but the look on Nora's face makes me pause. She hasn't denied anything. Surely, she should be denying it...*right*? This can't be fucking real.

Fake.

It wasn't fake.

Nora isn't like that. She wouldn't hurt me like that.

But why does she look guilty?

"Tell me it isn't true, Rose."

Shaking her head, she obliterates my recently mended

heart.

29
NORA

Taking a few steps back, his eyes bounce from Taylor to me. Ultimately, they land on me. The devastation in them is enough to steal my breath.

Betrayal is written in every facet of his face. He looks like he's been punched in the gut. "Tell me it isn't true, Rose," he pleads, his voice catching in his throat.

Trying to hold back tears, I shake my head, wishing it wasn't true. The urge to fall to my knees and beg for his forgiveness is overwhelming. The world around me fades away until it's just him—the look of devastation on his face something I'll never be able to forget.

His eyes widen. It's in this moment I learn how quickly a person can go from the highest highs to the lowest lows. With my own eyes I'm watching him fall apart. I have a front row seat to the breaking of his heart—and it's all my fault.

"This is a sick fucking joke, right? Tell her you would never. That isn't you, Rose. You wouldn't be so cruel.

Fucking tell her!" His voice raises in denial, causing Taylor to smile.

The tone of his voice does nothing to faze her; she's got such a look of accomplishment on her face. I want to slap it right off her. She's taken my truth and shared it with Nash before I got the chance.

"Nora?" His voice breaks, and it feels like a sledgehammer to my heart. But I made my bed, and unfortunately now I have to lie in it.

It hurts to even look at him, to see the damage I've done to him. No matter how hard it pains me to see this, to see him slowly fall apart, I make sure I look him in the eye. It's the least I can do. My lip quivers. "I'm sorry." The words come out scratchy, emotion sitting like a frog in my throat.

The crowd on the other side of the wall starts to chant his name. They're so loud, rattling the whole earth below our feet.

Pulling at his hair, he turns away from us, beginning to pace back and forth manically. I'm wondering if soon he'll end up ripping out the strands of his hair with how hard he's pulling at it. When he turns around, it's another shot to the heart to see his red-rimmed eyes.

"You're just like her," he mutters, shooting Taylor a dirty look. "You weren't supposed to fucking be like her!" My eyes dart to his fist, watching him clench and unclench it in anger.

"Nash," Taylor begins, not getting the chance to finish her sentence.

"Get lost!" he yells, pointing toward the exit.

She opens her mouth as if she wants to argue with him, but the look on his face makes her change her mind. Without looking back at either of us, she leaves, leaving me alone with a raging Nash.

He doesn't look at me, choosing instead to turn around to face a wall. The muscles underneath his shirt bunch together with tension. I watch him take a deep breath in. Still facing the wall, he says, "Everything in my life is a damn lie."

A stage manager makes their way toward us, but after seeing the look on Nash's face, they scurry away, mumbling something into their headset.

Looking toward the ceiling, I try and stop the tears from falling. "It wasn't a lie, Nash."

He laughs, facing me once again. I almost preferred him staring at the wall; at least then I didn't have to see the pain all over his face. His eyes are red, a vein in the middle of his forehead protruding in anger. "It was all a fucking lie! You slithered your way into my heart just to fucking break it. If that isn't a lie, I'm not sure what is."

He looks so heartbroken. It's in the way he stands, his shoulders slumping over and curving inward. In the tight grip of his hands. In the manic look of devastation in his eyes.

"It became real to me, too. I fell for you. I wanted to tell you last night, but you stopped me." My words come out jumbled as I try to get out as much as possible before he stops listening.

His arm shoots up. "Don't blame your deception on me, Nora. I've done a lot of things I regret in my life. But I've never set out to hurt someone...especially for the sake of money. You understand that's what you did, right? You broke me because they wanted more money." He sighs, looking up at the ceiling. "What a fucking sick joke my life is."

The tears fall from my eyes then, sliding down my cheeks until I taste the salt on my lips. "I didn't think I stood a chance," I confess. "I thought I would never even have a conversation with you. I thought I'd just be able to be a dancer on your tour, without anything else happening. I didn't expect you to be—"

"Be what?" he interrupts, his arms folding over his chest defensively.

"I didn't expect you to be *you*! I thought you'd be the guy the tabloids talk about. I thought you'd continue to fuck your way through top models. I didn't think I had a chance. I didn't—"

His eyes follow the line of tears down my cheek. "You spin such beautiful lies, Rose. I wish I believed you. You really did fool me. I didn't expect you to be so calculating."

My eyes rake over him. The sight of him breaks every part of me. Watching him break is in return shattering my own heart. I sigh, my mind racing with any kind of excuse that could ease the pain, knowing deep down there aren't any. Finally, I shrug, not knowing what else I can do to prove to him my feelings are genuine. "If I thought the feelings would've been real, I would've said no."

Laughing, he shakes his head at me dismissively. "Would you have, though? I'm not so sure, Rose. I'm not sure of a damn thing anymore."

Taking a step closer, I reach out to touch him. As soon as my hand hits the sleeve of his jacket, he pulls away as if I burned him straight through the leather. "The feelings were real. It was all real. The only thing that wasn't is that I didn't get picked for this tour because of my talent."

"Yeah, you got it because of your capability to break my fucking heart. Jesus," he breathes, rubbing the back of his neck, "my team really got me. They chose well. That innocent look of yours, that sweet demeanor...I fell for it. Fucking hard. But it was all a fucking lie. A scheme for money," he says in angered disbelief.

"I'm sorry." My eyes beg him to forgive me, to understand that I fell just as hard as he did.

"Well, it worked. I fell in love with you." His voice shakes, ripping my heart in two. "This betrayal is sure to get some good lyrics out of it. Consider me fucking inspired. I'll make sure to have my people send you royalties from the songs you worked so hard for." Taking a deep breath, he regains composure. Straightening his shoulders and rolling them back, he becomes a whole new Nash. *This* is the Nash I was expecting before I knew him—the look of indifference, the cocky tilt to his lips. His mask is falling back in place.

I've lost him.

Walking up to me, he gently moves the hair from my face. We're supposed to be on stage, but my feet stay planted, waiting to see what he'll do next.

Grasping onto both sides of my face, he pulls my head forward, burying it against his chest. His lips skim my forehead as he speaks the words that destroy me. "I wish it was real, Rose. I love you, with every part of me, with parts of me I didn't know existed. But I wish I never had to see your fucking face again."

Pulling away, he stares at me for a few moments longer before backing up. My body feels cold, already missing the warmth of his touch, knowing things will never be the same. We might have to put on a show for the crowd of screaming fans, but I'll never have his touch the way I used to. He'll never be mine again.

His steps are angry as he makes his way to the stage. Before he can go under, he starts barking orders. Grabbing the shirt of the nearest assistant, he pulls them in close. "Get me a fucking drink. Now."

"Nash!" Monica yells, beelining toward us in her stilettos. "You're late. We need to start the show. Now."

Nash laughs, greedily taking a bottle of vodka from the assistant. I don't know how the assistant found liquor that fast, but I find myself wishing it wasn't something so hard. The lips that have caressed every inch of my body now wrap around the top of that bottle. His throat bobs up and down as he takes significant gulps from it.

Wiping his mouth with the back of his hand, he smirks at Monica. "Sorry I'm late. I was too busy figuring out that the people closest to me are all fucking backstabbers." His eyebrows furrow. "You know, Monica. I always thought you were cold and calculating. But I didn't expect you to be fucking heartless. I trusted you despite knowing how cold you can be. My mistake."

Monica sighs, throwing me a dirty look as if this is my fault. I don't even have it in me to argue and let her know it was Taylor that broke the news to him in the most brutal way.

Nash takes another long sip of vodka, his grip tight around the neck of the bottle. Making his way to her, he hands over the bottle. She takes it without complaint, surely thinking the same thing I am—that this is about to be a disaster. There's a good amount of liquor running through his veins right now, which means the show we're about to perform could go up in flames.

"We've been through a lot together, Monica, and I know you've been ruthless in making sure I have a solid career. But I never thought you'd plan to destroy me to make money."

She opens her mouth to respond, but he doesn't give her the time of day. Instead, he struts to the door that leads below the stage.

Knowing I need to make my way to my mark, I give Monica an apologetic shrug. "Taylor came here and told him. Apparently, you guys sought her out first."

I leave Monica standing there, smoke almost billowing from her ears in anger. I'm sure she's running through different scenarios on how to fix this, but I already know it's too late.

We all got what we wanted. We broke Nash with our plotting. The only question is, what will be the consequences of our betrayal? He may have a broken heart, but the look on his face tells me it's way deeper than that. It seems like we didn't just break his heart, we crushed his soul. And I'm fearful of what'll happen next.

It turns out I don't have to wait long to see the fallout from our betrayal.

Nash spirals before all our eyes.

He's losing it in front of a crowd of people, and there's nothing any of us can do but to keep performing. As soon as Nash came up on stage on the lift, a cup in hand, I worried his drinking wouldn't stop, even to perform. I have to hand it to him, he was still able to perform with the alcohol coursing through his body. But by *Preach*, he's consumed enough for it to be obvious that he's toasted.

I'm standing behind him, waiting for him to start the song when he begins to speak into his mic.

"This song was one I wrote when I had my heart broken by both my girlfriend and someone I thought was my best friend. I wrote the whole album while nursing heartache." He stops to take a sip from his drink. He wobbles a bit before regaining his balance. "Turns out, I had *no* fucking clue what heartbreak was then. No fucking clue."

Sadly, he looks over his shoulder at me. The look on his face, destroys me. It's defeated, angry, sad, all wrapped in a heart piercing look from those blue-green eyes. "Now I do. And it fucking *sucks.*"

Looking back to the crowd, he adjusts the strap of his guitar, checking to make sure it's tuned correctly. "Want to know the worst part of all this? I thought for once, people were loving me for *me,* for who I wanted to be. In a twisted, heart wrenching turn of events, it was made clear they only want me when I'm broken."

"Nora Mason, everybody." The crowd cheers, somehow missing how fucked up this whole situation is right now. He extends a hand my way, an introduction to the crowd I don't want after the speech he just gave. He doesn't give me time to react. He starts the song, and for three minutes and forty-six agonizing seconds, the two of us pretend that both our hearts aren't broken and beaten.

At the end of the show, we're taking our final bow when my skin begins to crawl. Looking out at the crowd, they're going nuts for Nash. It's one of the loudest shows we've had, and it blows my mind. It's clear to anyone with a set of eyes to see how completely wasted he is, his ramblings throughout the show not making a lot of sense. But the crowd...loves it. The realization makes me want to throw up.

I know tomorrow there'll be countless articles rehashing Nash's demise, thriving off the fact that he's so broken. Society is sick, being more entertained by a broken celebrity than a healthy one.

The stage lights go black when Nash's words come back to haunt me. He's right, everyone likes him more when he's broken. It's the saddest realization.

30
NASH

Having to be near her is fucking torture. Night after night, we have to pretend that there isn't an ocean of lies and deceit between us. I thought I knew heartbreak when I saw Taylor in bed with my best friend—someone I considered my brother. But that feeling pales in comparison to the hole I feel in my heart now. It doesn't help that we still have to be in each other's worlds.

After giving Monica the verbal lashing of her life, incredibly hurt by her part in the whole ordeal, she made a point that there would be too much bad press if Nora wasn't suddenly on tour with us, especially after I made a drunken fool of myself when I learned of the betrayal.

Not wanting to be around Nora any longer than I had to, I made a deal with Monica. Nora could stay and finish up the North American leg of the tour, but I wanted her replaced for the second half of it when we were overseas. I didn't care who they got, but I didn't want her traveling with us. I didn't want to look at her night after night and face the fact that, despite her betrayal, I still love her.

A makeup artist is stuffing tissues in the collar of my shirt, fussing with brushing something over my forehead as I dread the interview that's about to take place. I'm biting back a complaint, trying hard to not to be a dick. I got a lot of backlash from the way I acted at my hometown show. I was piss drunk, ranting and raving about things they still don't understand. All the people calling me out would've probably acted the same way I did if they found out the first person they let in for years had bad intentions from the first time they met.

One of the worst parts of the whole ordeal is that Nora was the one thing in my life that felt like something *I* had control over. The rest of my life is heavily planned out and under a microscope. Nora felt like the first thing I chose for myself, and the universe laughed in my face, because she ended up being just another piece of my life that's been planned out—for the sake of sales.

"Close your eyes for me," the makeup artist instructs, still lightly running a makeup brush over my face.

Nora sits next to me, her own makeup artist working on her face. We're sitting on a small loveseat in the middle of a set. Every time she pulls down her dress to cover more of her thighs, her elbow brushes mine, making me want to scream. The press still thinks we're more than friends, even though I've been spotted out with other women since Nora ripped my heart out. Each time, Monica tears me a new asshole over the image I'm allegedly creating when the press thinks I'm dating Nora and cheating on her. It feeds into the image they already have of me.

I wish I could tell every last bit of them that Nora is the one who pushed me away. Her actions made her have no say in who I spend my time with. Even after all she did to me, the press is unaware, even though drunk me made it pretty clear at the hometown show. They're still unbelievably fascinated with her. I could probably tell them what she did, and I don't think they'd believe me. It's the bed I've made for myself over the years, and I'm going to fucking lie in it. But it doesn't mean I have to like it.

I'm only doing this interview because I didn't have it in me to argue further. Plus, I'm a masochist. I wanted to pretend, if only for the cameras for a small period of time, that Nora and I were still that couple that the world fell in love with. It's almost too easy to pretend that she hasn't caused so much hurt in me.

"Cameras rolling in one minute," someone shouts from my left.

The host of the nightly news, Piper Matthews, takes a seat across from us. She smiles, although the smile doesn't quite reach her eyes. I've done interviews with her before. She's savage, completely ruthless in some of her questioning. She'll ask questions as if she's owed an explanation of your whole damn life. She's tried to corner me many times into answering questions about my personal life, rehab, my parents—if it's been a part of my life, she's wanted to know about it.

"Y'all ready?" she asks. Her fake, sweet southern accent sets off my bullshit alarms.

Nora straightens in her seat, giving Piper a timid smile, a quiet "*yes*" coming right after.

I've got to give it to my Rose, she can act. I suppose I already knew that by the way our whole relationship was centered around her acting skills. Her body leans slightly toward me as if we don't have any problems.

I still sit awake at night, trying to figure out if I think she was telling the truth when she said she loved me too. With the tears running down her face, her eyes pleading with mine to understand, it seemed like she wasn't lying. But how could I trust that, when everything we were had been founded on her leaving me?

"Nash?" Piper asks, as the cameraman starts a twenty-second countdown.

"As I'll ever be," I mutter under my breath.

"Ten...nine..." the camera man counts down, switching to his fingers once he reaches three.

Suddenly, all cameras are pointed at us, the lights bright against our faces.

Piper looks at the camera, giving it a toothy smile. "Tonight, I get to sit down with Nash Pierce and the girl who's not only stolen the hearts of people around the world, but Nash's as well. Welcome to the show, Nora." Piper fixes her eyes on Nora, waiting for her answer.

"Happy to be here." Nora smiles, seeming completely at ease with all the rolling cameras.

"Nash," Piper begins.

I smile, already fully aware of what she's about to ask me. I've been trained by the best publicists; I can almost always guess what I'm about to be asked in interviews. They're all cliché and want to know the same damn things.

"Can you tell us how you found Nora? It seems like a fairytale love story. Her joining your tour, the two of you becoming close..."

Her words die off, a tactic they use so I fill in the blanks.

"Well, I didn't find Nora, my team did." *Oh, if only you knew the truth behind these words, Piper,* I think, not lying at all. My team did find her—it just wasn't through auditions, it was through socials—to find me someone acceptable to hand my heart over to. "But the first time we met was at auditions."

"Did she catch your eye from the beginning?" Piper crosses her ankles.

I smile, throwing my arm over the back of the couch, which is also over Nora's back. Piper eats it up, giving us a huge smile. "Yeah, you can say that." Looking at Nora, I wink, giving the cameras exactly what they want.

She smiles hesitantly, probably waiting for me to lose my shit and tell the world about what she's done.

My eyes find Monica's over Piper's shoulder. She gives me a nod, the look of approval for Monica-speak.

"What was it like, Nora? Catching the attention of someone like Nash?"

Nora swallows slowly, looking at me for a moment before fixing her attention on Piper. "He wasn't what I was expecting," she starts.

"Tell us more." Piper is eating this shit up, feasting on every word Nora and I feed her.

Oh, the pretty lies, I think, remembering the words I told Nora.

Nora shifts her weight from one hip to the other. The movement causes my fingers to brush over her shoulder. I have to touch her every night on tour, but even the smallest hint of her skin against mine reminds me of all the times I got to touch every delicate inch of her, the way it felt to have her come undone under my touch.

"The Nash the world sees is not the same Nash that those closest to him see." Those beautiful eyes of hers focus on me and I'm sucked in. "Getting to know him has been...epic. He's captivating."

I swallow, trying not to fall into her deception once again.

"Sounds like you think really highly of him. Could we assume that the two of you are in love?"

Breaking the trance between me and Nora, I face Piper. "I think that's something we'd like to keep private."

"Nora, you seem to have just popped up on our radar. You went from posting videos on your social media to dating America's most eligible bachelor. Can you tell us a little about yourself?"

"Oh, I'm not that interesting, Piper. I grew up in your typical small town, but I had dreams that didn't fit in that small town. After I graduated, I moved to LA to follow those dreams. The rest is history."

"Well, it seems like your town really lost a special talent. While doing some research on you, we found this beautiful piece of art you performed while still in high school. Could we roll a clip of that please?"

The screen behind us lights up with a video of Nora on stage. She has on a white outfit, her body gliding effortlessly. I'm drawn to the video on stage when Piper speaks again. "This is my favorite part."

It jumps to Nora being pulled at by multiple people, them ripping off layers of her clothing. She's left in nothing but a small leotard. Out of nowhere she somehow gets ahold of what looks like paint, and her hands drift all over her body, leaving streaky handprints in her wake.

The music she's dancing to is sad and dark. My eyes find her, wondering why I've never seen this video of her. My stomach falls to my feet when I look at her. All the blood has drained from her face, and she stares at the video with an agonizing look on her face.

Even after the screen goes black, she stares into the distance, her mind clearly not with us.

"When I first saw that video, it took my breath away. You were deliberate with every movement of your body. It was so beautiful, so haunting. Tell me, did the dance have anything to do with the expulsion of your high school's basketball star? It says that you attacked him for what he did. Your ex-boyfriend?"

"What the fuck?" I say, my hand falling to Nora's thigh. She jumps, looking at me with fear in her eyes.

"I can't, I can't, Nash," she mumbles, tears welling in her eyes.

"You okay, honey?" Piper asks, leaning forward.

"Don't fucking talk to her," I snap, completely unaware of why Nora is so shook-up right now, but my mind goes to the worst. I have no idea what has her reacting this way, all I know is she isn't okay right now, and I need to get her out of here.

"You guys agreed to sixty minutes," Piper reminds us, standing up when I do.

Stepping in front of Nora, I look down my nose at the vulture of a talk show host. "We agreed to the questions outlined ahead of time. This," I say, pointing toward the blank screen that started this, "wasn't agreed upon. My team will be taking all the footage."

"You can't do that," she interjects, visibly upset.

"Oh, I fucking can. You guys are god damn vultures.

We're leaving."

I pull a shaking Nora off the couch and guide us away from the stage. We don't stop until we're out in the parking lot.

Stopping on the asphalt, I turn to face her. "Nora?" I ask cautiously.

She looks up at me, mascara running down her cheeks. "I left all that behind. It wasn't supposed to come out. No one was supposed to know…"

Grabbing her by the shoulders, I try my best to soothe her. "Know what, Rose?"

Her painted bottom lip trembles as she looks me dead in the eye. "I tried to cover it up for her. It was supposed to be me…"

"What do you mean it was supposed to be you?"

She looks at me, tears falling freely from her eyes. Her voice shakes as she answers me. "He assaulted her. My sister. He almost raped my sister thinking she was me."

For someone who makes a living off stringing words together to create something beautiful, I'm at a complete loss for any. Her reaction to the trauma is visceral. It's clear that the situation Piper brought up was traumatic for Nora.

I don't push her for more answers, not wanting to make her relive any of it if she doesn't want to. The two of us stand in the middle of the backlot of the studio. I want to hug her, to show her that she doesn't have to go through this alone, but I also don't want to cross any boundaries.

"Can I hug you?" I ask, hesitant to touch her if she isn't in the right mind space for it.

Rubbing her tear-stained lips together, she nods, closing the distance between us on her own.

"My ex and I had just broken up. He'd cheated on me again and I was done dealing with it. It was a few weeks after our breakup that my parents went out of town, so I decided to have a party. My sister's two years younger than me, a sophomore at the time, and I'd convinced her not to go to her friend's and party with me. It was always my sister that was the better dancer. She was so passionate about ballet that she almost never had fun. She was incredibly disciplined. I told her to let loose this once, telling her our dance teachers would never find out."

Her shoulders shake in my arms as she takes a deep breath in, trying to steady her words. "My ex showed up, and I was pissed; we got in a fight a few hours into the party. I thought he left, but then as the night was winding down, one of my friends said he'd gone upstairs..."

There's a distant sound of a car honking as she collects her thoughts. "My sister had gone to bed in my room that night. It was deeper into the house and not as loud. She spent maybe an hour with us before she decided she had to go to bed. I told her she could go to my room. I thought it would make her feel better. But he went in there, and he was drunk, not that it gives him any excuse. He thought it was me in that bed and without asking, he began to assault her. If I hadn't found him, I think he would've gone all the way."

Swallowing, I try and speak through the anger. All I see is red, thinking about this fucker. "You found him?"

She nods against my chest. "I found him with his pants down, Lennon bawling and pleading with him to stop. I lost it. I grabbed the first thing I could find, a floor length mirror by my door, and hit him with it. I couldn't stop, I kept trying to swing it until broken glass was everywhere. If he wasn't so drunk, he would've been able to overpower me, but I stunned him. The only reason I stopped was because I was pulled off him by one of his teammates. As I was pulled off him, he looked at me and told me he thought it was *me* saying no. My world collapsed when I realized it was supposed to be me dealing with that trauma, not her."

"Fuck, Rose," I begin, words failing me. I can't even begin to fathom what her sister and her went through. There's got to be some emotional trauma on her part, being told that this guy thought it was her and not her sister. I'm an older sibling as well and understand the responsibility you feel to take care of your younger sibling. The guilt she feels for what happened to her sister is palpable between us.

"Luckily, one of my dad's best friends was a cop. They took it seriously when we told them the story. My scumbag ex obviously got in trouble with both the law and the school, causing his family to move away. Even with him gone, charges were pressed against him. There were still people at our high school that thought it was Lennon's fault this all happened. It changed my sister. She'd always been quiet, preferring to speak through dance than with words. After that, she didn't want to dance at all. She lost all interest. So, I decided to dance for her. That's what my showcase was, to one of *your songs*, telling the story for her. Every shitty human in our small town needed to understand the trauma an assault victim has to work through. They needed to know what it can do to someone and that she was a *victim*. It wasn't her fault. It was his."

"For a long time, I thought it was my fault, but even my sister didn't blame me. Still, our relationship changed. *She* changed. And I let her process it however she needed to. Which ended up in her bouncing from place to place, trying to find where she fits into the world. She got her GED and we speak occasionally. She was always my best friend, but now we're acquaintances. I keep dancing in hopes that one day she'll find her love for dance again, and it can be the thing to help mend our broken relationship. Before that night, dancing was just a hobby for me. Now it's something more. I started posting videos of me dancing online in hopes it could encourage her to do something she loved again."

Tears soak my shirt as she sobs against my chest. Her hands fist at the fabric between us. I let her cry, not being able to come up with words to justify what just happened to her—and her family. The dance Piper just cornered her into watching was her way of seeking justice for what happened to her sister. It was her way of coping with the damage that's been inflicted on them.

I want to go back into that studio and rip every single person involved a new one, but it feels more important to support her in this moment. I'm trusting my team to do whatever it takes to make sure the interview that just happened never sees the light of day.

Letting Nora work through her emotions as needed, I simply hold onto her. It doesn't take long before she's taking a few deep breaths, her hands slowly unfisting the fabric of my shirt.

Taking a few small steps back, she looks at me. "I was going to tell you one day; I just didn't know how to bring it up. It is something I've just wanted to...forget." Her last words are said quietly.

"Hey, you don't owe anyone that story."

"I know I don't, but it still doesn't change that I did want to tell you. I just didn't know how. And then..."

Her words drift off, the both of us knowing what the *"and then"* was.

Because no matter how bad I want to be there for her right now, there's still so much brokenness between us. Just because she hurt me doesn't mean I can't be there for her when she needs it. I decide not to discuss her past anymore, letting her talk about it more only if she wants to.

"Want to get out of here?" I ask, pulling out my phone to see where Sebastian is.

Using the sleeves of her dress to wipe her eyes, she shrugs. "Don't you hate me?"

Biting my lip, I let out a defeated sigh. "This would be a lot easier if I hated you, Rose."

Matt and Sebastian pull up next to us, both of them giving Nora sympathetic looks as she climbs in. Even though my team will make sure an audience never sees the footage from today, it doesn't erase the fact that half the people she works with daily all saw what happened in there.

After this, she may not be too upset about leaving the tour. She'll probably be thankful one day that we didn't get any deeper into a relationship, that way she'll soon be forgotten by the media. As someone in the public eye, the press will dig up every one of our dirty little secrets, making them seem way worse than they really are when they expose it to the world.

There's no excuse for the hurt Nora has caused me, but I can't help but feel a little guilty that her past got brought up today because of her affiliation with me.

I hold her the entirety of the car ride, knowing that the second we arrive back to the venue, we'll go our separate ways and I'll go back to wallowing in the pain she's caused me. I'll go on pretending that the heart she broke doesn't still beat for her and only her.

31
NASH

It's the last night of the North American leg of the tour. Which means it is also the last night with Nora on tour. She agreed to leave the tour, saying she'd like to take a step away from the spotlight a bit after what happened with Piper.

I'd envisioned meeting the halfway mark with Nora by my side so many times. What I hadn't expected was for us to go our separate ways after taking the final bow. Being near her, touching her, it has been torture each and every night, my mind at war with the feelings that still creep up when it comes to her. I'm so pissed off at her that I don't ever want to look at her again, but I'm also in love with her.

Once the show was over, I was so pissed about the situation we were in that I didn't say a word to anyone. I went straight to my dressing room, my lips wrapped around the bottle of vodka before the door was even shut. Unfortunately, the alcohol did nothing to help my aching heart, the buzz from the vodka doing nothing to dull the pain. All it did was make me feel worse about myself. It was a reminder that nothing can bring me the same high I felt with Nora. I know I need to let her go, but I'm not ready yet.

Standing at her hotel room door, I know before I even knock that this is a mistake. This won't do anything but cause me more heartache and confusion. But it doesn't stop me from knocking on her door, holding my breath as I wait for her to answer.

The alcohol is still running through me, but only slightly, my head aware enough to understand the mistake I'm making. The door swings open, a surprised Nora standing on the other side. She has on a long-sleeve T-shirt and nothing else. A hollow feeling develops in my stomach when I realize it's one of the T-shirts that's sold at each one of my shows, the logo for the current tour embroidered over her heart.

"Nash?" she asks, her eyes skirting over my appearance. I haven't changed since the show, my shirt disheveled. "What are you doing here?"

Taking a deep breath, I stare her down, allowing myself to really look at her for the first time in a while. Her hair stands up in different places, making it look like I may have woken her up.

Before losing my resolve, I answer her. "After the show..."

"Everyone knows what you've been doing after the shows, Nash. You don't have to remind me," she interrupts, referring to the photos of me heading to different clubs with women.

I don't bother to tell her that nothing has happened with any of those women. I've only been taking them out in the hopes that Nora would see and it would maybe hurt her a fraction of the way she's hurt me.

"After the show," I repeat, "I was *alone* and realized something. You had months to plan out a goodbye, knowing it was evident before we even met, and yet, I got the worst goodbye possible. I want a better goodbye,

Rose."

She looks at me dumbfounded. "What does that even mean?"

"It means if this is going to be the last time, I see you, I want to make it count." Stepping into the doorway, I crowd her, aware of her every move.

"Nash, we shouldn't. It isn't right. We can't—"

A sad laugh escapes my chest. "Oh, so now you're worried about what is right? Too late for that."

"If I could go back and change things, I would."

My eyes assess her every move, trying to decipher if she's telling the truth or not. She looks me in the eye, not cowering away. I wrap a piece of her curled hair around my finger. "Now that's something we can't do. No matter how much I wish we could."

"I didn't mean to—"

I stop her, not wanting to hear any more of her lies, or her truths at this point. I don't know what to believe from her mouth by now, so I prefer to hear nothing.

She opens the door, allowing me into her room. I take in the modern space around her. It's smaller than my penthouse suite, but still nice.

Making myself at home, I walk all the way in until I take a seat on her bed. "Your mouth has told me nothing but lies. I want to hear from your body one last time. Maybe at least that was real."

She crosses her arms over her middle. "You want to fuck me?"

My fingers play with the studs on the sleeve of my leather jacket. It takes me a minute to think of a response. I struggle with how honest I want to be with her. "Maybe if I know it's the last time, I'll be able to move on."

Her spine straightens with my words. If I knew better, I'd say there appears to be hurt in her eyes. "I should be easy to forget."

Laughing, I shake my head. "I've written songs about you, you know."

Her lips fall open as she walks closer to me. She stops,

resting against the corner of the wall a few feet away from me. "Nash..."

"I think this album might be the best one because of you. You did a number on my heart, Nora. I couldn't have come up with a better plan myself. I did need another broken heart to be able to connect with my lyrics. Maybe one day I'll thank you, but today isn't that day. Today I'm still so fucking mad at you. But today I'm also still so damn in love with you."

"I don't deserve your love, Nash." My eyes track the path of a lone teardrop falling from her eye.

"No, you don't," I say sadly. "But that doesn't help the fact that you have it."

The two of us are silent, neither one of us knowing how to act around the other. There's so much tension in the air, with every inhale I find myself needing her more and more.

Looking her in the eye, finding those hazel eyes pinned on me, I confess that I want to be able to hurt her like she hurt me. "I hope my songs follow you everywhere you go. I hope you hear them on the radio, and you're reminded of me. Sometimes I hope you hurt like I do, and that makes me such a sick fuck."

She closes the distance between us, running a hand over my cheek. I lean into her touch, relishing in the feel of her skin against mine once again. "Would it help if I told you I love you too?"

I look at her eyes, wanting to climb into that mind of hers to sift through the lies and truths she's told. Giving her a sad smile, I answer. "No, it wouldn't, Rose. How can you plan to hurt someone you love?"

Her hand stiffens against my cheek. She doesn't give me an answer, instead she leans in, her lips hovering over mine. "Is this what you want, Nash?"

Hesitating, my mind reviews all the different reasons this shouldn't happen. Tasting her again will just be a relapse for me. Whatever mending my heart has done since the truth of her betrayal came to light will be ruined.

But at this point, I'm not sure any healing has even happened.

It doesn't take long for me to make up my mind. I capture her lips in mine, letting my hands tangle in the long strands of her hair one last time. Our bodies mold against each other, her tongue eagerly entering my mouth.

Spinning us around, I let our bodies fall against the bed. I take my time running a hand over the curves of her body. If this is the last time I have with her, I want to make it count, savor it for as long as possible.

"Off," I tell her, lifting up for long enough to get her sleep shirt off. Underneath she wears no bra and a thin pair of panties.

"You're killing me, Nora," I tell her, my eyes raking over her near-naked body. I watch in fascination as she takes a shaky breath in, her breasts rising and falling in anticipation.

"I'm sorry," she says underneath me. Her hand slides under my leather jacket and T-shirt. Looking into her eyes, I know she's sorry, but even her apology doesn't make up for what's been done.

"It's my turn to talk," I instruct, holding my finger over her mouth to let her know to stay quiet. "I'm so fucking furious with you, so *hurt* by you," I say, leaning over her. My hand swipes the tendrils of her chestnut hair off her shoulder. I'm met with her soft, bare skin. "You were the last person I ever thought would hurt me." My lips roam over her exposed skin, the beat of her pulse thumping against my lips.

She tries to pull at my jacket to remove it, but I don't let her. Right now, I'm saying what I came here to say, and she's going to have to listen.

My finger lazily drifts up her stomach, her lean muscles flexing beneath my touch. "You betrayed me in the worst possible way, Nora. My heart feels like it's been stripped from my chest and laid out for everyone to examine." I point to the spot on her chest that covers up her beating heart. I lay my palm flat against it, relishing in the way the beat starts to pick up.

"Yet, despite it all, I'm still in love with you." Leaning down, I take one of her peaked nipples in my mouth.

A moan falls from her lips, the sound filling the otherwise quiet room.

"I still want you with every part of me." I feather kisses down her stomach. Nora squirms underneath me, her hands fisting around the white sheets. "Even the parts you hurt. Maybe the broken parts of me are the pieces that love you the most." My fingers hook into the underwear on either side of her hips. I tug, pulling the panties down and letting them get lost in the tangle of sheets.

Before leaning close to taste her, I look up to find her propped up on her elbow. She watches me carefully, her cheeks flushed under the yellow hotel lights.

"But I don't trust that you feel the same way. Now I'm left in this mindfuck of a situation. Loving you despite the betrayal, but not being able to trust you because of it."

She opens her mouth to say something. "I—"

Before she can say anything else, my mouth molds to her core, no longer wanting to have a conversation. I bared my soul to her. I told her that even after all the hurt and pain, I still want her more than anything else in the world. I still love her. I've laid it all on the table, unsure of what I want except a better goodbye.

Words are useless for us now, the both of us speaking with our bodies. I bring her to the brink of release before removing my mouth from her. Kissing my way back up her body, I take her mouth in mine. Our kisses used to be slow and romantic, but tonight, they're untamed and wild. Deep down, we both know this has to be the end of us. I'm not sure I'll ever be able to trust her again, which sets us up for nothing but disaster. We have to end, but one more night together won't cause any more hurt. Or it will, the two of us too reckless to care.

Nora's fingernails dig into my back as she pulls my

body against hers. Her teeth scrape against my bottom lip, causing a short sting of pain. Shocking me, Nora places both hands on my chest, pushing me away. I'm about to ask her what she's doing when she gestures for me to lie down. Following her lead, I scoot back until my shoulders hit the headboard. She pushes my jacket off, stripping off all my layers until I'm left shirtless. Moving on to my pants, she quickly undoes the button and fly of my jeans, pulling both my jeans and briefs off in one motion.

The two of us are completely naked, and for some reason, I feel way more exposed to her this time than I have any other time. Maybe it's the confessions I've made, maybe it's the knowledge that there's a good chance this'll be the last time I ever see her like this. Whatever it is, I'm extremely turned on. She doesn't have to do much to get me ready. Her knees come to rest on either side of my hips, her legs fully straddling me. She lines her center up with my dick, rolling over it, making me throw my head back.

Her hips move back and forth in a tantalizing rhythm. I want to enter her so bad, to grab her hips and take the lead. But I'm also turned on by having her in control. Her hands come up to rest on my shoulders, her fingers kneading into the back of my neck. Our eyes meet at the same time our bodies connect.

She starts off slow, riding up and down as if she has all the time in the world. Her lips find my throat, her lips and tongue leaving their mark. "I love you too," she says next to my ear, lowering herself until I'm as deep in her as possible.

The two of us moan at the same time, reminded of how good it feels when our bodies collide.

Unable to hold myself back a second longer, I grab each side of her narrow waist. I use the leverage to pump in and out of her quickly. I let her have the illusion that she's in control for a few minutes before I flip her over until she's on all fours. Pulling her hips against me, I enter her once again. My fingers wrap in her hair as I push as deep as I can, her encouraging moans pushing me too close to the edge.

Our bodies meet in the in-between of making love and fucking. We can't go slow and gentle like we used to, the both of us aware that we shouldn't do this again, but there are too many feelings between us to just fuck.

I'm on the brink of coming, pushing in and out of her until I'm confident she'll still be able to feel me tomorrow. Her body slackens as she reaches a climax. The way my name falls from her lips as she finds her release has me finding my own. I pull out of her swiftly, making sure not to empty inside her.

The two of us fall into the mattress, trying to gather our breath. Sex with her is just as good as I remember—better even. Which makes what I have to do now even harder.

Not wanting to stay and hold her close to me, I climb off the bed in search of my clothes. I'm debating on saying the hell with logic, to climb back in bed with her and mold her body to mine for one last night. But deep down, I know that my heart can't handle that. I can't stay and cuddle with her, fearful I'll never be able to leave if it happens.

She turns over, nodding slightly when she sees me gather my jeans from the floor. She pulls on the sheet until it covers her. "So just like that..." she mutters softly, a sad look on her face.

I stare at her as I pull my jeans on, wishing I had any idea what was going on in her head right now, wishing I could go back in time and remove us from the situation we're in.

"Yeah," I answer, pulling the rest of my clothes on.

"I didn't mean to hurt you," she whispers, so quiet I almost don't hear it. By the way she doesn't look at me, instead staring at the bed in front of her I wonder if it was something she even meant for me to hear.

"You know what hurts the worst? I've always thought

no one could actually love me because I've felt like such a shell of a person for years. There wasn't much of me to love. But then you came along. The worst part about this all is that you made me feel like I could be loved. I need to get my shit together, Nora. And I can't be near you to do it. You clearly fuck with my head."

Crawling across the bed, I cradle both sides of her head in my hands. I pull her forehead to my lips, swallowing to keep my emotions in check. I let myself linger there for a few moments, savoring feeling her skin against mine. All too soon, I pull away. "I'll always love you, Rose."

I'm opening the door when I hear a sob rip through her chest. The sound has me nearly turning around to comfort her. My hand pauses on the doorknob, my head trying to work through what to do. I realize that I can't comfort her through this. I love her, but this is her own doing. For my own sanity, I have to walk away, I have to move on.

I walk out the door, letting it slam behind me. I only make it a few steps before my own emotions get the best of me. Still haunted by the sounds of her cries, I slide down the wall of the hotel hallway, cursing the universe for giving me the love of my life, only to make her the person who would betray me the most.

32

NORA

FOUR MONTHS LATER

Darkness envelops the space around me as I flip off the lights to the dance studio I've worked at the last few months. Rifling through my purse, I find my car keys and head toward the parking lot. As soon as I step out the door, the dry LA heat warms my skin. The sun has begun to set, leaving the bustling city around me in an orange glow. Two little girls play on the sidewalk in front of the sandwich shop next door. It looks like they've set up a doll beauty shop, the two of them braiding the hair of their dolls. The owner of the shop, Maggie, watches from the doorway with a serene smile on her face.

The two little girls remind me of me and my sister when we were kids. She could always braid so much better than I could, making me so angry as a child. My sister and I have begun to talk more recently. She's currently in Washington working at a hotel, but she said when she gets the chance, she wants to come to LA to visit. It's a steppingstone toward a better relationship for the two of us.

After the interview with Piper, and telling Nash about what had happened in high school, I realized I needed to do a better job of reaching out to her. I'm the older sister and I should put in the work to mend our relationship, so that's what I've been doing. Surprisingly, she was all for it. We're taking baby steps, but a baby step is still a step.

Getting in my car, I find a text from Riley saying she is also on her way home. Tonight, we have big plans to watch the music awards. It's the first time Nash has performed there in two years. He's been teasing new music on all his socials for weeks now, and there's a pit in my stomach at the possibility of his performance tonight involving lyrics about me.

It's been over four months since I've seen him. In the beginning, I could barely leave my bed, too upset with myself and what I've done to be a functioning member of society. Riley eventually had to stage an intervention, forcing me to get out of bed and wash my hair. For a long time, she had his socials blocked on my phone, knowing I was too obsessed with stalking him online. I felt like I deserved to see him with girl after girl. It was a way of punishing myself for how much I hurt him. Every time I saw his arm wrapped around the waist of a beautiful girl, it felt like salt in the wound. I didn't blame him for moving on at all, but that didn't mean it didn't hurt.

When I finally got to a healthy place where I didn't cry about him daily, I caught up on every single thing he'd been up to recently. I only felt worse all over again when I learned how bad he was handling things. Night after night, he performs under the influence of something. Sometimes he begins the show slurring a bit, but for some reason, people love it. I've read some articles that even go as far as saying they're some of his best shows. It's crazy to me how, in one line, they'll talk about how he's unhealthily drunk and in the next, how they think it was his best show *because* of it. No wonder he has a hard time staying sober. Aside from being backstabbed by those closest to him, he has the media telling him he's at his best when he's three shots to the wind. It reminds me of a line he said at the show that went to shit. He'd said, "*They only want me when I'm broken*," and he was dead on.

It's sad. I'm sad for him. I'd reach out to him if I thought it would help, but he made it clear that he no longer wanted anything to do with me, and I have to respect that.

We haven't spoken a word since our night together on my last night of the tour. It was a night that left my head—and my heart—spinning for weeks. I wish I could've convinced him of my feelings for him, but his pain was too fresh to see past my deceit. I can't blame him for walking away; it was the plan all along. I just hadn't expected it to hurt the way it did, that final goodbye making things worse.

It's awkward while Riley and I eat dinner. She knows how anxious I am about this performance. I twirl the noodles around on my plate, too nervous to eat. My stomach is in knots. The two of us sit on our couch, both anxiously waiting for the announcement of when he'll be on. Right as they make an announcement that he'll be performing after the break, I panic.

"I can't do this," I tell Riley, hiding my face behind a pillow.

Her hand rubs my shoulder. "You don't have to watch it, Nora. We could turn it off."

Pulling the pillow down slightly, I meet her eyes. "I can't *not* watch it."

She nods, biting at one of her nails. The TV plays a trailer for a movie releasing next month, but all I can think about is what Nash will sing about. What will he say about me in his lyrics?

"I broke his heart, the least I could do is listen to the songs he created because of that."

Before I'm ready, the logo for the award shows pop up on the screen. It's time for him to perform, and a million little anxious butterflies take flight in my stomach.

My eyes are glued to the TV as I watch his face pop up onto the screen. There's a ping in my heart when I see his face, remembering all the times I feathered kisses over his skin. I want to die when I take in his outfit, remembering a time when the man on the screen was mine. He looks incredibly sexy. He wears a suit as black as night. There's a leather strap going down both arms, adding a bit of edge to it. As if he wasn't alluring enough, he's got nothing on underneath the suit jacket. His chiseled chest and tattoos peek out, and it's devastatingly hot. He has so much sex appeal. I think the only times he's looked better is when he was naked in bed with me. When the camera pans out, I notice a pair of black biker boots covering his feet, adding his own personal touch to the outfit.

Dancers I came to know so well from tour stand behind him on stage. All of them decked out in red and black. The screen behind him is as dark as his suit.

I hold my breath, waiting for the song to begin. Troy beats on the drum behind him, getting the song started, and then I feel the sting of regret for what I've done to Nash all over again.

Was I a pawn in your game of chess?
At this point, I'd expect nothing less
I tried to hate you, you know it's true
But the only thing I hate is how much I love you
You think you could've given me a better goodbye?
Now I'm left chasing that high

Oh Rose,
We were doomed from the start
You were sent to destroy me
Why couldn't you fall?

Oh Rose,
I've tried hating you
But all it did is make me love you

But how can we love with no trust?
I want love for the both of us
You want nothing from me at all
I told you I didn't want to fall

You're beautiful, Rose
Your thorns sure do stab
Blood running down my hand
I find myself still wishing I was your man

Oh Rose,
We were doomed from the starting gate
You were sent to destroy me
Why couldn't you fall?

Oh Rose,
I've tried hating you
But all it did is make me love you
But how can we love with no trust?
Can I love you enough for the two of us?
You want nothing from me at all
I told you I didn't want to fall

I didn't know my heart was flammable, baby
Thought you were sent to save me
Turns out you came holding kerosene
Lighting up the fragile part of what was left of me
We burn, burn, burn, baby
We're done, done, done, baby

Tears stream down my face as the red rose on the screen behind Nash wilts, all the petals falling to the ground. The screen goes black, only one stage light still illuminating Nash. He runs a hand through the curls at the top of his head, staring straight at the camera. My stomach lurches, feeling like he's looking straight into my soul. There's no doubt that song was about me. I'm not shocked. He told me to my face he had written songs about me, I just wasn't fully prepared to hear them for the first time. I wasn't ready to hear the pain etched in every one of his lyrics.

"Okay, well, that was..." Riley says next to me. I feel her watching me carefully, but I can't do anything but continue to stare at Nash on the screen. He gives the crowd an apprehensive smile as numerous famous people give him a standing ovation.

I thought my stomach had dropped as low as it could get, but when a gorgeous woman, an actress I think, comes up next to Nash, I feel sick all over again. The way she smiles at him, it makes it seem like they're familiar with each other. She easily leans her body toward his, fanning herself with her hand as she interacts with the crowd.

I don't hear a thing she says, my head still rushing with the lyrics he just sang. I'm busy analyzing each and every word when the words from the woman on the screen catch my attention.

"Catch Nash's new album, *Founded on Goodbye,* this fall!" Throwing her blonde hair over her shoulder, she looks toward Nash. "And if that song *Rose* is any indication of what that album will sound like, I'm sold."

Nash nods, murmuring a "*thank you*" into his microphone. All too soon, he's gone from our screen, the show moving onto the next award.

Riley scoots on the couch until she's pressed up against me. Her arm comes to wrap around me, pulling me into her chest as the tears really begin to fall. "Aww, Nora," she coos, rubbing my hair for comfort.

"I don't even know why I'm crying," I say into her hair. "I knew what I was getting into, I wasn't the one who was blindsided."

She continues to play with the strands of my hair. I used to pay her and my sister to brush my hair when we were kids, loving the feeling of someone playing with my hair. "That doesn't mean it didn't hurt you too. You did something shitty, but you also fell in love. It's okay to be sad about it. It's okay to miss him."

Her words send me over the edge, a waterfall of tears breaking through my chest. It's been a while since I cried about Nash, my sobs now making up for lost time. I've known for months I hurt Nash but hearing it in a song makes it more real. Knowing that people love the song only makes it worse, which is something I feel bad about. I just hate that it took all of us betraying him for him to write something people appreciate again.

"I miss him so much, Riley." It's true. There's not a day that goes by where I don't wish I could call him and tell him about my day or ask him a random fact about himself. I miss watching him joke around with Sebastian and his bandmates, some of the only moments where he's at ease enough to *really* laugh. I miss tracing each one of his tattoos, pestering him with questions about what they mean. I miss late nights with him, getting lost in each other.

I miss so many things about him that it overwhelms me. And it's hard to know that if I didn't hurt him, if I just told him the truth the second we became friends, that maybe I wouldn't have to be missing him at all.

It all fucking hurts. And I feel guilty that I knew it was bound to happen all along.

"We need tacos," Riley declares, getting up from the couch. She stands in front of me, motioning for me to get up.

I groan, settling myself deeper into the couch. "I can't! I'm too busy crying."

Moving her head from left to right, she thinks through my response. She reaches down and grabs me by the wrist, pulling me off the couch. "Yeah, well, if we're going to cry, we're going to do it into a pitcher of margaritas."

I try and escape her grasp, but she's too strong and I don't have it in me to fight with her. I let her drag me to our favorite place, quite literally crying into my margarita while there.

When I climb into bed hours later, I finally get brave enough to check my phone. I've been avoiding it all night, knowing once I open it, I won't be able to stop myself from listening to his new song over and over until I've cried myself to sleep.

I have to blink a few times, making sure it isn't the alcohol in my brain playing tricks on me when I see a missed text from Nash.

Nash: People love the new song. Tell me, was it worth it?

My heart pounds against my chest as I wonder if I should respond to him. He told me he wanted nothing to do with me, but clearly, he's wanting *something*. I just don't know *what* he wants from me. Does he want me to say it was? Because it wasn't, and I'm over telling lies.

Nora: Never.

Nash: I wish I could forget you. I wish I could hate you. But all I seem to be doing is loving you.

I don't respond at first, racking my brain with what I could say to him to ease his pain. My brain is fuzzy from the tequila, making it harder to think of something to say. I don't get the chance however, because a text comes in as I try to come up with some sort of answer.

Nash: You take the memories; I'll keep the heartbreak. I just don't want to remember you. To remember us. Goodbye, Rose.

Putting my phone down, I fall into my pillows, wishing things were different, wishing I hadn't hurt him, and wishing I could just be there for him again, showing him how amazing of a person he is.

But I can't change anything, no matter how much I want to. All I can do is hope that he gets better, that he forgives me one day.

I hope our goodbye isn't what ruins him when it was supposed to be the thing that rebuilt him.

33

NORA

SIX MONTHS LATER

I wipe my clammy hands on the denim of my jeans for what feels like the hundredth time. Sitting on the hood of my rental car, the sun beats down on the exposed skin at the nape of my neck. I spent at least an hour perfecting my hair into beachy waves this morning, but after waiting in the parking lot for thirty minutes, I had to put my hair up in fear I'd sweat right through the outfit I spent hours picking out.

When ordering the rental, I got the news that I only had two choices for a vehicle. I could take a mammoth sized truck or a minivan. I opted for the minivan. About two minutes into the drive, I began to wonder if I should've gone with the truck when I realized the air conditioning was only blowing hot air. The circulating Arizona air did nothing to help cool me the hour drive it took me to get here. I hadn't thought about what I'd do when I reached my destination. After getting off the phone with Monica, I booked a red-eye flight and ended up in the middle of nowhere, Arizona.

I've been sitting on the hood of the minivan for hours, where I'm currently listening to my sister rattle on about a new friend she made at a Zumba class, when the large gates of the facility open.

"Len, it's happening," I say, panicked.

"Do you see him?" she asks from the other line.

"I can't do this," I tell her, sliding off the car.

"You've got this, Nora," she says. "Call later with updates!" The line goes dead, and I'm left watching Nash get closer and closer to where I stand.

I've pictured this exact moment in my head for almost a year, but now with Nash standing in front of me, I'm utterly speechless. The last time I saw him in person, he was walking out of my hotel room. I had stayed in bed, so many things running through my mind. I wanted to apologize, to beg for his forgiveness, to tell my side, but I knew all of it would be futile. What I did was something we couldn't come back from. If there was *any* chance of hope that Nash would look at me again and not see betrayal, I had to give him space first. So even though it broke my heart to stay quiet, even as he kissed my forehead, whispering that he'd always love me, I'd done it. For him. Because I didn't deserve him then. I know I don't deserve him now. But there's been enough time and space between us now, that I just want to be able to tell him how sorry I am for everything.

It takes him a moment to notice me. He's too busy thumbing through his phone to really pay attention to the world surrounding him. A nurse in a pair of sage green scrubs captures the rest of his attention. They speak and it seems friendly, an easy conversation being held between the two of them. I miss when the conversations between me and him were easy. Now, they're filled with angst and regret. I absentmindedly wonder if anything has transpired between the two of them in the six months he's been at this facility, but I soon realize that's none of my business.

He's in the middle of saying something to her when he

looks up, his eyes crashing with mine.

Oh my god. I forgot what it was like to have his attention on me. Those blue eyes are relentless, tracing a line from the top of my head and all the way down my body. He doesn't look surprised to see me. In fact, he shows no emotion at all. I'm desperately trying to read his face, his body language, to gauge his reaction to me being here, but I can't get any kind of read on him.

Whispering something to the nurse, and to my jealous disappointment, he gives her a hug. The hug looks strictly platonic, but that doesn't mean it doesn't hurt just a little, watching him wrap those arms around somebody else.

She retreats toward the brown building, the gates closing shortly after her.

Nash takes a deep breath before walking my way and stopping in front of me. "It seems my countless hours of therapy are being put to the test before I even leave the property," he says, putting both his hands in his pockets. His hair is shorter than the last time I saw him. It's cropped closer to his head, his hair at the top barely long enough to be able to curl.

Taking a deep breath, I try to gain my composure, the apology I rehearsed in my head the whole way here completely forgotten now that he's in front of me.

He rocks back on his heels, looking around the parking lot. "Tell me, Nora, was there no one else available to pick me up from rehab?"

"Wellness Center," I correct, thinking of all the tabloid headlines about Nash in the last six months. To put it lightly, he had a very bad spiral after everything transpired between us. He performed every show clearly under the influence until one day he fell off the stage completely, landing himself in the emergency room with a concussion. He was able to finish the last couple of shows he had left, but the second the tour ended, there were reports of him checking himself into an unknown treatment center somewhere.

I tried calling Monica for months, trying to figure out

where he was so I could send a letter, but she was tight lipped. Eventually I annoyed her enough to convince her to tell me when he'd be leaving a center, that way I could apologize then.

Which leads to this moment right now.

Nash is about to speak, but I cut him off, needing to get these words off my chest before I lose my nerve.

"Nash, I'm sorry," I say. My heart now hammers against my chest and I can feel the sweat gathering on my neck. "What I did to you, there will never be enough words to describe how incredibly sorry I am for it. I got lost in the appeal of finally following the dream I had for myself, for my sister, that I lost all sense of my morals. And I hate it. I hate what I did to you *so* much, because you didn't deserve it. You needed someone to show you all the good in this industry and instead, I showed you every dirty, ugly thing about it. And I'm sorry. So. Freaking. Sorry." My voice cracks even though I'm trying like hell to keep it together.

I look up from my shoes, meeting his eyes once again. "There were countless times I wanted to come clean and tell you, but honestly, I was scared to. I was a chicken. I didn't want to lose the way you looked at me. For the first time in so long, I felt safe with a man, and to my shock, I was falling for someone. I was falling for *you*."

My eyes roam his face, taking in what's familiar and what's changed. I take a second to gather my words, not knowing how long he'll give me to explain myself. "I got lost in the lie, and in the process, I began lying to myself. I'd pretend I got on your tour the way everyone else did, by talent, and that by some miracle, you'd developed feelings for me. I got so lost in my feelings for you that by the time I remembered all the deception it took to get me there; I was too afraid of losing you. I know that isn't any excuse, and I'm not even trying to make an excuse for myself. There is none. What I did to you was such a shitty thing to do and I'm so sorry for it. If I could take it back, I would. Even though it would mean that I wouldn't have met you or loved you, I'd take it back because knowing that I knowingly hurt you, it's awful."

He shakes his head, his eyes scanning over me. I'd give anything to know what he was thinking, to know what comes to mind when he looks at me. He runs a finger over his lip. "You came all this way to say that?"

I laugh nervously, realizing how crazy it seems. I push a few stray hairs out of my face, making sure I can see him. "Yes. I didn't know if I'd ever get another chance. I jumped on a red-eye plane to apologize again. I just needed you to know that I'm so sorry for hurting you, and that even though I hurt you, I did have feelings for you. I fell for you so hard that I became selfish. I couldn't lose you and, in those feelings, I didn't come clean. I'd do anything to take it back, to be with you again. But in the time we've been apart, I've realized that sometimes no matter how much you love someone; it doesn't make you right for them. I understand that, so I know our ship has sailed. I just needed you to know everything was real—and that I'm sorry for what I did."

Nash looks like he's about to say something, but the scraping of tires on asphalt has us both turning our heads. A large black SUV pulls up, Sebastian opening the door of the passenger side.

"Sorry, boss. We were supposed to be early but there was traffic. I tried calling you but—" Sebastian's words cut off when his eyes land on me. "Oh," he says, moving his head up and down. Matt opens the door to the driver's side, slightly narrowing his eyes when he sees me.

"Yeah, I was getting ready to give you a call," Nash says to Sebastian. He looks away from me, stepping around me to go say something to Sebastian I can't hear. Both Matt and Sebastian get busy loading bags I didn't know had been brought out. I must've been too busy trying to profess my love and apologize to Nash to notice.

While the two of them load the car, Nash comes to stop in front of me once again. This time, our bodies are closer. We're so close I can see both the blue and green in his eyes. I can see the slight tic of his clenched jaw. It's the closest I've been to him since our last night together. I want to reach out and touch him so bad, but I don't think that's something I'm allowed to do anymore.

"Thank you for coming, Rose." One of his knuckles brushes over my cheek, slightly caressing my neck. "It's so fucking painful to see you, to look at you, but I'm now in a better place. I can deal with the pain. It's actually good to see you."

"Ready, Nash?" Matt says from a few feet away from us. It's clear that Matt is aware of what I did to Nash, and he's not Team Nora.

I nod my head slowly, knowing that is my hint to get lost. I've said what I came here to say, now I need to let him go—for good.

Trying not to let any tears fall, I swallow slowly. I look up at him one last time, memorizing every single detail of him. The unruly hair, now a little more tame than it used to be, the eyes that look more blue or green depending on his surroundings, the cleft on his chin, a place I'd kissed many times. I commit every single thing to memory, thankful that if only for a moment in time, I got to know this man, to love this man.

My hand caresses over his prominent cheekbones, savoring his skin against mine one last time. "I hope you get everything you ever want, Nash Pierce. You deserve it. You deserve it all." I turn around and run back to my car, not brave enough to look at him again. I wish I could drive away in something cooler, but my life has come to using a minivan as a getaway car.

The backs of my thighs stick to the hot leather as soon as I try and slide into the car. I fumble with turning the car on as fast as possible, the dash in front of me going blurry with unshed tears. I thought I was done crying over Nash, but I don't know if I'll ever get to a point where I don't shed a tear when I think of him.

He was my great love—my rain show. A love that comes once in a lifetime, but not the kind I could keep forever.

Speeding away from the rehab facility, I hope that last exchange was closure enough for the both of us. The end of me and Nash was sad enough to write a breakup song about.

He once told me I could keep the memories, that he didn't want them anymore. I wanted to tell him that was fine. I'll take the memories and the heartbreak—they're the only two reminders I have anymore to prove that at one point in time, we were us.

34
NASH

Matt speeds to the airport as I sit in the backseat, staring absentmindedly out the window. We were supposed to stay for a night before traveling back to LA tomorrow, but after seeing Nora as soon as I left rehab, I made a change to the plans. Watching her walk back to her car not too long ago, I knew that I still loved her. Seeing her waiting at the gates for me confirmed the many talks I'd had with my therapist in rehab. Despite it all, I was madly in love with her. It was only hurting the both of us for me to pretend that I hadn't forgiven her.

As soon as Matt pulls up to the lane people can unload from to get to their gate, I'm rushing out of the car. Both Sebastian and Matt yell after me, warning that everyone will notice me. I don't have time to tell them I don't give a fuck who sees me right now.

I have to get my girl.

Running through the airport, I pull my phone out of my pocket, checking the text from Monica once again.

Nora left me standing in the parking lot like a bat out of hell. I hadn't known a minivan could speed away so quickly. She hadn't given me much time to react to her apology, to her confession of love. As soon as she was out of sight, I was calling Monica, trying to get details on where Nora was heading.

Lucky for me, Monica is ruthless when getting information. She had the flight details for Nora fifteen minutes after I'd called her.

"Oh my god, it's Nash Pierce!" a girl screams from a few feet away from me. As soon as she notices me, people around the airport all get loud.

"He hasn't been seen in *months*," someone says from behind me. "They said he went to rehab."

I avoid all their curious gazes as I run through the busy airport, scanning the signs to find Nora's gate. I weave in and out of bodies, people trying their hardest to get to me. Finally, I make it to the entrance to her gate, but there's a TSA guard standing in front of it.

My hand reaches into my back pocket, pulling out my wallet. I slap my driver's license onto his desk.

"Ticket?" he asks, his outrageously long beard reaching his large belly.

Nodding, I flip through my phone until I pull up the message that holds a plane ticket for the same flight as Nora's, thankful that Monica has a tendency to think of it all.

A large crowd starts to make their way toward us, making me nervous. "Hey, think we could move this along a little faster?" I ask sheepishly, motioning to the swarm of people with their phones aimed at me. "Soon this airport is going to be a circus, paparazzi trying to get the first photo of me post-rehab, and before that happens, I'd like to go get my girl."

The guy, Steve I find out after reading his badge, picks up speed. "I remember young love. Go get her." He hands me my license back, pointing to the entrance to the gate.

"Thanks, man!" I yell over my shoulder, not wanting to

waste any more time.

I'm met with security, something I haven't had to go through in years. The agent clearly doesn't give a rat's ass who I am because she yells at me to take off my shoes and put my belongings in a tray.

My arms tap against my thigh nervously as I wait in line to go through the full body scanner. I'm trying not to make eye contact with the people whispering my name. I clearly hadn't thought my plan fully through. I didn't anticipate having to go through security.

It's my turn to walk through the scanner. Putting my arms above my head, I wait for it to scan me. The guy working the machine motions for me to step out. I'm given the thumbs up to continue on. I'm putting my shoes on as quickly as possible, sliding my phone and wallet into my pockets with urgency.

Ducking my head down, I jog toward her actual gate, praying that she's there. When I make it to her gate I finally look up, my eyes scanning over the people waiting until I find Nora.

She sits directly in the middle of a mass of people, unaware as to what's going around her. Headphones are in each of her ears, her eyes focused on the phone in her lap. Her lips silently sing along with whatever song is playing through the headphones.

I make my way toward her, ignoring the people that are beginning to notice me. Stopping in front of her, I grab her phone, finding my newest single playing—one I wrote about her.

She looks up, alarmed, her eyes widening when she realizes it's me. Pulling at the cords of her headphones, she takes a cautious look at our surroundings. "Nash?" she says incredulously. "What the hell are you doing here?"

I'm aware of the growing crowd around us, but I don't care. All I care about is the woman sitting in front of me. Her phone vibrates in my hand, but I ignore it, too focused on her. She stands up carefully, placing her purse in the chair behind her.

"Nash..." she repeats, her tone unsure.

"Did you ever think about asking me what I want?"

Her mouth opens in shock.

"Well?" I ask.

"What do you want, Nash?" she asks timidly. Her arm nervously crosses her middle and her eyes keep darting over my shoulder to the people saying my name around us.

"Look at me," I say quietly, letting my knuckle run across her jaw. "What I want is...you," I answer simply. "When you left, you said you hoped I got everything I ever wanted. Well, Nora, what I want is *you*. You just didn't give me time to tell you that."

Her eyes widen in shock. She blinks a few times, probably taken aback by my admission. We both know I shouldn't want her anymore, that what she did was wrong in so many ways. But our love is still right more than it is wrong.

"Nash," she whispers, so low I barely hear it over the crowd around us.

I step close enough to her to see the start of a sunburn on the top of her nose. Flyaway brunette hairs line her forehead, a mass of a bun sitting on the top of her head. "I know I shouldn't still love you. What you did to me, it was the worst thing someone has ever done to me. But despite all the betrayal, my heart is yours, Nora Mason. I've spent so many days trying not to love you only to realize I'll only ever love you. It took a long time for me to process that truth. Because I'm not going to lie, I hated myself for still loving you for a while. I thought that it was weak for me to love you after everything you did. But after unpacking all my shit with my therapist, I realized my love for you made me stronger. It made me learn to forgive, something I wasn't really capable of before. You want me to get all I ever wanted. Rose, what I want is you."

"How could you possibly still love me?"

"Because I'm crazy?" I joke, with a tilt to my lips.

"We shouldn't..." she begins, her words drifting off when I reach up and run a thumb over her cheek, letting my hand rest against her cheek.

"You're probably right. But since when do I give a damn about what I should or shouldn't do? The love I have for you is real. I need time to build the trust again, but I want to do the work, Nora. I want to figure our shit out and give this a chance. I think I'd regret it for the rest of my life if I didn't try a relationship with you. If I didn't try and trust you again. So, can I trust you?"

She takes a huge deep breath, not bothering to hide the tears that stream down her face. She smiles, the smile lighting up her entire face. It's breathtaking. "I'll do *whatever* you need in order to trust me again. I fucking love you, Nash Pierce. I'll spend the rest of my life proving how much I love you. I promise."

I smirk. "Then get the fuck over here, Rose."

Her body catapults against mine, almost causing me to lose my balance. People around us cheer, but I'm too lost in her to care that our reunion is most definitely going to be blasted everywhere. I lift her off the ground, her legs wrapping around my middle as she wraps her arms around my neck.

"Is this real?" she asks, tears pouring from her eyes, a large smile on her face.

My lips find hers, planting a small peck against her lips. "It's so damn real. I love you. You're mine. You and me, Rose."

She laughs, burying her face in the crook of my neck. "You and me and the mass amount of people watching us right now."

I laugh with her, realizing just how many people have gathered to watch us. "Let them take their pictures and videos. I don't give a fuck if it means that you're mine again."

"I'm so yours, Nash Pierce. I'm yours for as long as you'll have me. I love you."

"You're my rain show," I whisper against her hair.

My words have her pulling away, her eyes trained on me. "You found it," she murmurs.

"I did." I'd been in rehab for about a month when I discovered she'd made notes in my song journal. I'd already written all the songs I wanted to put on the *Founded on Goodbye* album and uploaded them in my notes that I share with my songwriting team, so I hadn't much need for my journal for a bit. I told my therapist how I hadn't looked at my song journal for a while and she told me to bring it to our next session, using this as an opportunity to face some of the demons I still had to deal with.

When I pulled it out of my suitcase, it automatically opened to her letter. I'd traced over the loops and curls of her dainty handwriting. My finger had brushed over the wet marks littered around the page, her teardrops. I had read her letter over so many times that I was late for my session. I couldn't stop wondering when she wrote these words—clearly a time before everything blew up in our faces.

After I had memorized her confession, her apology, I searched through every page of my journal. As I flipped through the pages, I realized she'd written me notes throughout the entire thing. For every lyric or poem I wrote about her, she had answered. My journal was proof of the love we both shared, our words keeping our love preserved forever.

I wanted to call her that night, tell her I found it and tell her that I wanted to try again, but after speaking with my therapist, we agreed it wasn't the healthiest thing for me to do at the time. I was in rehab for a reason. I'd gone off the deep end, partially from what Nora had done and partially for things I'd been dealing with for years. For me to be in a healthy relationship, I had to figure my own shit out first. I had to learn to forgive, to let go of any resentment I still had toward her for what she'd done.

It'd been a long, grueling six months. I had to face

parts of myself that were ugly and battered, but I did it. I've now been six months sober, and I've never felt better. My mind is in a good place. My health is in a good place. Now that I have Nora in my arms, my *heart* is in a good place.

"It was my way of telling you how I felt," Nora utters, breaking me from my thoughts. Her legs unwrap from my middle, her feet finding the floor shortly after. Even though she's on the ground, we still hold each other tightly. Her arms have replaced her legs around my middle, her fingers grasping tightly to the back of my shirt.

"Loving you is beautiful, exhilarating, epic, Nora Mason."

She bites her lip, happy tears welling in her hazel eyes.

"You're my rain show, baby. The love that is one of a kind, so damn epic it only comes once in a lifetime."

"It's special," she finishes for me.

My nose nuzzles against hers. "It's ours."

"Ours," she repeats, standing on her tiptoes to plant a kiss on my lips.

"Ask for a confession, Rose," I tell her, kissing the top of her head, breathing in the familiar scent of her. The scent that reminds me of home. *She's* my home.

"Give me a confession."

"I'm ready to get the fuck out of here. Public displays of affection aren't normally my thing," I gesture to the people huddled around us, "and this is as public as we can get."

"I'll follow you anywhere," she says, grabbing her bag while taking hold of my hand.

"I love you, Rose. No more goodbyes."

She leans into my chest as we make our way through the airport, trying to dodge the mass amount of people calling our names. It's the most at peace I've felt in a long time, since that sunrise in bed with her at the cabin. "No more goodbyes," she promises.

EPILOGUE

NASH

ONE YEAR LATER

Hearing the crowd sing along with me is a feeling that'll never get old. I stop singing, letting the crowd around me fill in the lyrics for me. Lyrics to *Founded on Goodbye* spill through the stadium. It's a surreal moment for me. I wrote these lyrics with a broken heart, but one that still beat for the woman standing on left stage. Looking toward her, I find Nora where she always is on tour—cheering me on from the sidelines. Her sister, Lennon, stands next to her, smiling wide.

My own lyrics surround me, and I take a moment to take it all in, to appreciate the place I am at in my life. I'm on another sold-out tour, the love of my life on it with me, but not as a dancer this time. When Nora and I got back together, she told me how she'd been working hard on mending her relationship with her sister and she wanted to focus on that rather than spend all her time in rehearsals and on stage. She said her sister was traveling around the country, doing what she could to enjoy every moment. I suggested inviting her sister on tour with us, and though it was a shock to Nora, Lenny said yes. The two of them are in talks of opening their own dance studio together in LA. They stay up late most nights, both of them hunched over design boards of what they envision for the studio.

The song comes to an end, the audience going wild. *Founded on Goodbye* has been my best-selling record by far, the public so invested in the love story between me and Nora that this tour sold out each venue quickly, setting records for half of them.

When I found out why Nora was truly on this tour over a year ago, I wasn't in a good place. I never imagined singing these songs about her, having her waiting backstage for me. But life has a funny way of working out, and with the both of us putting in the effort to making our relationship work, we're in as good of a place as ever.

Which is why I want to ask her to marry me. Tonight.

I've had the ring for months; I've just been trying to find the right time to ask her to be mine forever. We're both so young, I know it could be reckless and foolish, but I don't give a damn what anyone's opinion is on it. I want her forever. I told her a year ago I never wanted to say another goodbye and I meant it. Putting a ring on her finger will seal that promise we made to each other. No more goodbyes.

When I learned that my hometown show was going to be a rain show, I knew this was the time to ask her. If I believed in all the fate and universe bullshit, I'd say this was fate. This venue is the place where it all came crashing down for me and Nora, and I think it's poetic to also make it the place for us to promise each other forever.

The rain beating on my back, the energy of the crowd, it brings the one-of-a-kind experience of a rain show. Rain is now our thing, and I can't imagine a better time to ask her.

Instead of performing an encore song, I do something different with this show.

"Colorado, do you mind if I switch things up a bit tonight?" I ask the crowd, getting my wet hair out of my face.

They scream and I smile, hyped for what's about to happen.

Turning to face Nora, I give her the biggest grin. "Nora, my love, could you join me out here?"

Her jaw drops, her eyes looking down at her outfit. She stands in the shelter, having managed to avoid the rain thus far. I nod, gesturing for her to come and join me on stage.

The ring box in my pocket suddenly feels incredibly heavy, the weight of what I'm about to do dawning on me.

Lennon pushes on Nora's back, forcing her forward. Thirty minutes before the show, I'd found Lennon, telling her my plan to ask Nora to marry me. She was all for it, helping me come up with some semblance of a speech. Nora carefully walks across the stage toward me.

When she reaches me, I sling an arm over her shoulder. "Colorado, say hello to my girl, you *may* know her."

They go fucking nuts, everyone very aware of who she is. We've graced the front page of many magazines, the paparazzi fucking animals when it comes to trying to get pictures of us together. It was a lot to get used to at first, but I've learned to care less about the media than I used to.

When I have Nora, nothing else really matters.

Turning to face her, I take both of her hands in mine. "Nora," I begin, "you came into my life at a point when I needed you most, I just didn't know it yet. You made me look at the ugly, bitter parts of myself. You were the first person to challenge me...the first person to see me for *me*. I think I fell in love with you the moment you told me you stole a rabbit as a kid."

"That was supposed to be our secret." She laughs, her cheeks blushing.

I smile. "Rose, we've been through one hell of a ride

together. We've both done things that we regret, but I wouldn't change a damn thing about our story. In the end, it brought me you, and you're everything I could ever want."

I reach into my pocket, pulling out the red velvet box I've been hiding from her for months.

Her hands cover her mouth. "Nash, what are you doing?"

Getting on one knee, I look up at the woman I'm so madly in love with. "You're my rain show, Rose. You're my epic adventure. The once-in-a-lifetime kind of love. I want to spend all of my fucking life kissing in the rain with you. I love you. You know I'm shit at asking for things," I smirk, "and I don't like to beg. But I'm on my knees for you. Marry me, Nora Mason."

The rain pelts down at both of us, mixing with the tears on her face. She nods enthusiastically, choking out a "*yes.*"

My hands are shaky as I place the emerald cut diamond ring on her finger. She doesn't even take time to admire the ring, instead she's falling to the ground with me, wrapping her arms tightly around me. It's hard to keep my balance as she throws her body on top of mine.

"I love you so much, Nash Pierce," Nora says, trying to speak over the rain and the crowd.

"I love you too, Rose."

I love her more than I ever thought possible, which is cliché as fuck, but the truth. She's the best thing that ever happened to me and I can't wait to see what life has in store for us. Our love story was supposed to be doomed before we ever laid eyes on each other. But when you love someone enough, we've shown that you can overcome anything. Our love story is like a rain show. It's a story they'll write all the fucking love songs about.

Holding this woman close to my chest, I'm the happiest I've ever been. She's my home, and I can't fucking wait to see what the rest of our love story has in store, our story nowhere near being done.

Nora and I are proof that even the best love stories can be founded on goodbye.

ACKNOWLEDGEMENTS

There are so many people who put hard work into Nash and Nora's love story. Being an indie author is not easy, but I'm fortunate to have the best team of people behind me who make all my dreams come true.

First and foremost, the girl who somehow has gotten two dedications out of me: Ashlee. I'll never, EVER be able to thank you for everything you do for me. Calling you my designer doesn't even skim the surface of how valuable you are to me. You're my best friend. I meant it when I said FOG wouldn't be what it is if it weren't for you. You were my sound board for so much of this story. The person behind the inspiration playlist and the enormous Pinterest board. You brought *Founded on Goodbye* to life with the cover, teasers, formatting images, etc. I love you long time.

To my husband. You're my rain show. I wouldn't be able to do this author thing if it weren't for you. Thank you for being you. I love you.

To my baby boy. Somehow I wrote this book when you were a newborn. Thank you for taking good naps and giving me all the newborn snuggles. I love you, Bubs.

Christina, I've said it once and I'll say it again, I LOVE YOU. Thank you for making me a better writer. You've taught me so much. I value your friendship and partnership so much.

Stevie, you were the person I didn't know I needed in my life. Thank you for all your time, keeping me organized, and for all that you do for me. I was a lost soul without you. I'm so happy fate brought us together.

You're stuck with me, babe!

To my betas. I value your feedback immensely. Thank you for getting Nash and Nora's love story in its rawest form and helping to make it what it is today. I wouldn't be able to create these stories without you. All my love and gratitude!

Tori, thank you for bringing my dreams to life with the fancy formatting!

Monty Jay, Kristin Turnage, and J.C. Hannigan, I'm so thankful that we were brought together. I've found forever friends in you. When are we booking our writing retreat?!

To the bloggers, bookstagrammers, booktokers, and people in this community that helped share the word about Nash, I'm so incredibly thankful for you. I've met so many people in the process of getting this book into the world. I'm so appreciative of the fact that you took the time to talk about my words on your platform. I notice every single one of your posts, videos, pictures, etc., and it means the world to me. You're the lifeblood of this community. Thank you for everything you do.

To the girls at Next Step PR, thank you for everything you did to help with this release. I appreciate it!

I have the privilege of having a growing group of people I can run to on Facebook for anything—Kat Singleton's Sweethearts. The members there are always there for me and I'm so fortunate to have you in my corner. I owe you so much gratitude for being there on the hard days and on the good days. Y'all are my people.

Lastly, to the readers. If you've made it this far, I wish I could envelop you in the biggest hug ever. I want to say THANK YOU for taking the time to read my words. I wouldn't be able to follow my dream and release books if there weren't people like *you* to read them. There is a numerous amount of amazing, badass, breathtaking books out in the world. The fact you chose mine from all of the options out there is incredible! Thank you! I hope you continue to tune in to the many more books I have planned.

Kat Singleton is an author who developed a passion for reading and writing at a young age. When writing stories, she strives to write an authentically raw love story for her characters. She feels that no book is complete without some angst and emotional turmoil before the characters can live out their happily ever after. She lives in Kansas with her husband, her baby boy and her two doodles. In her spare time, you can find her surviving off iced coffee and sneaking in a few pages of her current read. If you're a fan of angsty, emotional, contemporary romances then you'll love a Kat Singleton book.

THE AFTERSHOCK SERIES

Vol. 1: *The Consequence of Loving Me*
www.books2read.com/TCOLM

Vol. 2: *The Road to Finding Us*
www.books2read.com/TRTFU

THE MIXTAPE SERIES

Founded on Temptation
www.books2read.com/FOT
Coming October 2021!

THE MIXTAPE SERIES

If you enjoyed *Founded on Goodbye*, you'll love book two, *Founded on Temptation*!

Founded on Temptation is coming in October of 2021, but you can preorder now.

Track 1: *Founded on Goodbye*

***Founded on Goodbye* Pinterest:**
bit.ly/FOGpinterest

***Founded on Goodbye* Playlist:**
spoti.fi/3uB6SWT

Track 2: *Founded on Temptation*
www.books2read.com/FOT

Email:
authorkatsingleton@gmail.com

Website:
authorkatsingleton.com

Facebook Reader Group:
bit.ly/katsingletonSWEETHEARTS

Free Download of
The Waves of Wanting You:
dl.bookfunnel.com/7buobclx4i

Facebook:
facebook.com/authorkatsingleton

Instagram:
instagram.com/authorkatsingleton

Goodreads:
goodreads.com/author/show/19920088.Kat_Singleton

Tiktok:
www.tiktok.com/@authorkatsingleton

Printed in Great Britain
by Amazon

65648025R00173